UNION

BY JOHN MULCAHY

Published in 2009 by ABDEF, Dublin, Ireland

Cover credits:

Robert Fagan (1761–1816):
Portrait of Anna Maria Ferri, The Artist's First Wife, c.1790–2
oil on canvas Tate Gallery, London (c.1790)

Detail. Francis Wheatley (1747–1801)
The Dublin Volunteers on College Green, 4 November 1779
oil on canvas 175x323cm
Courtesy of the National Gallery of Ireland
Photo ©National Gallery of Ireland

ISBN 978-0-9563172-1-6

Designed by John Power
Colour reproduction by Des Fry at Typeform
Printed by Nicholson & Bass

CONTENTS

Historical characters in order of appearance

BROWNE, John Denis (1756–1809). Third Earl of Altamont and first Marquess of Sligo owned extensive property around Westport, County Mayo and in Jamaica. (page 20 & epilogue)

STEWART, Robert (1769–1822). Second Marquess of Londonderry, better known as Lord Castlereagh. Elected to the Irish House of Commons in 1790 at the age of 21 in an election that cost his family £60,000. He was the principal architect of the Act of Union under the administration of William Pitt. Afterwards British Secretary for War in 1805 and British Foreign Secretary from 1812 until his death in 1822. (page 37 & epilogue)

CORNWALLIS, Charles (1738–1805). First Marquess and second Earl Cornwallis. Capitulated to American forces at Yorktown on 19 October 1781. Governor general of India 1786–1794. In May 1798 he was appointed Viceroy and Commander-in-Chief in Ireland. Died in India 5 October 1805. (page 47 & epilogue)

LAKE, Gerard (1744–1808). English general who earned a reputation for excessive cruelty in Ireland 1797–1800. He served under Cornwallis in the American wars and was at the Yorktown surrender in 1781. Appointed army commander in Ireland on 23 April 1798 just one month before the outbreak of the Rebellion, he was victorious at the Battle for Vinegar Hill in June. He was routed by Humbert in Castlebar in August but had his revenge at Ballinamuck a few weeks later. He was brought into parliament for Armagh in 1799 by Castlereagh to vote for the Union. (page 47)

HUMBERT, Jean Joseph (1775–1823). French general appointed in 1798 to command a diversionary expedition to Ireland. With his flotilla of three frigates, one brig and 1060 men he landed at Killala, County Mayo on 22 August 1798. (page 48 & epilogue)

O'DONNELL, Colonel (1760–1799). Eldest son of Sir Neil O'Donnell of Newport, County Mayo, a man of very large fortune. He commanded the Mayo regiment. His impassioned speech against the Union motion on 22 January 1799 was, in fact, his maiden speech in the House but as a result of it he was deprived of his regiment. (page 64)

MAGEE, John (c.1750–1809). Owner/editor of the *Dublin Evening Post*. His paper consistently opposed the Union. (page 87)

GRATTAN, Henry (1746–1820). Leader of the Irish parliamentary opposition 1775–1797. Vigorous advocate for parliamentary reform and Catholic emancipation. Dramatically returned to the House to oppose the Act of Union on 16 January 1800. However, like John Foster, he was later elected to the House of Commons in Westminster and took his seat in 1805. (page 88)

BINGHAM, Charles (1730–1799). Second son of Sir John Bingham who had married a grand niece of Patrick Sarsfield, the Jacobite general who had been created Earl of Lucan by James II in 1691. Charles Bingham was created Baron Lucan of Castlebar in 1776 and Earl of Lucan in 1795. (page 89)

BINGHAM, Richard. Eldest son and heir of Charles Bingham. He succeeded to the Lucan title in 1799. (page 89)

FOSTER, John (1740–1828). Baron Oriel. Last Speaker of the Irish House of Commons. First elected in 1761. Called to the Bar in 1766. Strongly opposed any concessions to Roman Catholics but opposed the Union to the bitter end. He was one of the few anti-Unionists who later secured a seat in the Imperial Parliament and in 1804 he was appointed Chancellor of the Irish Exchequer. (page 98)

FITZGIBBON, John (1749–1802). Earl of Clare and Lord Chancellor of Ireland from 1789. Consistently opposed Grattan's attempts to reform the Irish Parliament and to grant concessions to Roman Catholics. His staunch support in the House of Lords for Castlereagh's strategies was an important factor in getting the Act of Union passed. (page 101)

BARRINGTON, Jonah (1760–1834). Called to the Bar in 1788 and elected to the Irish House of Commons in 1790. He opposed the Act of Union in 1800 and in his *Rise and Fall of the Irish Nation* (1833), he recorded the details of the votes cast in the final session. His *Personal Sketches of his own Time* (1827) give a racy account of Irish society at the end of the 18th century. (page 106)

Historical characters in order of appearance

DE QUINCEY, Thomas (1785–1859). Philosopher, poet and author of *Confessions of an Opium Eater*. He met Howe Peter Browne, son of Lord Altamont, in Bath and later visited him at Eton. In 1800 he travelled to Ireland as guest of Browne and was present at the last sitting of the Irish House of Lords. (page 143)

DOWDALL, William (c.1767–1812). Natural son of Mr. Walter Hussey Burg who was patronised by Henry Grattan after Hussey Burg's early demise. Imprisoned after the 1798 Rebellion in Scotland, Dowdall was an ally of Robert Emmet in 2003. (page 161 & epilogue)

EMMET, Robert (1778–1803). Youngest son of Dr Robert Emmet who lived on St Stephen's Green, Dublin. Joined the United Irishmen while at Trinity College Dublin but was not active in the 1798 rebellion. Fled to France after a warrant was issued for his arrest in April 1799. Returned to Ireland in October 1802 determined to organise a Rising. (page 162 & epilogue)

EMMET, Thomas Addis (1764–1827). Elder brother of Robert Emmet and distinguished barrister who defended many nationalists in court. Secretary of the Supreme Council of the United Irishmen, he was imprisoned after the 1798 rebellion in Fort George in Scotland 1799–1802 and after his release moved to Paris. After Robert Emmet's Rising in July 1803, he emigrated to New York where he died in 1827. (page 162)

RUSSELL, Thomas (1767–1803). An ex-captain in the British army, he was a friend of such Northern radicals as Henry Joy McCracken and Samuel Neilson. Was active in recruiting for the United Irishmen and after the rebellion of 1798 was sent to Fort George in Scotland. Released in 1802 he went to Paris where he met Robert Emmet and followed him back to Ireland. He was Emmet's chief lieutenant in the North but was no more successful than Emmet in effecting a Rising there. Early in August 1803 he returned to Dublin in an effort to effect Emmet's release but was arrested on 9 September and was publicly executed on 21 October. (page 162 & epilogue)

LAWLESS, Valentine (1773–1853). Second Baron Cloncurry sympathised with the United Irishmen organisation and was imprisoned in the Tower of London from April 1799 – March 1801. While his country residence was at Lyons House in County Kildare which his father had built, the *Personal Recollections of Lord Cloncurry* (1850) include the story of his city property called Mornington House on Merrion Street in Dublin. (page 168)

BYRNE, Miles (1780–1862). Born in Wexford, he joined the Society of United Irishmen in 1797 and fought at Vinegar Hill in 1798. After the Rebellion he hid out in the Wicklow mountains until joining Robert Emmet's conspiracy in 1803. (page 175 & epilogue)

WOLFE, Arthur (1739–1803). First Viscount Kilwarden, of Forenaughts, County Kildare. Progressively appointed solicitor-general (1787), attorney-general and a member of the Privy Council (1789). In 1798 he was appointed Lord Chief Justice of Ireland. He supported the passing of the Union in 1800. On 23 July 1803, on being summoned to attend a meeting of the Privy Council in the city, his carriage was attacked on Thomas Street and both he and his nephew who was travelling with him, were murdered by the insurgents. (page 176)

SIRR, Henry Charles (1764–1841). Town-major, or head of police, in Dublin in 1798, the year of the great rebellion. He took part in the capture of Lord Edward FitzGerald on 19 May 1798 and in 1803 he organised the arrest of Robert Emmet and other leaders. (page 178)

YORKE, Philip (1757–1834). Third Earl of Hardwicke. Lord Lieutenant of Ireland 1801–1806 and was thus in Dublin during the Emmet rising. Became a supporter of Catholic emancipation, to which cause he adhered until it became law in 1829. (page 187)

McNALLY, Leonard (1752–1820). Barrister at Law popularly known as 'McNally the Incorruptible' he was, in fact, a government informer. One of the first members of the Society of United Irishmen, he appeared in court on behalf of Wolfe Tone, Napper Tandy and Robert Emmet, the latter at his trial on 19 September 1803. After McNally's death on 13 February 1820, his heir claimed a continuance of the secret service pension of £300 per annum that his father had enjoyed since 1798. It then emerged that McNally, while taking large fees to defend the United Irishmen, had also accepted large sums to betray them. (page 206)

BOOK I

Chapter I

THE PRESTON PICNIC

The West of Ireland 1798

BRENDAN O'REILLY lay on his back gazing up at the great white clouds floating in from the Atlantic. Immediately above him a skylark fluttered into the summer sky soaring, higher and higher to its own serenade. The day was unusually warm and Brendan felt drowsy after the splendid picnic they had enjoyed, lounging around the large linen tablecloth spread out on the sandy turf. He now lay a little apart from the rest and, thanks to the wine, his mind wandered in a haze like the clouds above.

Brendan was a young gentleman of leisure and the only son of Mr. William O'Reilly, the wealthiest merchant in Westport. His mother was determined that he should not follow his father into trade. "And why should he?", she used to ask rather grandly. To please his father, Brendan had studied at the King's Inns and had been called to the Bar. But although an avid student, he didn't take to the law. He found it too dry. He was happy to be back in Mayo while he considered his future prospects. His mother fondly hoped that he would become, as she put it, "a man of letters". Lately, that idea was growing on him.

Brendan would never forget the details of that extraordinary day, a watershed between the lazy pleasures of his youth and all the troubles that were to follow thereafter. A delicious repast of cold poached salmon was washed down with a choice Chablis. Pamela Preston, in a flowing white muslin dress, was effervescent as always and the centre of attention. Margaret O'Reilly, Brendan's sister, was chatting on about her wedding plans. Pamela's father, old Bonaventure Preston, the Master of Murrisk, was grumbling about the unsettled state of the country to his brother, Captain John Preston, who was slightly tipsy after the lunch.

The picnic had taken place on Bartra Head, a narrow neck of land that juts out like a finger into the immensity of Clew Bay. At its furthest point, which is more than a mile from the shoreline, the promontory widens into a flat headland that stands barely twenty feet out of the sea. This low-lying table of mossy grass and tiny wild flowers is almost entirely surrounded by water. Beyond it are the small islands of Inisheeny and Inisaugh that look like giant stepping-stones in the bay. And far out to sea stands Clare Island, a stout bastion against the Atlantic. Captain John, lately retired from Jamaica, chose this idyllic spot for the summer Preston picnic. Every year the excursion took place on the last Sunday in July, so that the family could avoid the crowds of common people who assembled in Murrisk for the annual Papist pilgrimage up to the peak of Croagh Patrick.

"Are there as many as last year?", old Bonaventure asked as he nodded towards the line of pilgrims winding their way to the top of the mountain.

"I wouldn't say so," Captain John replied. "It's too fine a day to miss the hay-making."

"Half of them never leave Campbell's shebeen," Bonaventure complained. "There won't be a man fit for work tomorrow."

"Devotion among the people is greatly to be encouraged," said the Captain. "It keeps their mind off other mischief."

Captain John Preston had just passed fifty when he returned from Jamaica, where he had acquired all the habits of a man well used to his comforts. He was a simple man at heart, but the fact that he was unmarried attracted a certain kind of speculation locally, as indeed did the source of his wealth. His life at sea had left him with a bearded countenance, but he kept himself fit and enjoyed all the country pursuits of a gentleman in retirement. He had a good stable and was a keen shot. His clothes came from one of the best tailors in Dublin and he sported a gold chain in his waistcoat and a Claddagh ring on his finger.

"I had a letter from Olive," said the Captain. "She was asking about Pamela again." Aunt Olive was the only Preston sister. She was widowed and lived in Dublin. "She wants Pamela in Dublin for the season."

"Time enough for her to be introduced to society," old Bonaventure hedged, as usual.

"But she would be in good hands with Olive," said Captain Preston. "And I might go up myself for a few weeks."

"I'll think about it," said Bonaventure, without any enthusiasm, and there the subject was left. Pamela was his pet and the only love left in his life. The thought of being parted from her, even temporarily, was distressful to him in the extreme.

Captain Preston hoisted his bulky frame off the rug and stretched himself. "I think I'll give *Jock* some exercise and shake down that big lunch," he said, then strolled over to where the servants were polishing off the remains of the picnic. "Saddle up *Jock* for me," he called over to Stephen Allen, his right-hand man at the Abbey. "And saddle *Nora* too. You can give her a stretch."

Stephen helped the Captain mount the big bay and then swung himself astride the mare. Together they slithered down the sand bank, leaning back in the saddles, and walked their mounts into the shallow sea. The Captain swore when

Jock began to play up and splashed him with water. The mare, too, was restless, tossing her head and prancing sideways and Stephen was pleased when the Captain turned *Jock* back onto the hard strand and gave him his head.

With a shudder, the mare set off in pursuit, her ears flat back against her head and her neck stretched out and down. *Jock* thundered ahead with powerful strides while the Captain stood in the stirrups leaning forward over his neck. The flying hooves sprayed great lumps of wet sand in the air, forcing Stephen to pull off to one side as they galloped down the long strand. Only when the Captain started to pull up near Curraghmore Point was Stephen able to draw abreast.

"You handle her well," the Captain remarked as they walked the panting horses back again. "But keep your knees tighter to the saddle. It's all right on the flat but the knees are everything when the going is rough."

Stephen was pleased with the remark simply because the Captain had bothered to notice. Everyone in the Barony knew that Stephen was a natural horseman. He could train them, shoe them and judge them at a glance. Neighbours often sent for him when they had trouble with a foaling or a horse gone lame. Stephen made it his business to have everything just right for the Captain. He cleaned his guns, kept his horses and polished his riding boots. The Captain always took Stephen with him when he went fishing or shooting and Stephen drove the Captain to Westport every Thursday in the family trap. To Stephen, the Captain personified everything a gentleman should be: courteous, accomplished and manly. And the Captain was particularly generous to Stephen. He passed on his old riding clothes and boots – and well before they were worn out. And when they went into Westport, he always gave him half a sovereign "to look after himself for the day."

~~~~~~~~~ ● ~~~~~~~~

While the Captain was gone, the ladies talked on about Margaret's forthcoming wedding, the dresses, the flowers, the guests and so on. Like Pamela, Margaret O'Reilly was also dressed in white, with a long full skirt and a short-sleeved blouse that kept slipping off her shoulder.

"How do you know when you're in love?" Pamela asked Margaret with a giggle.

"I haven't the faintest idea."

"But you must. You're in love, aren't you?"

"I suppose so."

"Only suppose?"

"Well, I've never been in love before, so how do I know."

"I thought you felt it in every fibre of your body?"

"So they say."

"Don't you?"

"Yes, I suppose so," said Margaret.

"Well, is Charles in love with you?"

"I wonder do men know anything about love," answered Margaret. "I mean real love. Men love themselves, their professions, their estates. We are only a decoration to their property."

"I would never marry a man who didn't love me," said Pamela, blushing slightly.

"Quite right too. But don't confuse love with infatuation. It's all too easy to be infatuated. I speak of a deeper love. A love you would die for."

"Yes, of course," Pamela agreed. Love was an emotion about which she had only dreamt, and she fell silent while envying her older friend.

Brendan glanced over at the girls. His sister Margaret was the more striking of the two. She was taller and of a stronger build than Pamela, with a fair skin set against her thick auburn hair which today was hanging loose over her shoulders. High cheek bones, that came from her mother, gave a structured distinction to her face, but the most arresting feature of her countenance was undoubtedly her emerald green eyes.

Pamela was more petite with soft brown eyes and an open countenance. She had a short nose, very small ears and long delicate fingers which Brendan had first noticed as she played the pianoforte. Nobody had ever seen Pamela lose her temper and she was endowed with natural good manners which endeared her to everyone she met. Pamela had barely entered Brendan's consciousness before his return from Dublin earlier this year. He was aware only that she was one of the young ladies who, like Margaret, attended Miss Meredith's Dancing School in Westport. But he had begun to see more of her after the June Ball in Robinson's Hotel to mark the end of the Law term. That night she wore her hair in ringlets. Today it hung loose in the breeze.

～～～～～ ● ～～～～～

Just as the clock in the stable yard struck four, a young woman with a shawl over her head knocked at the front door of Murrisk Abbey. The Preston house was situated between the road and the sea and the short avenue swept down through banks of overgrown rhododendron. The remains of the ancient Friary of Murrisk could be seen from the front of the Preston residence. The Friary had been established in 1457 with a grant of lands to the Augustinian monks by Thady O'Malley, the clan chief who had long ruled the area around Clew Bay. After the suppression of the monasteries, the Prestons had been granted 500 acres of the Augustinian lands by King James I.

"Could ye spare a wee cup of water mam, or a drop o' buttermilk?" said the beggar-woman with a northern accent.

"What business have you coming to the front door?" rejoined Sarah Barton, who had been in service with the Prestons for over thirty years and was as cantankerous as her master.

"God bless ye mam, I'm a stranger in these parts. No offence meant, to be sure, but I don't know any better."

"There's not a drop of buttermilk left in the house with all the callers I've had this day," said Mrs. Barton.

The woman looked crestfallen and Mrs. Barton left her in suspense for a moment. "Come across to the dairy, then," she relented, "and I'll see what I can find for you."

Mrs. Barton enjoyed the exercise of her little power but she never turned away a beggar from the door. So she led the way across the deserted yard and filled a mug of buttermilk for the stranger. She also ladled some into a can to bring back to the house. The woman took the drink slowly, interspersing every gulp with invocations to the Almighty and calling eternal blessings on the house and on Mrs. Barton for her goodness. Mrs. Barton called off the dogs which had been barking and sniffing around the stranger and with that the young woman made off up the avenue again, pulling the shawl around her shoulders as she went. The housekeeper did not close the hall door until she was well out of sight.

Hugh O'Malley had been hanging around Campbell's shebeen among the pilgrims since early morning. He was a strong build of a lad with a freckled face and a great mop of red hair. Some said that his real father had been the curate in nearby Lechanvey partly because the priest too had a head of red hair. But there was another reason for this rumour. O'Malley had disappeared from the parish some years ago and word was that he had been smuggled out to France. Certainly when he reappeared he seemed to have acquired some education. He spouted radical opinions in every pub and was regarded with suspicion by the authorities. Although he kept very much to himself, he was said to be a United man.

Just before four o'clock, O'Malley slipped out of Campbell's and pulling a knitted cap down over his hair, headed down the back lane to Prestons. As the stable clock struck four, he quietly unlatched the back door of the house and turned into the old gun-room, which doubled as the armoury for the Murrisk men of the South Mayo Militia. The militia had been issued with guns, flintlocks and powder to deal with local unrest and as a precaution against the constant threat of an invasion from France.

O'Malley quickly shoved a dozen muskets into a deep sack. He then let himself out the back door and retraced his steps up the lane where a donkey with baskets strapped to its sides was tied up. O'Malley put the sack into the empty basket and covered it with turf. Outside Campbell's, he handed the animal to a waiting gasún and strolled back into the shebeen. Nobody had even noticed his five-minute absence. All had gone according to plan.

It must have been about half-past four when Mrs. Barton noticed that the door to the gun-room was ajar and that the muskets had been taken. Alarmed, she ran outside but could find no one to help. She shuffled over to the clock tower in the yard and pulled on the bell-rope again and again until she was out of breath. Old Bonaventure was the first of the picnic party to hear the tocsin. "There's something amiss at the house," he cried, as the whole party rose in alarm and strained their eyes back to Murrisk. "Stephen, bring me the mare – fast. John, you come with me. Mr. O'Reilly, let you look after the ladies," the Master ordered as he dug his heels into his surprised mount and departed at a gallop.

Chapter II

LORD ALTAMONT

"DELIVER THIS into *Lord Altamont's own hand," the Master instructed Stephen as he gave him a hastily written account of the past hour at Murrisk Abbey. "And ride for all you're worth."

Mounted for this emergency on the Captain's big black *Hamilton*, Stephen had galloped furiously over the five miles into Westport – much to the consternation of the pilgrims crowding the narrow road. Stephen was pleased to have been given this commission. Despite his bold exterior, inside he was troubled by insecurity. Stephen had been born at Murrisk Abbey. His mother, who had been a parlour maid in the big house, had died in childbirth. He never knew his father. Mrs Barton's sister had reared him on the estate and Captain John had paid his fees at the Protestant school in Westport. But he had to make his own way in the world and signs on it. He was not just the best horseman in the Barony: he was as good a sailor as there was in the Bay. He had spent long hours harvesting the Preston mussels and sailing them down to the Quay at Westport. He knew how to navigate the currents and to cope with the tides. Of course he had to put up with the "bastard" tag when he was a young fellow, but it was several years since anyone had dared to mutter that taunt in his hearing.

Now he was standing with a footman inside the door of Lord Altamont's book-lined study in Westport House. It was the first time he had ever been inside the Big House.

"Damn Preston, the bloody fool," Lord Altamont muttered under his breath, as he read of the theft of the guns. But he was really angry with himself. He should have anticipated the danger. He should have given explicit orders for the safekeeping of the muskets.

"Mr. Preston will be with your Lordship within the hour," Stephen volunteered, uncertain whether or not to speak in this intimidating presence.

"And what is your name, young man?"

"Stephen Allen, sir."

"Good. You have done well. But mark you mention this business to no one," he said as he dismissed the messenger.

But Stephen decided to have a good look around the estate while he had the opportunity. Mounting *Hamilton,* who was now cooled down and groomed, he walked the big horse around the ornamental lake at the back of the house down to the extensive outhouses and stable yards and stopped to admire some of his Lordship's prize cattle which had been imported from England.

"Can I help you, sir," came a pointed call from across the yard.

"No, I have just been with his Lordship," Stephen replied rather grandly.

So he moved off slowly to the rear gate of the estate which leads onto the harbour quay and there he met Brendan O'Reilly coming in off the Murrisk road.

The two men dismounted for a few minutes, the better to have a quiet chat.

"You must have a fair idea who stole the guns," Brendan said.

"I have my suspicions all right but it's too early to say positively. There's half a dozen of them boyos who could be up to it. But I'd say Lord Altamont won't be too long in finding them."

"What worries me is that they picked on the Prestons. They could have struck a dozen other places in Mayo. I'd fear there's something personal in this."

"Exactly my own thoughts," said Stephen. "But I'd better be off. I must report to Captain John."

<center>~~~~~~ • ~~~~~~</center>

Lord Altamont scribbled a cryptic command to his brother, Denis Browne Esquire, High Sheriff for the County of Mayo, and another to Tom Lindsay, the High Constable. Both were to attend him immediately. Then he settled his heavy frame into an old wing chair while he contemplated the seriousness of this development.

John Denis Browne, the third Earl of Altamont, didn't like surprises. He was a man who believed in controlling affairs, and his life was singularly devoted to looking after his own business. Not for him the life of the absentee landlord, wasting abroad what rents his agent could squeeze out of the tenantry. Lord Altamont lived in Westport and he worked in Westport. And signs on it. His own estate, which extended over 100,000 acres, was a credit to his husbandry and the great work initiated by his grandfather, the first Earl. Like his grandfather, the present Earl was devoted to experiments in the rotation of crops – potatoes, barley, oats, flax; in the reclamation of bogland and in the employment of the abundant seaweed as a natural manure. He had gone to great expense in introducing the best breed of English cattle to Westport, and his stables were deservedly famous throughout the West. He had been a keen horseman in his youth, but his damned weight now kept him out of the saddle. Except when the business of Parliament required his presence in Dublin, he spent most of his life here, in his study, receiving reports, writing letters and generally keeping his finger on the pulse of the county.

He had come into the property in 1780 – when he was only twenty-four – and it was no exaggeration to say that he had transformed the whole area since. Of course the country had been enjoying a period of unusual prosperity, but Westport itself had improved out of all recognition. Lord Altamont had spent long hours with his architect designing the new town, even diverting the river to create the much admired new Mall along its banks. But it was his establishment of the linen industry in the district which really brought about the most marked improvement. His Lordship had built houses in the town and let them at reasonable terms to weavers. He gave them looms and lent them money to buy yarn. He even bought the produce they could not sell.

But his real interest – apart from doting on his only son and heir – had always been in public affairs. The Brownes had monopolised the parliamentary representation in Mayo for almost half a century – and his Lordship meant to keep it that way. How else could one control everything that stirred in the county?

Within the hour, four men were seated around Lord Altamont's large desk. Denis Browne, overweight like his older brother but lacking the latter's subtlety; Tom Lindsay, tall and lean, sallow-skinned, brown-eyed, Cromwellian. Denis Browne was the flamboyant exponent of law and order in Mayo. Tom Lindsay was its cold executioner. Bonaventure Preston was the last to arrive and felt none too happy in this company. He was a plain country squire and he felt a fool over the loss of the muskets.

"We have two priorities," said Lord Altamont as soon as they were all seated. "To seize the thieves and to recover the guns. But first," he addressed Lindsay "send an order immediately to all Militia Corps Commanders with specific instructions on the storing of arms. All arms must be secured with double padlocks. The keys to these must be kept by the Commander only. Windows to such stores must be protected with iron bars. Add any other precautions as you think fit. Perhaps the flintlocks should be removed from muskets? See that the order goes out to all Commanders in the county by nightfall, and you, Denis, arrange an inspection within two days. This is a serious business and we don't yet know what other treachery is planned."

"Now, Mr. Preston," he said, turning towards Bonaventure. "Tell us in detail everything you know of today's unfortunate occurrence. And please omit no detail that may be of relevance."

Old Bonaventure went over the whole story again, from early morning until he heard the stable-yard bell pealing. Several times he was stopped and questioned by Tom Lindsay who was taking notes. Finally, and rather shamefacedly, he told of finding the gun room ransacked and the muskets gone.

No, the door was not locked.

No, the window was not barred.

No, special precautions had not been taken while they were out on the picnic. Bonaventure cringed while Lindsay rammed home the obvious. But Lord Altamont was in no mood for recriminations.

"Well, gentlemen," said his Lordship, as soon as he heard Bonaventure's detailed account. "I think we can conclude three main points from what we know so far. Firstly, that a Northern woman is at least an accomplice to this dastardly business. Secondly, that there is at least one other person involved, a local person who knew the house and the significance of the day of the pilgrimage. Thirdly, that we are most likely dealing with a conspiracy of Defenders or United Irishmen whose purpose in taking these guns can be well imagined. However, I don't wish to alarm the whole county before we have made progress. Thanks to your swift reaction, Mr. Preston (old Bonaventure had connections throughout the county, and even in Jamaica, that were useful to Lord Altamont. His Lordship didn't want him embarrassed by this incident) we may be able to nip this business in the bud."

He took from the wide drawer of the table a list of all known immigrants from the North in the Westport district.

"There cannot be too many women on this list who come close to the description we have," he said to his brother. "But I want them all questioned immediately – I mean by tonight. Have them account for their movements since dawn today. Have statements taken and witnessed by the head of each house. Draft in whatever extra constables you need from Newport or Castlebar. Lodge the dozen most likely suspects in the militia barracks. We must find this woman before she has a chance to slip through our fingers. And then bring her here to me. I will deal with her personally."

After he had dismissed them, Lord Altamont lingered on in his study. He didn't like this business in Murrisk. This was no small theft to be taken lightly. He recognised it for what it was – the action of well-organised men with murder in mind. For several months past the country had been ravaged by open insurrection. Thousands had been killed in Kildare, Wicklow and Wexford but happily the rebellion had not spread west of the Shannon. To date, the West had been spared the horrors of pillage and anarchy, but this business did not bode well. There would be Papists behind it, of course. Always Papists.

The Brownes themselves had been Papists, once upon a time. Colonel John Browne, who supported King James II at the Battle of the Boyne, had been the last of them and nearly lost everything for his pains. His son, Peter, had conformed to the Established Church and set the family fortunes on their long and steady improvement through the 18th century. Peter's son, John, was the present Earl's grandfather, and his prototype in so many respects. Then came Peter, the second Earl, who lived to enjoy the title for only four years, but who made one great contribution to the family's welfare in marrying Elizabeth Kelly.

She was the only daughter and heir to Denis Kelly of Lisduff in County Galway, Chief Justice of Jamaica. He left his daughter a considerable plantation in Jamaica which enlarged the Browne coffers ever since. At this time, Lord Altamont's estates in Co. Mayo yielded him an annual income of almost £20,000. It was said that his Jamaican property was no less lucrative

~~~~~~ • ~~~~~

By the time the High Sheriff rode up to the barracks on John's Row next morning, ten Northern women had been rounded up and locked in the barrack's guardroom. No explanation had been given them. Nor had they received any refreshment. No bedding had been provided during the night. But they had all been questioned intensely about their movements.

"I'm pretty sure it's the one called Sadie McCafferty," the High Constable told him. "She admits she was in Murrisk yesterday."

"Has she been in trouble before?", asked Denis Browne.

"Not that we know of. She's in service with Mrs. O'Reilly on the Mall."

"Convey her immediately to His Lordship and make sure she is guarded well."

~~~~~~ • ~~~~~

When Sadie McCafferty was shown into his study, Lord Altamont did not look up. He didn't savour this kind of activity but he wanted quick results and he was fully aware of the power of his intimidating presence. From under his heavy eyebrows he noticed her small delicate frame, her thin high-boned face and the fear in her eyes. But without any preliminaries, he launched into the interrogation.

"Your name?" he demanded peremptorily.

"Sadie McCafferty, yur Lordship."

"Where do you live?"

"Wit Mrs. O'Reilly on the Mall."

"Married or single?"

"Single."

"Any family?"

"Only me mother now."

"What's your occupation?"

"I'm in service wit Mrs. O Reilly."

"When did you come to Westport?"

"Last year."

"Religion?"

"Papist."

"Whom do you know in Westport?"

Sadie paused and Lord Altamont waited. Then, for the first time since she had entered the room, he lifted his head slowly, very slowly.

"Answer my questions directly," he ordered in that deep tone that carried all the authority of his position.

"I knows Patsy Joyce and Mary O'Connor and Deirdre Malley."

"Who else?"

"Well, I knows Father Egan and Father Kelly," she said cautiously now, "and … a few of de lads."

"What lads?"

"Well I don't know them real well like, but der's Pat Gibbons and Luke Power and Mick Gavin …"

Most of this information had already been provided to Lord Altamont.

"All of these people will now be held suspect," he announced, rising slowly from his chair and pacing a full circle around her while the implication of this statement bore in on poor Sadie. Then leaning over the desk until his jowl was quite close to her face he demanded, "Which of them was involved in stealing the guns?"

"Guns!", said Sadie with evident alarm. "Wat guns?"

Lord Altamont was slightly surprised.

"The guns stolen from Mr. Preston's residence at Murrisk yesterday at exactly four o'clock," he shot back.

The girl's face now totally collapsed and Lord Altamont could see that the reason for the whole alarm had dawned on her for the first time.

"Guns," repeated Lord Altamont, bringing her back to earth. "The missing guns."

"I know nuttin of guns. I swear to God, Yur Lordship. I don't know wat you're talking about," said Sadie desperately.

Lord Altamont had come to the same conclusion but he pressed on with the interrogation.

"I hope you realise that you are implicated in a most serious crime – the punishment for which is transportation at least. However, if you can help us – if you identify your accomplice for us – I promise to use my influence on your behalf. It's entirely up to you now. On the other hand, if you persist in your present course, the consequences must affect all your friends and relations. Even your mother."

At the mention of her mother, Sadie started again. Lord Altamont knew that the family had fled to Westport to escape the Orange pogroms in the North.

"I've told you, I know nuttin of any guns," she continued.

"But you were in Murrisk, yesterday?"

"Yes."

"And you did knock at the front door of Murrisk Abbey at four o'clock?"

"Yes."

"Who put you up to it, then?", asked Lord Altamont directly staring straight into her face.

Again there was a pause, but this time Lord Altamont was all consideration. He put his warm hand on her shoulder.

"Take my advice, young lassy, it's your life or his. He doesn't deserve your consideration – or is it your love?" There was a mocking tone in this last remark.

"No one put me up to it. I just wanted a glass of buttermilk," she lied.

Now Lord Altamont dropped all pretence of politeness.

"You're wasting my time, you miserable slut," he spat out, "and you deserve no consideration from Lord Altamont. You're sheltering a scoundrel, a thief, and a potential murderer. Do you realise the consequences? You'll probably be strung up with him and your mother transported back to Armagh. Expect no mercy now from Lord Altamont. I was kind enough last year to allow you to settle in this town. But you have betrayed my trust. You have signed your own death warrant and consigned your own mother to misery."

Such arguments were too strong for Sadie McCafferty. As Lord Altamont had anticipated, she suddenly broke down in tears and blurted out all she knew. She told him how she'd come down off Croagh Patrick when this fellow got talking to her. They were chatting and laughing for a while, when he asked her – as a favour like – to knock at the front door of the big house down the lane. Nothing else. Just to chat up the housekeeper for a few minutes.

"What was his name?"

"I dun know."

"What did he look like?"

"He was a fine strong fellow with red hair."

"You knew he was up to no good," Lord Altamont said.

"I just wanted to plase him," Sadie replied pathetically.

Lord Altamont could see that Sadie was no further use to him. Evidently the man had been clever enough not to disclose his name. But at least they had a good description and it didn't take too long for the High Constable to narrow down the list of suspects near the top of which stood the name of Hugh O'Malley.

<center>~~~~~~~ • ~~~~~~~</center>

Hugh O'Malley had been sharing a shack with two Northern lads since they came to Westport. It was a roughly made construction that leant against the back wall of a warehouse on Westport Quay. One kick of Tom Lindsay's boot shattered the door of this feeble construction and the next moment the three men had been dragged outside.

"Which of you is O'Malley?" demanded the High Constable, although he recognised O'Malley immediately from the description. None of them replied.

"Take away the redhead," ordered the High Constable brusquely as he turned his horse back towards the barracks.

Tom Lindsay was waiting for them at the barracks. It was late and he had no inclination to waste the whole night breaking down this suspect. He knew he must get a quick result for Lord Altamont so he decided on the direct approach.

"We know everything about you O'Malley since you came back from France. What you've been up to with your United friends and how you stole those muskets in Murrisk yesterday. Now, I'll be blunt. We want those muskets back. The odds are that you'll be swinging from a rope before the end of the week. And you'll deserve it. Your only chance is to co-operate fully with me. If you value your life, you'll answer my questions directly. If you don't, you're a gone man."

Hugh O'Malley had often thought of a moment like this. He knew he must tell them nothing. He knew his only chance in the world was that the lads would get him out of here. He must hold out.

"I don't know what you're talking about," he blurted out. "I know nothing about muskets. I was in Campbell's pub all day yesterday. Ask Owen Campbell himself. He'll tell you."

"We know all about that," replied the High Constable coldly. "But you weren't in Campbell's at four o'clock. You were at the back door of Mr. Preston's residence stealing the muskets."

But still O'Malley refused to say a word.

"You're a foolish man, O'Malley," the High Constable spat out. "I tried to give you a chance – but you won't take it. Well if you won't co-operate with me, you're out of my hands. You deserve what's coming to you."

And with that he called in two constables who frog-marched O'Malley to a shed in a remote corner of the barrack yard. The constables were big fellows and their heavy boots crunched menacingly on the gravel. But neither of them spoke a word. They were men with a job to do. And it wasn't the first time.

They closed the heavy door of the shed behind them and one of them lit a candle. O'Malley instinctively backed against the wall while the bigger man spoke at last.

"For the last time, will you tells us where the muskets are?", he asked. But the words were hardly out of his mouth before he slammed his heavy boot down onto the prisoner's bare foot. O'Malley doubled up in pain as the second constable hit him hard in the kidneys. Then a savage punch to his stomach knocked him gasping and reeling to the floor. After that they kicked him in the testicles, on the shins, on his back, everywhere, grunting as they buried their heavy boots into his squirming, jerking, bleeding body.

Later he couldn't remember how long this punishment had continued. Perhaps only a minute. Perhaps five. He couldn't recall. But it seemed like an eternity while he begged them to stop, crying, moaning, gasping for breath until his system could take no more and he lapsed into unconsciousness.

Much later again, he found himself alone in utter darkness. There was a hammering of anvils in his head and even to draw a breath was agony. He coughed once and felt the sticky taste of blood in his mouth. He lay still, fearful of moving a single joint, and tried to remember had he told them anything. He hoped he hadn't. But he couldn't be sure.

Early in the morning, Lord Altamont received a personal report from the obviously fatigued High Constable.

"We tried everything, my Lord, and I mean everything. But not a word."

"What's your opinion?", cut in Lord Altamont. He suffered from gout – as had his grandfather – and he had felt the imminence of an attack since the previous day.

"Guilty without a doubt," said Tom Lindsay firmly. "I could see it in his eyes."

Lord Altamont shifted himself slowly and lifted his left foot onto a footstool. He disliked everything about this business but he was damned if he was going to let them get away with it. The word was all over the Barony by now. People would be watching for his reaction. Yes, he'd have to make an example of O'Malley.

"Then let the Grand Jury deal with him," he said. "Maybe the smell of the rope will loosen his tongue. And remove him to Castlebar jail where he will be secure until after the trial."

Before he left, the High Constable discussed some details that would be mentioned in evidence. Nothing was to be left to chance. If an example was to be made, it had to be well made.

Chapter III

THE O'REILLYS
OF WESTPORT

THE NEWS OF the theft at Murrisk spread quickly through the town of Westport. While insurrection and military repression had been widespread in other parts of the country since May, the West of Ireland had remained remarkably calm. So the theft of the muskets was considered highly alarming. There was outrage among the respectable community in the town and in church the following Sunday, Fr. Egan delivered himself of the strongest possible condemnation of "the diabolical work of those who conspire to encourage a visit from the French." But in several pubs down on the quay, there were nods and winks as the story of the raid was told and retold until it began to assume heroic proportions.

In the O'Reilly household, however, the theft of the muskets created huge embarrassment.

"How could Sadie get mixed up in such a business?", wailed Mrs. O'Reilly. "She's a disgrace to us all. She'll be out of the door tomorrow."

"She's the best maid we've had in years," said Margaret.

"Lord Altamont will expel her from the town, anyhow," Mr. O'Reilly pronounced.

"She appears to have been a victim of circumstances," Brendan interjected.

"She had too much time off," Mrs. O'Reilly countered, before diverting into complaints about her ironing.

"She can't stay on in this house and that's for sure," Mr. O'Reilly concluded, and that was that.

The news which Brendan had brought back from the picnic was as disturbing to his father as it was to Lord Altamont, but for different reasons. The prosperity of the O'Reilly family was of fairly recent origins. Old Paddy O'Reilly, Brendan's grandfather, had kept a public house and general provision store down at the quay. He also had a schooner in the bay. The boat was employed in a regular provisioning business to the islands, particularly to Clare Island, but it also joined in the lucrative off-loading of contraband from France or Spain, as the opportunity arose. Old Paddy O'Reilly spent a lifetime making money but he never spent a penny on himself. However, he left a tidy fortune to his son, William, when he passed away just a week before his seventy-seventh birthday.

On the strength of this inheritance, Mr. William O'Reilly had acquired new premises in the town, at the corner of Quay Street and Church Lane. At first he lived over his new shop. But, as the business thrived and his children were born, he had purchased the largest house on the Mall, more becoming to a man now considered one of the wealthiest merchants in Mayo.

In the early years of the herring boom, Mr. William O'Reilly had seen the opportunity of getting into salt which he imported in rock form from Cheshire and ground and purified down at the quay. Next, he started a small manufactory making barrels for the salted herring and soon he had to expand this business because of the demand for barrels and firkins for the export of everything from pork to oats and butter. Then, just a few years ago, he had opened the first brewery in Westport and it was the brewery that made his fortune.

The family discussion about Sadie was interrupted by the arrival of John Palmer, a young solicitor who wished to see Brendan privately.

"I'll come straight to the point," he told Brendan when they were alone in the study. "I'm here to ask you to represent Hugh O'Malley at his trial. He is to be arraigned before the Grand Jury and not a single King's Counsel on the circuit is willing to represent him. Even your future brother-in-law, Charles Bourke, will not take the brief.

Brendan was taken aback by this request.

"I am the least experienced barrister in this area," he replied, while the difficulties of the situation ran through his mind. "And you must know that I was with the Prestons at Murrisk that day?"

"Of course, I do," said the solicitor. " And I see the difficulty. But O'Malley deserves a fair trial like anyone else and it's a scandal that no counsel is willing to represent him."

"Well, I agree with you there. Indeed it is quite disgraceful."

"The only evidence against him is the say-so of your Sadie – an immigrant from Armagh who has been terrified out of her wits. Of course they want to make an example of someone and O'Malley is an easy target. He's known to be a hot-head and the authorities would like to see the back of him. But he has never been in trouble before. They beat him to within an inch of his life in the barracks but they couldn't get a confession out of him. Even the lowest in the land is innocent until he is proved guilty."

Brendan paced the length of the study.

"You know that any effort on my part will make no difference to the outcome?"

"Probably not, but one has to try."

"The jury will all be Protestant?"

"Of course."

"Presumably all tenants of Lord Altamont?"

"That would be usual."

"And who will be appearing for the prosecution?"

"Probably Richard Synott. He usually gets these cases."

"The most experienced counsel in the West!"

"Of course he's experienced – but he has a weak case here."

"Any witnesses?".

"None that I know of."

"Identity?"

"Only what Sadie told them: that a red-headed Northerner had sent her to Preston's front door."

"And no confession?"

"My client swears he never said a word."

Brendan still demurred.

"You're really putting me in a spot here"

"You're the only person I could ask."

"Aren't you taking a risk yourself in taking a case like this?"

"Well, it won't add to my popularity in certain quarters but I am only upholding the Rule of Law."

"Well, give me a little time. I'll have to think about it. My own family is my first difficulty – but it's the Prestons I would be really worried about. Old Bonaventure has been seriously embarrassed in all this. He wants to see someone swing for it and he certainly won't appreciate any interference on my part. But leave it with me. I'll contact you very soon."

～～～～～ ● ～～～～～

Brendan knew that there was no point in discussing the proposal with his father. It was entirely understandable that Mr. O'Reilly would be opposed to any involvement, whatsoever, with the likes of O'Malley. As for his mother, she was already hysterical on the subject of Sadie and the very mention of O'Malley would be the last straw. That left his sister Margaret who, as he had long recognised, had a sound head on her shoulders. Later in the day, Brendan told her of John Palmer's request and sounded out her opinion.

"I can think of several reasons why you should NOT accept the brief," she said, "I presume no one else would take the case?"

"Exactly."

"So the whole profession will resent you taking the brief too?"

"I'm not worried about that."

"Father will be embarrassed and mother will be ashamed to show her face at Mass."

"Yes, that is a big consideration."

"So why are you hesitating? Why are you even thinking of taking the case?"

"I'm not anxious to take it. In fact, I don't want it at all. I didn't look for it. It came to me."

"Well, the Prestons will not look at it like that."

"No, I suppose not."

"And Pamela may not come to my wedding."

"Would she take it so personally? I am only doing a professional job."

"Of course they will all resent it. Look at it from their point of view. This man has not just stolen the guns. He has humiliated Mr. Preston in the eyes of Lord Altamont. They won't be satisfied until O'Malley is hung, drawn and quartered. And for you to intervene on his behalf! They will be utterly furious, I can assure you."

"Do you think I could explain to them?"

"No I don't. Do what you have to do but don't apologise to anyone. Anyhow the irony is that it won't make any difference. Whatever you do, O'Malley will be found guilty. He is certain to hang."

"Possibly so. But again, that's not the point."

"So what is the point? You seem to have your mind made up already."

"The point is me. I may be the most junior barrister in Mayo and, of course, one of the very few Catholics in the profession; but the problem has landed on my lap. If I refuse to represent O'Malley, I must admit to being a coward: to be afraid of what people will think of me even though I am performing my professional duty. I think it comes down to this: can I live with the possibility of O'Malley being hanged because I was afraid to lift a professional finger for him? Yes, that's my problem."

"Well, that's not how Pamela will look at it. She regards you as a friend. Perhaps something more than that. And you are going to take sides against her and her family. That's how she will see it. And so will all the Prestons."

"I know," Brendan conceded, looking quite dejected.

"Still and all," Margaret said, "I never realised I had such a brave brother."

And with that she gave him a peck on the cheek.

"Whatever you decide, your little sister will stand by you."

Chapter IV

HUGH O'MALLEY'S TRIAL

THERE WAS A huge interest in the O'Malley trial, which was held in Castlebar on the following Saturday. Outside the court as the crowd waited for the judge to arrive, Brendan kept his distance from the other wigs on circuit who were loudly chatting and exchanging raucous laughter.

The Prestons arrived in a trap driven by Stephen, with Bonaventure, Captain John and Pamela dressed more formally than ever he had seen her. Perhaps it was the small bonnet perched on her head. She looked very much the young lady

The trial did not occupy more than one hour's duration. There was evidence from Mr. Bonaventure Preston concerning the quantity and location of the guns. Mrs. Barton recounted the happenings on the day of the robbery and Owen Campbell confirmed that the prisoner had been in his public house that day. But Campbell denied that he had seen O'Malley leave or return around four o'clock. Sadie McCafferty was also persuaded to give evidence. She told in a halting voice that was little more than a whisper, of being asked to knock at the Preston's front door.

"And is this the man who sent you on that fateful errand?", asked the prosecutor, pointing accusingly at Hugh O'Malley.

"Yes," she answered almost inaudibly and without even lifting her downcast eyes. The whole world had collapsed for poor Sadie.

The final witness was Petty Constable Alex Dale. He gave evidence that he had been on duty in Murrisk that day and had seen the accused on or about four o'clock. He recalled him distinctly because of his bright red hair.

"He was carrying a heavy sack on his back at the time," the constable swore and the jury was duly impressed. So was the High Constable.

Brendan O Reilly was nervous as he took the floor and surveyed the forces ranged against him. He knew the cards were stacked against his client. The jury had been well chosen and was entirely Protestant. The judge glowered down at him conscious, no doubt, that he was isolated from his legal colleagues. He glanced up at Pamela but she looked as severe as the rest of the family. He was very much on his own as he gathered his thoughts and prepared to do battle. The strongest point in the Defence was that no one had seen O'Malley taking the guns so the evidence was completely circumstantial. His best hope lay in discrediting Constable Dale whose story was obviously concocted, presumably by the High Constable.

"Constable, you gave evidence that you saw Hugh O'Malley carrying a heavy sack outside Campbell's pub."

"That is correct, my Lord," he replied, facing the bench.

"And at what time was that?"

"At about four o'clock, my Lord."

"How did you know it was four o'clock?"

"Because the clock in Preston's yard had just struck four."

"Did you hear anything else from Preston's yard?"

Constable Dale hesitated. He had been briefed by the High Constable about the time but …

"Answer the question directly. Did you hear anything else from Preston's yard?"

"Nothing that I can remember."

"Did you not hear the bell tolling in Preston's yard some time later?"

"Oh yes, I did sir," he lied, "I had forgotten that."

"So you did hear the alarm being sounded?"

"Yes, I did."

"Well, if you heard the alarm, why didn't you go down to Preston's?", Brendan asked the constable while he faced directly to the jury. There was silence in the court. It was obvious that Constable Dale didn't know what to say but he was cunning enough to say nothing.

"I put it to you again Constable, why did you not go down to Preston's when you heard the yard bell tolling in alarm?" But still the constable held his silence.

"I put it to you that you are lying to the court and that you were not at Campbell's pub at four o'clock. I put it to you that you never saw Hugh O'Malley and you never heard the alarm from Prestons."

"Oh! That is not true, my Lord," the constable blurted out, now totally confused. "That's not the way it was at all."

"Then tell my Lord and the jury – in your own words – why you did not investigate when you heard the bell tolling from Preston's?" Again the constable hesitated and Brendan let him squirm. But suddenly the Judge intervened to save him from further embarrassment.

"We have heard the constable's evidence," he intoned. "It is up to the jury to decide whose word to take in this whole account." After an absence of only ten minutes, the jury found the prisoner guilty and Hugh O'Malley was capitally convicted.

Immediately O'Malley was led down, Brendan gathered up his papers and headed out of the court. He was disappointed but not surprised by the verdict and he had no wish to discuss it with anyone - especially not with the Prestons. But at the bottom of the steps from the Court House, there was Stephen holding the Preston horse and trap.

"Well, he got what he deserved " said Stephen "despite your best efforts."

Brendan stopped in his tracks. He should have ignored the comment but he was stung by the mocking tone and was still full of tension from the hearing.

"Wouldn't you be better advised to mind your own business," he replied grandly and, pulling his gown tight around him, proceeded to follow John Taylor across to Robinson's Hotel.

~~~~~~ • ~~~~~~

Outside the jail in Castlebar, on the wall facing onto the square, there is a narrow shelf or veranda at a height of about ten feet above the roadway. The floor of this steel structure is, in fact, a trap door which is controlled by a bolt inside the prison wall. Above, a gibbet sticks out at right angles to the grey stone face of the prison. As this was the most commonly used place of execution in Mayo, Hugh O'Malley was greatly surprised to find himself being conveyed under escort back to Westport after the trial. Of course, it didn't matter where the hanging was to take place but he knew that his chances of rescue from the Westport barracks were infinitely better than from the well-guarded prison in Castlebar. And his hopes were now entirely in rescue.

It was Lord Altamont who had decided to shift the hanging to Westport. He was determined to show – in as public a manner as possible – the fate that awaited all rebels, Defenders, United Irishmen, or any others who threatened the peace in Westport. He ordered a scaffold to be erected in the centre of that open area at the confluence of James Street, Shop Street and Quay Street in Westport which is called the Octagon. The time of execution was set for eleven o'clock on Wednesday morning – the Fair Day in Westport.

"Let them all see what happens to traitors and rebels in this county," he said. "There'll be no repeat of the Wexford rebellion in Mayo," he told the High Sheriff.

~~~~~~ • ~~~~~~

On Wednesday morning, they put the prisoner seated on an open cart, his hands tied behind him, his mop of red hair clearly visible to all and sundry. Alongside, six constables marched in uneven step. Mounted ahead of him, the High Sheriff and the High Constable rode side-by-side. It was an unusual sight for Westport and most of the citizenry turned out to see it approach from John's

Row, down Quay Street towards the Octagon.

From over the shop in Quay Street, Brendan O'Reilly looked out on the pathetic procession.

"This is meant to impress the populace," he said to his father, "but it may have a very different effect."

"An example had to be made," said Mr. William O'Reilly. "If they got away with this, what would they be up to next?"

"But they did get away with it," said Brendan. "They still have the guns "

"Well, it is a good warning to the rest of them," Mr. O'Reilly replied. "It will make them think twice before they plan any further adventures."

"I imagine revenge will be uppermost in their minds after this," said Brendan, to whom the sight of Mr. Denis Browne swaggering in his saddle was not the most pleasing.

"So what would you have done?", his father asked.

"Oh, I don't know," said Brendan. He never did. He liked arguing the toss but was never really convinced of any one side in an argument. "I think something less than hanging would have been more appropriate. They'll make a hero out of him now. It's a bad precedent for this town. I fear it will lead to much more trouble."

The clock on the market house was striking eleven as the procession made its way down Quay St with the High Sheriff forcing his way through the curious crowd.

"You should have drafted in more constables," he complained to the High Constable as his horse played up in all the commotion.

"The Fair Day's the problem," the High Constable replied. "The country people have never had such a spectacle."

But, even as he spoke, the crowd was suddenly scattering in all directions as an enraged bull came thundering down a side street, heading directly for the procession. And following close behind it, a herd of bullocks was stampeding out of control. There was panic on all sides but O'Malley was the first to see his chance and quickly sprang down from the cart. He dodged between the screaming crowd and, within seconds, was among friends and well hidden from the pursuing constables. By nightfall, he had been spirited away to Clare Island.

"By God, they'll pay for what they did to me," Hugh O'Malley swore to a small group of the lads who had organised his escape. "Mark my word, they'll rue this day."

"Altamont's the right bastard," one of them echoed.

"Yes and Tom Lindsay and Denis Browne. They all have it coming to them now. But we'll start at the beginning which is back to Preston," said O'Malley. "And I have an older score to settle too."

Hugh O'Malley was thinking of the day his father had been drowned. "Only for Bonaventure Preston, your father would be alive today," his mother had cried. "Mr. Preston put him off the oyster beds where he had every right to fish. Hadn't the O'Malleys fished there for generations?" The oyster beds were in Murrisk sound.

"Why was he put off the oyster beds?", the young boy had asked his tormented mother the day they brought back the bloated corpse.

"Because Mr. Preston wanted them all for himself," she replied bitterly. "That's why. That's why your father had to go fishing off beyond Clare Island. And that's why he was drowned."

The line of logic was indisputable to Hugh O'Malley. Old Preston had murdered his father and done his best to have him strung up by the neck. That was the first score to be settled.

~~~~~~ • ~~~~~~

Later that evening, Lord Altamont wrote an account of the whole affair to *Lord Castlereagh, the First Secretary in Dublin Castle. He expressed confidence that the guns would soon be recovered and didn't even mention the escape of Hugh O'Malley. But he dwelt in great detail on the difficulties caused by the influx of immigrants from the North and suggested a complete review of the security situation in view of the persistent rumours of a French invasion.

Lord Altamont's deepest ambition was to obtain an advancement in the peerage not, let it be said, for his own personal satisfaction, but for the sake of his only child, Howe Peter, whose mother (a daughter of Earl Howe, Admiral of the Fleet) had already spent much of her life at Court. Lord Altamont had not the least desire to leave his estates in the West of Ireland but he dearly wanted the advancement for his son and heir. This was part of his motivation in serving Lord Castlereagh so faithfully both in Mayo and when he was in the House in Dublin. The other was simply that he enjoyed the exercise of almost absolute power in the county, and he had no intention of letting the Binghams of Castlebar, or Sir Neal O'Donnell of Newport, or any of the other gentlemen of the county, prise it away from him.

But little did he realise how profoundly the long established tranquillity of his existence was to be so violently disrupted.

Chapter V

MARGARET'S WEDDING

AFTER A SLEEPLESS night, tossing and turning and worrying about what lay ahead, Margaret was drowsing on her wedding morning. She was under no illusions about her husband-to-be. He was marrying her for her money. Everyone said Charles Bourke was a brilliant lawyer and that a great future lay ahead of him. And the Bourkes were one of the oldest Catholic families in Mayo. Charles was already making his mark on the Western Circuit where the availability of a Catholic barrister was working to his advantage. But he was not well provided for and it would be some years before his income came to match the demands of the life to which he aspired. In this respect, Margaret O'Reilly had to be considered quite a catch. And Charles Bourke was pragmatic enough to acknowledge this. Margaret would also be presentable in Dublin society, which was important for a young barrister starting out on his career.

For Margaret, the real attraction in the marriage was the opportunity to move to Dublin. She longed for life in the capital, which she read about in the *Hibernian Magazine*, and followed its accounts of balls and soirees at the theatre with avid interest. Such were her thoughts as her brother entered her room and drew back the heavy curtains.

"Perfect day for a wedding," Brendan announced cheerfully as Margaret quickly pulled the linen sheet over her head. "Your breakfast is just coming up."

"What time is it?", Margaret asked.

"Oh, Just after nine. No hurry. But there is one big worry on this great day."

"What's that?"

"Well, will she or won't she?"

"What are you talking about?"

"Will Pamela come to the wedding or won't she?" Brendan laughed.

"Of course she will," said Margaret. "Didn't her aunt Olive send her a lovely new dress from Dublin?"

"I wish it was as simple as that. None of the family spoke to me after the trial – or indeed since."

"Oh, don't be ridiculous. It's not your fault that O'Malley escaped. And I'm sure he'll be behind bars again very soon."

"But while he's at large, they must be worried."

"If he's in Mayo he'll be found. If he's not, he is no threat to them , guns or no guns."

"Well, let's hope so. Ah, here comes your breakfast."

⁓⁓⁓⁓ • ⁓⁓⁓⁓

Almost seventy invitations for the wedding had been sent to friends and acquaintances of the two families and acceptances had been received from most of them. But in addition to this, a large number of tenants, customers, servants and employees had to be accommodated. Mrs. O'Reilly was determined to make this a memorable occasion in Westport and no expense had been spared. Fortunately, it was a warm August day and, long before noon, the whole Mall was crowded with smartly turned-out carriages, many decorated with favours and ribbons, and all sporting the finest horses in newly polished harness. A big crowd had gathered outside the church to view the carriages and the gentry in all their finery.

Back at the house after the ceremony, over one hundred people crowded into the O'Reilly residence, with the quality mounting the front steps to be greeted by the receiving line in the hall. The lower orders entered the side gate to the garden where long trestle tables, decorated with garlands of evergreen bowers and favours of all colours, had been laid out.

Brendan stood outside on the street directing some of the guests while keeping a look-out for the Prestons. At last he spotted Stephen driving the Preston chaise as he gently manoeuvred the two black ponies along the crowded Mall.

"I'm delighted you could come," Brendan blurted out as he helped Pamela to alight, before shaking hands with the Captain. Pamela was wearing her new empire-style dress of pale cream satin, her hair gathered above her head and interwoven with a string of pearls

"You look wonderful," he whispered to her. And he meant it.

Pamela smiled broadly as she moved ahead with her uncle towards the receiving line in the hall.

Two large drawing rooms, interconnected by folding-doors, had been practically denuded of furniture except for some chairs and some small tables along the walls.

Soon the wine was flowing and the guests, most of them needing no introduction to each other, were getting into the humour of this festive occasion. Father Egan arrived late from the church but just in time to hear the bride's health proposed by the best man. Charles replied with a typically pompous speech that was, however, roundly applauded. After that the toasts grew loud and furious and the gentlemen were in flying form by the time they moved across the hall where lunch was being served.

Out in the garden, four long trestle tables, each set for a dozen couples, were barely sufficient to accommodate the long list of retainers and country people that Mr. O'Reilly had insisted should be included in the celebrations. The men from the salt-works were there with their women, together with all the workers from the shop and several others from the Quay. There were at least a dozen tradespeople among the company and several labourers from O'Reilly's farm of land on the Newport road. Stephen too had been directed to the garden area, although he looked very elegant in a well-cut suit, presumably handed down by the Captain. He felt overdressed among the common company and he wondered would he feel out of place in the house as well. It was the most formal celebration he had ever attended.

At around three o'clock, the principal guests foregathered in the drawing room for the cutting of the cake, and the French window which gave out on to the balcony at the back of the house was thrown open for everyone in the garden to see the ceremony. Now it was Brendan's turn to say a few words and he invited Pamela on to the balcony so that everyone had a good view of the proceedings.

"There is an old Irish saying," said Brendan in a loud voice "which is more appropriate to this occasion than anything I could compose myself. So with it, I toast my new brother-in-law and my dearest, dearest sister."

"Slan agus saol agut
Bean ar do mbin agut
Teac gan cios agut
Agus bas in Eireann."

"What does it mean?", asked Pamela Preston who always had trouble with the native language.

"It can be translated as follows," Brendan explained.

"Health and life to you
The woman of your choice to you
A house without rent to you
And may you die in Ireland."

After the toast, Brendan took Pamela aside for a quiet word.

"I must explain about the O'Malley business."

"I thought you were very good in court."

"But seriously. I hope I didn't offend the family. I felt I had to do it – from a professional point of view. No one else would defend him."

"But Papa says he's now roaming the countryside with a small armoury of guns."

"Is he very angry with me?"

"Well, he was cross at first. But I think he understands a bit better now."

"You mean you spoke for me to him?

"Well, he talked of nothing else for a few weeks," Pamela laughed.

"And what about the Captain?"

"He's the practical member of the family. He and Stephen have been preparing for all eventualities at Murrisk Abbey. It's like a fortress now."

"Oh God. I am sorry."

"It's not your fault. You didn't help him escape. Anyhow, I'm sure he will be caught again soon."

"Should I talk to the Captain?"

"Perhaps not. He seems to be enjoying himself with that lady in the corner."

"Well, let's go into the garden?"

<hr />

Late in the afternoon, the newly weds prepared to take their leave. Mr. O'Reilly had arranged for the Dublin coach, which normally left from Robinson's Hotel across the Mall, to make a detour to the house for the bridal couple. The guests assembled on the steps and down onto the Mall and the crowd from the garden swarmed out in a wider circle to bid the couple God Speed for the last time. Margaret came down to the hall dressed in an all too crushable cherry velvet costume with matching bonnet.

"Good luck, little sister," whispered Brendan as he kissed her goodbye. Then Margaret was borne along towards the carriage, shaking hands and exchanging kisses on all sides. Mrs. O'Reilly hugged her for the last time and her father helped her into the coach where Charles was already ensconced. All the guests stood waving and smiling and cheering as the coach slowly moved off through the throng. As the coach rounded the end of the Mall, Margaret caught a glimpse of her mother at the bedroom window, alternately waving a small white handkerchief and dabbing it to her eyes.

<hr />

After the departure of the bridal couple, the party went on apace. The big hayloft over the stables at the end of the garden had been made ready for dancing and most of the common company repaired there to dance, to sing and to enjoy the music. Three fiddlers and two accordions made up the orchestra and it wasn't long before the whole building reverberated to jigs and reels and waltzes with the occasional rendering of a polka or polonaise – just to show how up-to-date Westport could be. Brendan invited Pamela to join the dancing and, as they entered the big hayloft, they were greeted with a hearty round of applause.

"Play that Polka again," Brendan called to the musicians and the crowd parted as he led Pamela to the centre of the floor. Stephen Allen watched them from the shadows. He had enjoyed an excellent dinner in the garden and had consumed several pints of O'Reilly's ale during the evening. He was feeling warm and mellow in himself and perfectly happy until Brendan started to dance with Pamela. At first, like the others, he admired the pure zest and elegance of the dancing couple as they faultlessly performed the polka up and down the length of the loft. But when they had finished and Brendan bowed to kiss Pamela's hand and everyone applauded, Stephen felt a pang of jealousy stab his heart. Without thinking about it, he found himself moving forward through the crowd and slowly crossing the floor until he stood directly in front of Pamela.

"May I have the next dance, please?" he heard himself saying. Pamela looked up in some surprise. Brendan too was taken aback but bowed gracefully and retired a step or two.

"But of course," said Pamela "I would be delighted."

And with that the musicians launched into the rendering of an Irish reel, and several other couples joined in the circle with Pamela and Stephen. At first they moved in and out, narrowing and then widening the circle all together. Then the group moved in a circular motion, first to the right and then back to the left, while they all tapped their toes and heels in unison. Then the circle broke up into couples and Stephen held Pamela tightly as the pace of the dance quickened up. He appeared totally in command but inwardly he was trembling. Pamela was wondering where Stephen had learnt such dancing but gradually she gave herself up to the music and the swirling and the whirling of the ever faster beat of the music. Finally it came to the climax of the reel and Stephen, tightening his firm arm behind her, lifted her off her feet completely and effortlessly swung her around in a full circle. Then he gently put her down and gave her a deep bow while the crowd raised the roof with their applause. But he didn't presume to kiss her hand.

Pamela was breathless as she made her way back to the house with Brendan.

Later on some of the guests, including Captain Preston, began to take their leave.

"I'm afraid we'll have to go," Pamela whispered to Brendan. "It's past bedtime for Uncle John."

"Well thank you again for coming," said Brendan. "And I hope you enjoyed the day."

"Of course we did. It was a wonderful party and Margaret looked so beautiful." Brendan escorted Pamela out to the carriage where Stephen was doing his best to get the Captain aboard. There was still a late evening light in the air as Brendan stood and waved until the carriage turned off the Mall.

In the dining room, the big mahogany table, now covered with trays of lemonade and of iced and sherry cobblers, had been pushed back against the window and several small tables had been set out for cards. In the back drawing room, the big window to the garden was closed again and quite a group was gathered near the harpsichord where Miss Jane McDonnell was playing. Some of the younger guests had gone to join the dancing in the loft and in the front room a group of men were discussing the disturbed state of the country in the wake of the recent rebellion in Leinster and the North.

"Well, let's drink to peace in the West," said Brendan determined to keep the party spirit going.

But even as some of the gentlemen were raising their glasses to this happy toast, they became aware of an unusual commotion outside on the Mall. Brendan moved to the hallway and saw an excited group gathered around Robinson's Hotel just across the Mall.

"What is it?", he called to a passer-by, who was however no wiser than the company inside. Some of the gentlemen then moved out onto the front steps, some standing on tiptoes, all looking over in the direction of the excitement and all asking each other the same question. Suddenly the group parted and a horseman came out at a gallop from the mail-coach yard.

"What is it? What is it?", they all shouted at him as he galloped past in the direction of Castlebar.

"It's the French," he called back. "It's the French. They've landed above in Killala."

Chapter VI

THE RACES OF CASTLEBAR

THE DAYS immediately following the French landing in Killala were ones of excitement and apprehension all over Mayo. Some said there were only a thousand of them. Others said ten thousand. A traveller from Erris swore that he had seen a whole flotilla off Blacksod Bay and this information was forwarded to Dublin Castle. Hundreds of men from all over the county were said to be joining the French but nobody was sure. Everyone was trying to guess in what direction they would march and how quickly the Crown forces would be brought up against them.

Mr. O'Reilly had read enough of the ravages of the French revolution to realise that no good could come to men of property from this violent invasion. But he was shrewd enough to keep his options open. To Lord Altamont he sent off a note offering whatever assistance (especially in provisioning) he could offer to His Majesty's forces during this emergency, not forgetting to pledge his undying loyalty in the usual fashion. At the same time he asked Brendan to ride over to Castlebar, a distance of fifteen miles, to appraise the situation there and report back.

"John Palmer will be well informed," he told Brendan, "but if there's any sign of the French come back immediately"

The following morning Brendan was about to set off when he met Captain John on the Mall .

"A capital party – the wedding that is," the Captain called out. My compliments to the family. And where are you off to?"

"Castlebar," Brendan replied. "My father wants the latest intelligence."

"Don't we all. A dastardly development. Could you take Stephen here with you? We all need to know what's going on."

"I'd be delighted," said Brendan who was anxious to build bridges with the Prestons.

"But don't delay over there. I need Stephen back at Murrisk as soon as possible."

By the time they got to Castlebar the place had already been transformed into an army camp. Whole fields outside the town walls were strewn with bivouacs and the paraphernalia of war. Word had already come through that the French had moved out of Killala, taken the town of Ballina and were expected to march south to Castlebar. The previous day, Major General Hutchinson, the military commander in Connaught, had marched up from Galway with Major General Trench and a large force of men. They saw the colours of the Kilkenny Militia and the Longford Militia and, closer to the town, the camp of the veteran sixth infantry regiment, perhaps two thousand men in all. And that was only the first impression. Passing into town, they came up to the fair green where they counted no less than eight heavy cannon and four lighter curricles drawn up in line ready to be repositioned at a moment's notice. Everywhere there were officers barking orders or galloping about with an air of importance. But surprisingly, they found the town's people very relaxed. The whole town seemed to be out of doors enjoying the excitement and observing the smartness of the military and their prancing horseflesh. When they arrived at John Palmer's house, however, they met a very different scene. The young lawyer was in a fever of activity, "preparing for the worst", as he put it.

Several men were battening up the lower windows while others were shifting furniture and stores all over the place.

"What word of the French?", Brendan asked him directly.

"Some say they number two thousand and that they are heading in this direction."

"Surely two thousand troops are no threat to the Crown forces fresh from their victories in Wexford? It seems a ludicrous force to be landed in the first place."

"Well, I'm taking no chances," Palmer replied. "This is a serious business and it could turn very nasty."

Stephen surveyed the house from top to bottom. Downstairs had been made ready as if for a siege. On the ground floor, tallboys and cupboards had been moved over against the shuttered windows which the workmen were battening on the outside, and several sacks full of stones from the river were ready to be placed behind the doors. Upstairs more provisions, candles, flints, buckets of water, ladders and an assortment of axes, slashers and other dangerous looking implements were carefully in place. Palmer, of course, had more reason than most to take extra precautions. The family house was at the very end of Bridge Street, in fact overlooking the river which formed the boundary of the town to the west and to the north.

"If the French ever do get here, they will like as not come over this very bridge," he told them while barely stopping in his work of supervising every detail of the preparations. "But the real fight will be above at Foxford. The French have to come through there on their way south and General Taylor is ready for them. He moved up there this afternoon with twelve hundred of the Yeomanry from

Sligo. And the Kerry militia and the Leicester Fencibles have gone up to reinforce him. I'll be surprised if the French ever get past Foxford. But I am taking no chances," he repeated.

Brendan felt a pang of disappointment. So near and yet so far. He hoped to get a glimpse at least of the French – this extraordinary detachment from the *Grand Armee* before which all Europe was tottering – and he wondered if he could ride up to Foxford. It was only nine miles distant. But Palmer wouldn't hear of it.

"Probably get yourself arrested," he scoffed. "Taylor is a tough man. Will put up with no nonsense. No, stay the night here, and see what the morrow brings. We should know a lot more by tomorrow."

Just then a detachment of mounted Fencibles came clattering down towards the bridge.

"That's General Trench moving the guns into position," said Palmer.

A few minutes later, a whole column of the Royal Artillery passed down over the bridge followed by the battalion guns, each now hitched to a pair of powerful ponies. And behind them came the tumbrels of ammunition clattering noisily on the cobblestones as they headed out on the Foxford Road. Brendan and Stephen followed them out of town for perhaps half a mile and watched as the guns were positioned astride the road from Foxford.

"God help the French," Brendan thought. "If they ever get past Foxford, they'll be blown to smithereens here."

~~~~~~~ • ~~~~~~~

Late that evening *General Lake and his suite arrived in Castlebar with instructions to assume overall command. He had ridden almost non-stop from Dublin and his humour was not improved by his first impressions in Castlebar. To General Lake's amazement, the town itself was entirely unfortified except for two curricle guns still positioned on the fair green. Despite the late hour, he called a council of war. He read out the details of his own appointment from *Lord Cornwallis, the Lord Lieutenant, and checked over every detail of the battle plan, the front line at Foxford, the siting of the guns and the disposition of the troops. Only then did this veteran rebel-hunter retire for a well-earned rest. And even that was short-lived.

Sometime in the middle of the night, Billy Dixon, a loyal yeoman from Barren, galloped breathless to the town gate with remarkable information. He claimed to have seen French troops coming south through the mountain pass of Barnageely. They were bypassing Foxford altogether. The night watch would not believe him at first but the guard was roused. Lamps were lit. Maps called for and consulted once again. The yeoman was cross-questioned intensely.

There are two possible routes from Ballina to Castlebar. The high road, indeed the only real road, runs east of the intervening mass of water, Lough Conn, and through Foxford. But there is another way to the west of the lake, which is nothing more than a mountain pass. Was it possible that the French were coming that way? Reluctantly, it was decided to wake General Lake.

"Damn, damn, damn," the General swore loudly. "Why were no pickets posted to guard that pass?" He slipped his watch from his waistcoat. It was exactly 4 a.m.

"Pray God we have time," he muttered as he pulled on his boots and strode swiftly to his waiting mount. He wanted to see for himself and within minutes he was galloping out into the morning mist.

The dawn was just breaking when General Lake came cantering back with the escort as fast as their mounts could carry them. There was no doubt about it. The French had taken the mountain road and were coming in the back way to Castlebar. The French *General Humbert was a clever fox. But there was still time. He ordered the general alarm to be sounded.

By five-thirty, fresh orders had been issued and new dispositions made. Major Alcock and Captain Shorthall worked wonders with the artillery. The six-pounders were drawn away from the Foxford road and repositioned on Sion Hill facing the mountain road less than a mile outside the town. To the left of the road were four of the heavy cannon and, to the right, two lighter curricles. By six-thirty, General Lake's forces were in position behind them, drawn up in two parallel lines with the cavalry in between. In the front line were the Kilkenny militia, a detachment of the sixth infantry regiment and the Prince of Wales Fencibles. Behind were the Longford militia, the Fraser Fencibles and the Galway yeomanry. It was a very strong defensive position and it was now the turn of the French to be surprised.

In Castlebar there was bedlam on the streets. A few merchants with their families managed to get out onto the Tuam road to the south. Others looked to their property and John Palmer's precautions of yesterday were emulated the length of Bridge Street and beyond. But few people really believed that the French would get past Sion Hill.

Stephen wanted to go abroad in the town but his host firmly refused.

"Our doors will not be opened before the end of this day," Palmer said firmly. "But come up on the roof if you wish. I have got a good eyeglass and you can see the action from there."

And it was from that vantage point that Stephen Allen and Brendan O'Reilly saw the famous battle for Castlebar, the latter's account of which afterwards appeared in the *Dublin Evening Post*, and was, in fact, the instrument for his finding employment with that paper.

~~~~~~~ • ~~~~~~~

"Take a look at this," said John Palmer, handing the eyeglass to Brendan. It was now about eight o'clock. "I believe we are going to see some action."

Brendan peered through the eyeglass just as General Humbert and his suite breasted a ridge about a thousand yards distant below Sion Hill. From there the French general examined the Royal position and the formidable force to which he was opposed. Strangely, the church bell of St Auden's Church of Ireland, which had been tolling all morning since the alarm was first raised, now fell silent and an extraordinary hush fell over the whole town and the battlefield itself. But this was short-lived. Soon after General Humbert had surveyed the scene, three columns of Blue (these were Irish insurgents in French uniforms) breasted the ridge and immediately the Royal artillery opened fire.

"They are falling like ninepins," Brendan cried as he saw the havoc wrought by the cannon. "The poor devils are being blown to bits."

Palmer took the eyeglass and observed the confusion in the Irish ranks. "They are retreating already," he said. "I knew they were no match for the Crown forces."

But soon the Blues advanced again, and again the guns struck the columns with similar precision. About fifty of the French, however, rushed forward and got under cover of a house, but the main body was obliged once more to retire and reform. Again they advanced, this time driving cattle ahead of them in the hope of gaining some protection from the withering fire of the cannon. But again the guns spat out in deadly fashion. The Blues fell back again, this time in disarray, leaving behind a terrible carnage of bleeding, groaning and dying bodies.

"It's all over," shouted Palmer. "It's a victory for the artillery. What can any troops do in the face of such murderous fire?"

Through the eye-piece Brendan saw dreadfully mutilated men and bodies, some limbless, some headless, oozing Irish blood onto ill-fitting blue French uniforms. Some were still alive and crying out piteously. But their usefulness was past. Nobody answered their pleas for help. He passed the eyeglass to Stephen whose eye settled on one poor peasant whose leg had been badly damaged and who was trying to regain the French line. He thought he had enough strength to hop at first but he soon collapsed on the ground again. Then he dragged himself on his good side, glancing back all the time in the direction of the guns. What he obviously feared most of all was a charge by the cavalry, and the dread of a sabre thrust gave him the strength to keep going. Then Stephen saw him raise himself again in an effort to stand, supporting himself now on an upturned musket. But the unfortunate creature caught the eye of a marksman positioned just behind the cannon and Brendan saw him suddenly throw his arms in the air as he was propelled forwards and upwards for a moment before falling dead.

Stephen put down the eyeglass, convinced that the French were finished.

"It is all over," Palmer repeated as he surveyed the scene with a detachment that surprised his friends. "I told you they never stood a chance."

But the French were not so easily discouraged. General Humbert had used his Irish adherents as cannon fodder while studying the dispositions of the enemy. His own troops he had kept in reserve. Now he switched tactics entirely and, out of view of the Crown forces, redeployed rapidly from his centre. He spread out his veterans in a single thin file, fixed bayonets and once again advanced over the ridge. Extended like this, the French were, of course, cruelly exposed to a cavalry charge. But the cavalry were not ordered forward and instead the defenders made their first but fatal mistake. Instead of allowing the enemy to close, the militia regiments opened a useless fire at a distance that was quite ineffective.

To Brendan's delight, the French then rushed forward and seized some hedges in front of General Lake's line and commenced extending rapidly with the intention of outflanking the Militia. At the same time, the two curricle guns that the French had dragged over the mountains came into play and wrought serious damage on the Kilkennys and the Longfords behind them. And this was the first flank to waver.

General Humbert had also sent a detachment to his right with the intention of joining the Newport road and possibly forcing an entry to the town from that direction. But the Longfords, suddenly spotting these Hussars almost behind them, took fright and started to retreat towards the town. This wavering became infectious and, within minutes, the Kilkennys were following them, leaving the guns exposed and undefended. Then, with a roar, the insurgents bounded up the hill and the French bayonets wrought terrible slaughter.

⁓⁓⁓⁓ ▮ ⁓⁓⁓⁓

The fiercest fighting now shifted to the bridge below Palmer's house. Brendan had seen a glimpse of the French Hussars off to his left; he had seen the Longfords and then the Kilkennys on top of Sion Hill waver under fire and then start to withdraw; and he had seen this retreat turn into a rout. And now, directly below him, he saw such scenes of horror and terror, of savagery and gallantry as he would never witness again.

"Surely they'll hold the town!", Brendan shouted as he watched the Redcoats streaming back across the river, some in total panic having discarded their arms, others supporting their wounded comrades as best they could, but all intent on one thing only – to distance themselves as far as possible from the pursuing French.

"If they don't hold that bloody bridge," Palmer cursed, "we're all in trouble." The lawyer entertained no romantic notions of the French and was beginning to realise the perilousness of his position.

But not all the troops succumbed to the general panic. Captain Chambers, who earlier had tried to stem the rout of the Longfords, now formed a small party determined to defend this vital entry to the town. Supported by a curricle gun, the only one saved from the battlefield, his men held back the advancing French until their ammunition ran out.

And now Brendan, for the first time, got a real taste of what battle is all about. The earlier movements of this bloody encounter had been at a distance and played out for him as if on stage. But now he could see the hand-to-hand combat, could hear the incessant crack of the guns above the roars and shouts of the men, could smell the acrid smell of the powder discharged. But it was the little incidents which remained in his mind afterwards – like that of the four Galway Yeomen trapped on the far side of the river. One by one they ran for the bridge. The first was shot down by French snipers now infesting the buildings facing the bridge, as was the second and the third. Brendan could see the fourth, crouching below the wall. He could almost feel his terror. Should he run or should he stay? Should he risk death now or take his chances as a prisoner of the French? Suddenly he burst forth and the bullets spattered off the roadway all round him. But this was a canny fellow. He pitched himself forward in an erratic bouncing gait, zigzagging this way and that, leaping and dodging as if his feet were on hot coals. And miraculously he made it to the other side. A great cheer went up from the town side as he reached safety – but the diversion was only momentary.

"For God's sake keep your head down!" shouted Palmer who was now lying flat under the parapet.

But Brendan was too tantalised to listen. He was now caught up in the sheer excitement of it all and he found himself cheering or gasping or groaning as his attention focussed momentarily on this or that part of the drama below. He could now see the swarthy faces of the French marksmen in the buildings across the river loading, aiming and firing with cool precision. For the first time, he felt in physical contact with these sons of the Revolution.

⁓⁓⁓⁓ • ⁓⁓⁓⁓

The Crown forces defending the bridge were now exposed to crossfire both from the roads leading to it and from the houses on either side. The men often fell back but they were rallied time and again by their officers. At length, most of the Royal Irish artillery who worked the curricle having been killed or wounded, the gun fell silent and the French were able to push forward a body of cavalry whose charge finally cleared the last vestiges of resistance. His Majesty's forces then fled the town from the south gate, leaving behind them at least ten guns, all their colours and ammunition, and several hundred men dead, dying or deserted. Such was their panic that they remained on the run until they reached Tuam twenty miles to the south – which is why this military encounter was ever after referred to locally as the Races of Castlebar.

⁓⁓⁓⁓ • ⁓⁓⁓⁓

That night General Humbert and his officers held a celebration which was attended by many leading Papists in the town, including John Palmer.

"As long as they control Mayo," he remarked to Brendan, "it's as well to keep on terms with them."

But neither Stephen nor Brendan joined the party. The mood had changed as they watched the wounded and the dying being brought in from the battlefield. They were carried in on open carts and hay bogies and on gun carriages: men in blue uniforms and red uniforms and no uniforms at all, some bandaged, some bleeding, some stretched out so stiff that it was hard to know whether they were dead or alive.

Very early the next morning the two men rode back to Westport. Palmer had learnt that General Humbert had no intention of chasing the Crown Forces south but intended sweeping east to threaten the capital. But whichever way he went hardly mattered to Stephen. The reality was that he was leaving behind him a state of anarchy in county Mayo.

As soon as Stephen got back to Murrisk, the whole family sat down to digest the alarming news from Castlebar. What it meant, in effect, was that the French were now masters of all Mayo, but, with so few troops on the ground, there was no one to enforce law and order in the county. Captain John's first impulse was to clear out while it was still possible to do so. He was particularly anxious for Pamela. But other counsels soon prevailed. Bonaventure argued strongly against flight and what finally persuaded him to stay put was the conviction that he could not desert his own people. Right out along the coast to Louisberg and beyond there were loyalist families depending on his leadership and his example. If he fled, the whole district would be left open to anarchy. But he agreed that Pamela should be evacuated to safety and Stephen undertook to work out a plan with some Protestant families in the area. Captain John turned his mind to improving the "defences", as he called them at Murrisk Abbey and Pamela remarked that he appeared to be in better form that he had been for years.

Chapter VII

REVENGE AT MURRISK

AFTER THE BATTLE of Castlebar, there was a period of great tension in and around Westport. Out in the country, the lads were quick to exploit the sudden collapse of authority and to settle a few old scores. As luck would have it, Lord Altamont was in Dublin and only his cellar had been rifled before the arrival of Captain Boudet from General Humbert's staff who posted a watch on the great house. However, Mr. Denis Browne, the High Sheriff, was not so fortunate. His fine seat at Mount Browne was gutted and its contents entirely destroyed. Palmerston House, the home of Sir Edmund Browne, was also severely damaged, as was Deal Castle, the seat of Mr. James Cuffe, the Lieutenant Colonel of the North Mayo Militia. Later a total of £8,903 was paid in compensation to about two score of gentlemen in Mayo for loss or damage to their property, furnishings and livestock. Lord Altamont received £719 for losses of wine, cattle, corn, provisions and side arms. Considering all the circumstances, the damage could have been very much more.

Captain John Preston had served in the Royal Navy for over twenty years and had seen action with Admiral Rodney when Martinique was taken in '62. He had also been commended by Earl Howe after the Chesapeake Bay expedition in '77. So he was not without military experience. His first initiative after the Castlebar rout was to move Stephen Allen in from the stable yard. He quartered him in the gun room, tutored him in the loading and firing of muskets, and, much to Stephen's delight, designated him as his deputy in all matters of defence.

Because of the danger to sheep, the dogs at Murrisk Abbey were normally locked up at night. The red setter, an old favourite, was allowed the comfort of the main house and had a basket in the big kitchen. But the Labradors and the Wolfhounds (a spotted variety specially bred by Lord Altamont) were normally confined to the stable yard. Now, however, Stephen left them out at night, tethered with long ropes. Naturally, they had been barking at anything that came within sight or sound of the house, and even Mrs. Barton had been complaining. But Stephen kept an eye to them while he did his nightly round after shuttering all the ground-floor windows and bolting all doors.

⁓⁓⁓⁓ • ⁓⁓⁓⁓

As soon as he heard of the landing at Killala, Hugh O'Malley and a few of his closest mates made their way north to join the French and his basic knowledge of the language made him immediately useful to the invaders. He was amongst those who guided General Humbert over the mountain pass to Castlebar and even managed to be decorated by the General after that stunning victory over the Crown forces. Cleverly, he also managed to lay his hands on a considerable quantity of the military supplies abandoned by General Lake's retreating army. These he sent to be hidden with the Murrisk muskets in a souterrain on an island in the middle of Moher Lake just south of Westport.

When General Humbert moved out of Castlebar, O'Malley summoned a few of the lads to meet him in a tavern on the quay in Westport. There he outlined the first stage in his plan to take control of the whole peninsula west of Westport itself – an attack on the Preston residence in Murrisk. But at first there were some objections to this particular target.

"Old Preston's not the worst of 'em," Johnny Gibbons objected. "Let's do the town first? I'd like to get me hands on Lindsay."

"That can follow," said O'Malley. "Once we clear out the Prestons, the whole county back to Louisburgh and beyond is as good as ours. After that we can move into the town."

"There's wimmin in dat house," said John Kirwan. "What about dem?"

"They'll come to no harm," O'Malley assured him. "As soon as they hear the first shots, they will be out of there like bats out of hell."

"So why use the guns at all?", young Kirwan persisted.

"Just to frighten them out," O'Malley replied. "It's the house we want burnt to the ground."

And so they finalised their plan.

⁓⁓⁓⁓ • ⁓⁓⁓⁓

The following night, just before midnight, six men met in the yard behind Campbell's pub. Each was carrying a musket fully primed and two ale bottles full of paraffin oil and a taper. Each man had his instructions. The drill had been gone over carefully. There were to be no mistakes. As a final touch, Hugh O'Malley smeared some mud on each man's face although it was a moonless night. O'Malley and two of his men went down the avenue heading for the front of the Preston residence. Johnny Gibbons and two others went down the laneway to the back. And Jack Kirwan with Jim O'Dowd went through the fields, skirting the yard, until they reached the haybarn. The attack was to start on the stroke of midnight. But they hadn't counted on Stephen's outer defences.

As soon as the dogs heard O'Malley's men approaching, they started barking and growling and pulling at the extremity of their long leads.

"At the first stroke of twelve, shoot the bastards," O'Malley ordered and his command was whispered from one man to the next. And just as the old clock in the stable yard began the chimes of midnight, six muskets rang out and the dogs fell squealing and whining to a bloody death. But they had served their purpose.

The house was now fully alarmed, and the men inside were reaching for their muskets before the echoes of the shots had died out across the bay. Outside, the men were reloading their guns – an exercise which, in the dark, took them much longer than expected. And this delay was of great advantage to the defenders. By the time O'Malley and his men were ready to light the tapers and rush at the house, the Prestons were well poised to receive them, Bonaventure at the front and the Captain with Stephen at the back of the house.

At a shout from O'Malley, the men ran forward all together carrying their lighted bombs. The Captain let them come until one dark figure was square in his sights. As he discharged the musket, he saw his man topple and fall. Stephen too fired but almost at the same moment he heard the shattering of glass as several incendiary devices burst into the upper windows. Bonaventure too had fired but his target had zig-zagged as he came on and the shot scrapeed over the man's shoulder.

"Pamela, quick – the sand buckets," the Captain ordered, as he ran along the corridor through the smoke that was already gathering at the top of the stairs. He pulled off his coat as he ran, beating at the flames and stamping on the smouldering carpet. Stephen emptied the sand buckets that had been stored along the corridor for exactly such an emergency, but the flames seemed to start up in every direction.

"They're coming again," the Captain warned as he saw the bobbing lights approach out of the bushes at the back, and again the defenders went to their guns. Captain John and Stephen crouched low down behind the window ledge and steadied their muskets on the crosspane. But Bonaventure lacked such caution born of military training. Standing in the middle of the window at the top of the stairs, he forgot that the flames behind him silhouetted his form to the front. Hugh O'Malley saw him there and, sending his two men zig-zagging with their bombs to the two extremes of the house, he advanced slowly in the total darkness until he could almost see into the old man's eyes.

For a moment O'Malley stared at him while he thought of his own father and his mother's oft repeated lament: "Only for Bonaventure Preston, your father would be alive this day."

In front of him stood his father's "murderer", a grotesque form appearing larger than life in the flickering light of the flames. O'Malley took careful aim and pulled the trigger slowly. Old Bonaventure never knew what hit him. He fell forward, through the shattered window and his body thumped heavily onto the flagstones below. He was dead before he hit the ground. It was not yet five minutes after twelve. O'Malley then whistled three times through his teeth. It was the order to withdraw.

The fire had now taken a good hold at both ends of the house and the old timbers were crackling and snapping as the flames jumped ever higher in the air. But over in the yard an even greater conflagration was raging. O'Malley's men had sprinkled oil all round the haybarn and around the bases of the three huge ricks of straw and along the walls of the old wooden buildings. Now the flames were crackling up all round them, shooting great fountains of sparks into the sky and lighting up the night for miles around. Later it was said that the glow could be seen even in Westport.

Captain John came bursting out the front door, coughing and choking, but with a firm grip on Pamela, who ran along beside him. Stephen rushed out behind him only to see old Bonaventure splayed out face downwards on the flagstones.

"Get the Master, Stephen," Captain John ordered, as he stumbled away from the house, still coughing and retching from the dense smoke that seemed to follow him out of the doors. "And get water, form up a chain, get all the men. The house must be saved."

And with that he collapsed on the lawn, still trying to clear his lungs and to comfort Pamela who was now hysterical. Stephen bent down to pick up the Master and his stomach heaved when he saw that the old man's face had been literally torn to pieces by the shot, the flying glass and the force of the fall. He slipped off his own coat and covered the old man's head and torso. Then he carefully lifted him in his arms and carried him down to the end of the lawn where he laid him gently on his back away from the glaring light of the fire. Since he could first remember, the Master had personified the security, the continuity, and the certainty in his life. It would be hard to think of Murrisk without the Master.

Then suddenly he heard a shout from the crowd that had gathered and, looking back, he saw Mrs. Barton standing in the landing window above the hall door.

"Jump, woman, jump," Captain John shouted to her but Mrs. Barton stood there as if transfixed, the flames and smoke billowing all around her.

"Jump, for God's sake, jump," he repeated, now springing to his feet. But still the old housekeeper stood there, frozen in terror.

The Captain hesitated no longer. Drawing one great breath he bounded in the front door and up the stairs to the landing. The crowd now surged forward, forsaking the water chain, seized only with the personal drama. For a moment an extraordinary hush fell amongst them and only the roar of the fire could be heard in the night air. Then the Captain appeared at the window behind Mrs. Barton and the whole throng burst into a fury of cheering and clapping and even waving, as if they were at the races. But the drama was not yet over. The flames were closing inexorably from the wings of the house and Captain John realised that he had no hope of retreating down the stairs again. Instead, he kicked out what remained of the window frame and, seizing the terrified and still resisting Mrs. Barton by the wrists, lowered her down the house front as far as he could stretch and then let her drop.

Despite the intense heat, Stephen ran forward and although he didn't manage to catch the old housekeeper, he broke her fall as she fell and they both tumbled to the ground. Within seconds he had pulled her to safety.

Now it was the Captain's turn. Again the throng looked up, mouths open, hearts beating as they waited, rooted in horror and apprehension for the man who had risked his life for the housekeeper.

"Get some ladders," Stephen shouted. And several young lads ran off together to the yard to find the ladders.

"Hold on," Stephen roared up to the Captain, cupping his mouth in his hands trying to make himself heard above the roar of the fire.

For a moment it looked as if the Captain would attempt to lower himself from the window-sill, but the flames were now licking all round him and he was unable to get a grip. There was a flower-bed to the right below and Stephen now saw the Captain set his eye on this, draw back for a moment and then propel himself forward as best he could. But the heel of his boot caught in the window frame and, instead of jumping up and out, the Captain tumbled straight down on to the flagstones below.

He landed with a thump that Stephen instinctively knew must be fatal, but he rushed forward to drag the Captain away from the burning building. There was still some life in him. The Captain opened his eyes. It was obviously an effort for him to concentrate, but for the moment he seemed to focus on the faces staring down at him.

"Stephen," he said more in a hiss than a whisper. Stephen bent his ear closer to the prostrate form.

"Get Miss Pamela out of here," the Captain continued with difficulty, and his eyes moved slowly to his niece. "Get her to Dublin....To Aunt Olive." He raised his hand. "And take my ring... my Claddagh ring..."

Stephen bent down even closer to the Captain but he couldn't make out another word. He felt the Captain's fingers tighten on his for a moment – and then he was gone. He whispered a prayer into his ear and then closed the lids on his eyes. Finally he eased the heavy gold ring from the Captain's finger and placed it on his own right hand. Murrisk would never be the same again.

Chapter VIII

THE FLIGHT TO DUBLIN

VERY EARLY the following morning, Brendan was awoken by his father in an agitated state.

"There's been trouble out at Murrisk Abbey," he said. "A big fire, I believe."

"Who brought the news?"

"Fishermen down at the Quay."

"I'll ride out immediately," Brendan said as the wildest thoughts raced through his head.

"I'll send some men after you. God knows what help they may need."

Brendan galloped out along the coast road. A heavy mist hung over Croagh Patrick, but long before he got to Murrisk he could smell the smouldering aftermath of the fire in the morning air. When he got to Campbell's shebeen he found groups of locals standing around in curious wonderment, but Brendan pushed his mount through to the avenue that led to the house. Or what had been the house. As he emerged from the wall of giant rhododendron lining the avenue, he was faced with only the gutted and roofless remains of Murrisk Abbey. Smoke was still rising from the interior but it was obvious that everything had been destroyed.

Brendan dismounted and led his horse around to the yard where he saw Stephen and Malcolm the farm manager and several of the farm-hands standing around.

"It's as bad as could be," Stephen told him directly. "The Master and the Captain are both dead."

"My God. And Pamela?"

"Thank God, she's safe. I'm taking her to Dublin as soon as she's ready."

Since day-break, Stephen had been trying to cope with the situation with Malcolm. They agreed plans for the immediate burial of the Master and Captain John in the nearby Friary and for word to be sent to Aunt Olive in Dublin.

Obviously it was unsafe for Miss Pamela to stay in Murrisk and they agreed that Stephen would get her to Dublin.

"Is that safe?", Brendan asked when informed of the plan.

"It's not without risk. But she can't stay here."

"She could come into Westport with us."

"Who's to say she would be safe in Westport? With those armed gangs on the loose, nowhere is safe."

"Still, the roads are even more hazardous."

"We have to take that chance. And, besides, it was the Captain's last command."

Stephen then told Brendan the terrible details of the previous night while Malcolm continued to saddle the horses.

A few minutes later Mrs. Barton appeared from the dairy with Pamela and Brendan could see that she was still in a state of shock – her appearance not enhanced by the boy's clothes in which she was now attired.

"I said to Stephen that you might be safer in Westport," Brendan said.

But she didn't reply. He wondered if she had even heard him.

"Keep your wits about you," Malcolm warned Stephen." And avoid the French whatever you do. Don't stop till you get to Ballinrobe tonight. Micky Roche will look after you there if *The Robe* is full. Don't let Miss Pamela out of your sight. And keep a close eye to the horses."

Stephen was only half listening to Malcolm. He was anxious to get going while the day was still fresh. He was confident he could get Miss Pamela to Dublin safely and God help any man who stood in his way. In his saddlebag he carried a blunderbuss fully primed.

"So let's be off then," he said almost brusquely as he swung his strong frame into the saddle and *Jock* began to play up on the cobbled yard. Pamela hugged good-bye to Mrs. Barton and Malcolm helped her to mount the mare. Finally she turned to Brendan:

"If you would be kind enough to see to the funerals, I would be much obliged to you. I hope to see Margaret in Dublin but, like my Aunt Olive, I never want to see Mayo again."

And with that they moved off.

Stephen made a brief stop when they reached Belclare, just outside Westport. They both dismounted for a few minutes while he checked the girths and stirrup leathers again and examined the shoes of both horses in turn. Then they skirted Westport and turned towards Partree, that little village that nestles between Lough Carra and Lough Mask on the Castlebar to Ballinrobe high road. Stephen did not slacken the pace. He was determined to reach Ballinrobe that night – a distance from Murrisk of about thirty miles.

As they approached Partree, however, they found the village devastated by the retreating army and totally deserted. Hardly a cabin on the road remained standing although the remnants of some were still smouldering. Stephen and Pamela rode side by side through the village, walking their horses as they looked warily around them. But there was not a soul to be seen. The few buildings at the cross-roads had been wrecked, their doors and windows smashed in. The street itself was littered with every assortment of rubbish and debris as if a hurricane had deposited the smashed contents of the village on the road. A dead horse, its legs grotesquely stiff in the air, lay near the cross-roads, a swarm of bottle flies buzzing all round it. The stench was awful.

"Do you think we should turn back?", Pamela asked tentatively. It was the first time she had spoken since leaving.

"Not at all," Stephen replied firmly. "There's no security in Murrisk now and we don't know where the French are marauding. We must push on to Ballinrobe. I want to get there before dark."

Pamela didn't question his decision. In fact she found herself reassured by his decisiveness.

And so they rode on, skirting Tooreen on their right, and crossing over the Keel Bridge at the point where Lough Carra flows into the great Lough Mask by an underground river. Everywhere they saw the devastation created by the retreating loyalist army, hedges broken down, fields of corn trampled to the ground, wheel-less carts discarded by the way, and the litter of desperate soldiers and their camp followers on all sides. It was almost seven o'clock when they finally reached Ballinrobe, tired and hungry, but silently grateful to have completed the first day of their journey.

Stephen dismounted and led the horses to each of the three inns that Malcolm had named but all of them were packed out with refugees from Castlebar. *The Robe* had been commandeered by the militia for the wounded and, although a lot of the refugees had already pushed on to Tuam, all the inns were packed to the rafters. It must have been a couple of hours later before Stephen found Mickey Roche, the horse dealer from Westport, in O'Reilly's ale-house. Mickey directed them to O'Donovan's, a small but clean-looking cottage on the Tuam Rd.

"Mention my name and they'll look after you. You can stable your horses at *The Robe*" he said.

Stephen did as directed. He stabled the two horses at *The Robe*, unsaddled them, rubbed them down, and watered them himself, before leaving them in the care of the yard-man who smelled so strongly of whiskey that Stephen most reluctantly gave him the customary sixpence. Then he walked down with Pamela to O'Donovan's where the name of Micky Roche did the necessary.

But disaster awaited them in the morning. Denis Murphy, the proprietor of *The Robe*, was a former Volunteer and proud of the quality of service at his establishment. But he denied all responsibility when an angry Stephen confronted him with the news that his mare had been stolen from the yard during the night.

"Read the notice for yourself," he said brusquely. "It's written up there in black and white. NO RESPONSIBILITY FOR ARTICLES OR ANIMALS LEFT ON THE PREMISES."

"And where were you all night, young man?", he asked rounding on Stephen. "Don't you know the whole town is full of brigands and deserters and scavengers of all sorts? It behoved you to look after your own property. Don't come blaming me for your own carelessness. You are lucky they didn't take the big horse while they were at it."

And with that he turned on his heel, muttering about the state of the country, and leaving Stephen feeling deeply ashamed. But Pamela was surprisingly good-humoured about it as they rode off, both now mounted on big *Jock*. Although she said she was stiff after the long ride yesterday, Stephen thought she was looking more cheerful. She showed more interest in what was going on and in the people they passed and she even began to tell Stephen about Aunt Olive in Dublin.

Astride the horse's rump, Pamela at first tried holding on to the back of the saddle but, especially when the horse was trotting, she found it difficult to maintain her balance. So she took a grip on Stephen's coat and tried to keep in unison with his rise and fall in the saddle. But it didn't work and she wasn't comfortable.

"Put your arms around my waist and hold on tight," Stephen ordered in a firm voice over his shoulder while putting *Jock* into an easy canter. She did as she was told and they swayed together with the steady motion of the horse. At first too she kept her face pointing forwards so that her chin sometimes just tipped his shoulders, but after a little while she turned her head and rested her cheek on his broad back, tucking into him as tightly as she could.

Stephen pretended to concentrate entirely on the horse and on avoiding the crush of travellers of every description now streaming towards Tuam. But in fact he was conscious of every movement of her body, every tightening of the delicious encirclement of his waist and every touch of her cheek on his back. Once, when *Jock* shied with a sudden start on the road, Pamela had to tighten her hold to maintain her balance. Stephen wished the animal would shy again and he hated those periods when they slowed to a walk and Pamela relaxed her grip for even a few seconds. Sometimes he thought that she tightened her hold on him unnecessarily and a surge of ridiculous pleasure ran through every nerve in his body. At others, he stole a glance at her long fingers entwined firmly together and he had to resist the desire to clasp them within his own. Then suddenly he had a wild idea and succumbed to it on the spur of the moment.

"You take the saddle now, Miss Pamela," he ordered as he pulled up. He threw one leg over *Jock's* head and slid to the ground. "It will be easier for you and will give *Jock* a change of weight," he added in a serious tone.

And before Pamela could consider otherwise, he had helped her to move forward into the saddle and had jumped up behind her. Stephen then took the reins so that Pamela was cradled between his arms while his whole frame protected her from behind. Now the proximity of her body, the fleeting touch of her hair and her inimitable scent were pure intoxication to him

And suddenly he was reminded of that terrible day last summer. Pamela was out riding with Margaret O'Reilly, and Stephen, who had been required to accompany them, was left with the horses when the girls decided to walk on ahead. They had been chasing butterflies above Leckanvy on the slopes of Croagh Patrick for barely ten minutes when Stephen first heard the screams. Both girls were screaming but Stephen could hear Pamela's cry distinctly. Hers was a shriek of real terror and it sent a cold stab through his heart. When he caught up with the girls, he saw Pamela on the far side of a little stream literally covered by a swarm of wasps. Pamela had disturbed a wasp's nest on the bank and the wasps had attacked her from all sides.

Stephen splashed across the stream and, grabbing hold of Pamela, pulled her back into a pool of water. She was still screaming hysterically and the angry insects now entangled in her clothes and even in her hair were stinging her furiously. Stephen submerged her almost completely in the mountain water and held her there until the wasps were all drowned. But she had been badly stung and was severely shocked. So he took her up in his arms and carried her gently down the hill. And as he held her close to his chest, her wet clothes clinging to her tormented body, her slender frame still convulsed with sobs, Stephen breathed in the aroma that was Pamela, her favourite *Rose of Damascene*. And from that time onwards, the scent reminded him not just of Pamela's terrible experience or of his own timely intervention (which was greatly praised in Murrisk Abbey) but of his own deep longing for her.

They arrived in Tuam in the afternoon, only to find that the situation there was worse than what they had left behind in Ballinrobe. Everywhere there was the same crush of refugees and army camp-followers and Stephen found himself doing the same useless round of the inns and taverns looking for accommodation. They got a hot meal at *The Jarlath* on High Street and then decided to push on some of the way towards Athlone. Everyone had a different story to tell about the French but all were agreed that Athlone was under government control and Stephen hoped that Pamela could get the stage coach to Dublin from there. Since the battle for Castlebar, all stage coaches west of the Shannon had been suspended.

They got as far as Moylough before Stephen found a place for them to stay the night. It was a small, modest cabin but clean and Pamela slept on a settle-bed beside the smoky turf fire. Stephen however slept in the stable. He was taking no more chances with the horse.

The next morning was blustery and threatening to rain but they made good progress before the rain started. And then it poured with a vengeance, blowing from the east right into their faces. Sometimes they took shelter when it came down too heavy but mostly they plodded on, wet to the skin, despondent and weary. They spoke hardly at all, nor did they feel the need to. Stephen was worried about Pamela being so drenched. Everyone always worried about Pamela's health.

Jock too was tired and was showing the strain of his double burden. Sometimes Stephen walked at his head to lighten his load and encourage him. Stephen often talked to Jock and stroked his nose or rubbed his soft chin and it was remarkable how the big horse reacted to such personal attention. He would throw up his proud head or swish his tail in evident appreciation. And afterwards he seemed to take new heart.

At last they saw the spires of Athlone in the distance. Stephen mounted up again, this time with Pamela behind, unashamedly tucking right into him as much for warmth as to cling on for balance. And thus they completed the last few miles into Athlone, which, at that moment, was the point of the greatest concentration of men under arms in Ireland since the Williamite Wars a hundred years earlier.

~~~~~~ • ~~~~~~

A few days had passed and Pamela was sitting up in bed with a large breakfast tray in front of her. Aunt Olive was still fussing and drawing out every last detail of the tragedy at Murrisk and Pamela's extraordinary escape to Dublin.

"I don't know what we would have done if I had not seen *Colonel O'Donnell," Pamela went on between mouthfuls of brown bread and marmalade. "You know him of course? From Newport Pratt on the other side of Westport? Well, we were utterly exhausted, drenched through and through and stranded at the gates of Athlone for hours before he rode by with a detachment of the Mayo militia. Of course, we didn't have passports and we might still be there but I recognised him and called out his name. Imagine his surprise when addressed by a dripping ragamuffin astride the back of a horse! However, he was gracious enough to approach and when I made myself known, he could not have been more solicitous. Really, aunt, I will for ever be grateful to Colonel O'Donnell."

Aunt Olive had been married for over forty years to the former Chancellor of the High Court, Lord Porter, who had earned the reputation of being the meanest man at the Bar. While he was alive, they had had a fairly miserable life together but his death had given a new lease of life to his widow. After his demise, she began to spend some of his accumulated savings, not in any ostentatious way of course, but in the selective entertainment of her friends among whom were counted the cream of Dublin society. Lady Porter was a big woman but surprisingly light on her feet and she loved dancing. She also had a weakness for large hats, the more elaborate the better. The past few days had, of course, been traumatic for her. She had never particularly liked Bonaventure and she hated everything to do with Mayo. But she had been close to her brother John. He always remembered her wherever he sailed in foreign parts and the most unusual gifts would arrive from places she had never even heard of. Two silk rugs which had been sent from India still hung in the judge's study. She felt they were too good to put on the floor. But Pamela's sudden arrival had quickly infused a new purpose into her life. She already had great plans for her niece. She couldn't wait to introduce her to the very best society in Dublin.

However Aunt Olive did not relish any part of Pamela's "horseback escapade", as she called it, and particularly those references to the young man, Stephen Allen. The very idea of a young lady in such compromising circumstances was too awful to contemplate. Aunt Olive had been shocked by the intimacy that seemed to exist between them on their arrival and one or two remarks from Pamela were enough to convince her that he must be got rid of immediately.

Aunt Olive had sent for Stephen to attend her and had acted firmly and decisively and, she believed, in Pamela's best interest.

"I want to thank you, young man, for your faithful service to my niece," she said. "We are greatly in your debt and I want you to know how much your good work was appreciated."

Stephen was standing in Lady Porter's first floor drawing room which looked onto Merrion Square, holding his cap in his hands. Still in deep mourning, Lady Porter was dressed entirely in black which perfectly matched the severity of her countenance. What Stephen didn't realise, of course, was that this was exactly the impression she had determined to convey for the purpose of this interview.

"Will you be returning to Murrisk soon?", she enquired, tilting up her chin deliberately.

Stephen was flabbergasted. "I hoped I might be of service to Miss Pamela here," he replied after a pause.

"I'm afraid that is quite out of the question," Lady Porter replied firmly. "As you have seen, we are well served in the stables here already."

Lady Porter was sitting erect beside the window at the far end of the room. She knew that Stephen was embarrassed but that's as she wanted it.

"I suppose I could return to Murrisk," he said tentatively.

"Of course, you shouldn't return to the West," Lady Porter declared. "There's nothing left in Murrisk and all west of the Shannon is under military control. You should look elsewhere. Why not the army or the colonies? There are so many possibilities for young men today." She paused. "Anyhow this will help. I have taken the trouble to write you a good recommendation." She held out a paper to Stephen and he approached awkwardly across the wide room.

"In appreciation of your service, I am also providing a substantial purse for you – fifty gold sovereigns, in fact. That should be more than sufficient for you to travel or find service elsewhere."

But as Stephen held out his hand to accept the purse, Lady Porter suddenly froze.

"Do I see a gold ring on your finger?", she asked inquisitorially.

"Yes, Lady Porter."

"Should I recognise that ring?", she demanded.

"Possibly," Stephen replied. "It belonged to Captain Preston."

"Exactly as I thought," said Lady Porter, barely able to contain herself. "Now, may I have it forthwith?"

Stephen stepped back a couple of paces.

"Captain Preston gave me this ring before he died," Stephen replied. "And with all due respects, Lady Porter, I treasure it more than whatever this purse contains."

Lady Porter was taken aback. She was accustomed to immediate compliance from servants and infuriated by Stephen's reply. But she couldn't fault his manners and his calm confidence somewhat intimidated her.

"Oh, well keep it," she said "and be off with you."

Stephen had left immediately and Lady Porter's coachman heard that he took ship the next day for some foreign part. Pamela had been surprised to learn of his sudden departure, but she was still so engrossed with her own tragedy that she thought of it less then than later. Aunt Olive, of course, indicated that it was entirely Stephen's decision. All in all, she felt, it was a job well done – or at least a danger eliminated.

~~~~~~ • ~~~~~~

Stephen left Lady Porter's house in a state of shock. He didn't even see Pamela. He felt humiliated and angry. All his life he had been in the service of the Prestons. Now he was literally out on the street. He wandered around for a while with no idea of where he was or where to go. He dropped into the *Silver Swan* on Burgh Quay and swallowed two quick whiskeys. Then he strolled along the wharf admiring the sailing vessels as he passed. On George's Quay, several lofty American schooners, some of them three-masters, were tied up to the South Wall. On the opposite side of the river, two revenue-cutters, designed for speed, were moored alongside the magnificent new Custom House. Further down the river, on City Quay, the wide hulled coal-tramps from England were discharging their black cargo. And, in the distance, Stephen could see the gulls hovering and swooping over the fleet of fishing smacks tied up at Ringsend. As the whiskey mellowed in his head, he was beginning to feel more expansive and continued along the river front with one hand in his pocket firmly gripping his purse of gold.

"Givus a penny, Mister," a small urchin begged him and Stephen tossed him a shilling.

On Sir John Rogerson's Quay, a large brig was unloading bales of faded yellow leaves from the state of Virginia and, further along, a British schooner was discharging barrels of rum from the West Indies. Stephen was amazed to see several negroes, enormous giants of men, manhandling the barrels as if they were baubles. And then he remembered what Lady Porter had said to him about the colonies.

"Perhaps the old bag wasn't so wrong after all," he thought to himself.

Just ahead of him, an elderly gentleman alighted from a hackney cab and went aboard the good ship *Expedition*.

"Bound for Jamaica," Stephen heard the porter tell some waifs who were helping with the trunks.

Jamaica? Bound for Jamaica? Stephen snapped out of his reverie. The destination conjured up all the romance that he associated with Captain John. He had heard so much about Jamaica from the Captain, about the sun and the sea and the fish and the fruits, that he felt he almost knew it.

"Did you say she was bound for Jamaica?", Stephen asked the porter.

"That's right, sir. She sails on the tide tomorrow."

Stephen looked at the *Expedition* and wondered that she could cross the Atlantic.

"How big would you say she is?"

"She's all of three-hundred and fifty tons burden and in fine fettle too."

"How long is the voyage to Jamaica?"

"Anything up to two months, I imagine. But ask Captain Powell if you're interested. He's the man with all the answers."

Stephen hesitated for moment while a thousand thoughts flashed through his mind. But what had he to lose? He squared his shoulders and bounded up the gangway.

BOOK II

Chapter IX

CAPTAIN JOHN'S WILL

Dublin, September 1798

"GREAT NEWS! Great news," Aunt Olive announced as she bustled into the morning room.

"The French are routed at Ballinamuck. General Humbert is taken along with most of his army. *Deo Gratias.*"

Aunt Olive put on her spectacles again and started to read from the *Freeman's Journal.*

"*Dublin Castle. 9th September, 1798. Advices have been received this morning from Johnstown, the headquarters of the Lord Lieutenant, which bring the pleasing and satisfactory intelligence that Lieutenant General Lake, having come up with the enemy yesterday morning, entirely defeated them. The French have surrendered at discretion. The Rebels who had joined them were dispersed and a great proportion killed or taken*"

"Oh, is it not wonderful news, my dear? Here, read the full account while I am out. I'll be back before lunch. I have an appointment with the solicitor."

Lady Porter had received a note from Mr. Alexander Hamilton, the solicitor who acted in Dublin for Captain John Preston, requesting her to call "on a matter of considerable importance." Of course she presumed it had to do with her late brother's will and she had dressed this morning in clothes becoming to the occasion, with a large black hat pinned tightly to her plentiful coiffure.

She took an instant dislike to Mr. Hamilton. He was a small thin man, almost bald, and had the unfortunate habit of never quite looking one straight in the eye. He had a passion for snuff as was all too evident from his soiled shirt-front, and Lady Porter immediately felt that there was something shifty about him. But then she had a prejudice against solicitors.

"They spend too much time listening to criminals," her husband used to say. "Some of it is bound to rub off."

Mr. Hamilton let her into his office, which predictably was covered with papers and documents on every available table and shelf.

"Too mean to employ a filing clerk," Lady Porter thought. She had seen his type before.

Mr. Hamilton made quite a performance of welcoming Aunt Olive, of setting her in a comfortable chair and of finding the particular document which was now to engage their attention; but eventually he was ready to start.

"You may be aware, Lady Porter," he said, "that I had the honour to act for Captain Preston for many years – and I have here his last will and testament. The estate is substantial and as you are his sister I thought it proper to advise you first of the contents."

Lady Porter shifted in her chair. She had, of course, expected to be remembered in her brother's will, but this solicitor seemed to be hinting that she was in for a substantial bequest. It was a pleasant surprise.

Mr. Hamilton then proceeded to read out the Schedule of Assets in the estate, item by item, and as he went down them Lady Porter's surprise grew to wonder and then to amazement. Her brother had died a very wealthy man indeed.

"…and last but not least," intoned Mr. Hamilton, "one thousand tickets in the Lottery."

"Tickets in the Lottery?" echoed Lady Porter. "My goodness, I never knew my brother had an interest in gambling." But in truth her mind was not on the lottery tickets but on the long list of Consuls and other government securities that John had apparently acquired since his return from Jamaica.

"Oh yes, the Captain always enjoyed a flutter," Mr. Hamilton replied in a patronising tone. "I had standing instructions to subscribe for one thousand tickets in each lottery. And I may say that the Captain was not unlucky in that regard."

Mr. Hamilton took off his spectacles and polished them carefully while Aunt Olive tried to remain patient.

"Of course there will be expenses in liquidating the estate," he said. "But, taken all together, it should realise a very substantial sum."

Lady Porter wanted to ask "how much?", but she restrained herself while the solicitor kept her in suspense for another while, murmuring on in legal jargon that they both knew meant nothing at all.

"I would estimate the final value of the estate to be in or around one hundred thousand pounds," he said finally, and Lady Porter couldn't resist an involuntary raising of her eyebrows. One hundred thousand in the funds was certainly a substantial fortune. She had never dreamt that her brother had done so well for himself in Jamaica.

"He is certainly a most fortunate young man," Mr. Hamilton continued, in a tone that was now full of kindness, almost deferential.

"YOUNG MAN, did you say?", asked Lady Porter, whose mind had been wandering in fanciful pursuit of the hundred thousand pounds.

"Yes, Mr. Allen."

"Mr. Who?"

"Mr. Stephen Allen."

"And who is Mr. Stephen Allen?"

"He is the sole heir, Lady Porter, the sole beneficiary of Captain Preston's will. I understand he is employed as a groom at Murrisk Abbey."

Lady Porter was not just shocked. She was flabbergasted, and all her reserves of propriety and caution in front of this canny solicitor were suddenly discarded.

"Why, that's impossible," she blurted out. "There must be some mistake. I don't believe it. I won't believe it. John wouldn't do this to his family. It's preposterous. Show me that document." And without further ado, she snatched the will from the solicitor's hand and began perusing it from top to bottom.

"The will is entirely in order, Lady Porter. It was executed only last year and witnessed, as you see, by myself and my late clerk, poor Mr. Henry. Captain Preston did mention to me his reasons... that is to say his relationship..."

"His relationship?", asked Aunt Olive aghast.

"His relationship to the young man..."

"Be frank, Mr. Hamilton," Aunt Olive ordered. "This is no time for beating around the bush."

The solicitor assumed a hurt air, as if the matter was really of such delicacy as to be unmentionable in front of any lady. But slowly, and with apparent reluctance, he pronounced the terrible truth.

"Captain Preston was the young man's father. I understand that his mother was in service at Murrisk Abbey some years ago."

Lady Porter lowered her head, not in embarrassment, but to hide her all-consuming fury. That her brother should have degraded himself in this fashion was bad enough. But that he should have compounded his sin with stupidity was altogether intolerable.

"I was hoping you could help me to locate Mr. Allen," interjected the solicitor.

"Me!", cried Lady Porter,"know the whereabouts of a stable boy?" Her tone was a mixture of hurt and outrage and she fixed her squinting eye directly on Alexander Hamilton. It was a white lie but uttered with such conviction that even old Hamilton was convinced. "For all I know he's with the rebels in Mayo," she added.

"Would Miss Preston know?"

"Most improbable." The lie was getting heavier now, but Aunt Olive had no intention of helping one little bit in locating young Allen. "She is lucky to be alive, poor thing."

This information seemed to interest old Hamilton and he continued cautiously.

"Of course I can understand your feelings in this matter," he began in a newly sympathetic tone.

"MY feelings?", interrupted Lady Porter. "My feelings count for nothing in this. I am thinking only of my niece. The poor girl has already suffered cruelly. Within a week she has lost both her father and her uncle; her home is destroyed and her property is threatened by the French and their rabble-followers. The poor girl has been forced to throw herself on the charity – yes the charity – of her old aunt. No, Mr. Hamilton, it is not my feelings that are at stake here. It is Miss Preston and her expectations, which were entirely justified and which I believe would concur entirely with my dear brother's true intentions if he were aware of the present circumstances."

Mr. Hamilton looked properly sympathetic, as if the burden were truly his and his sympathies lay entirely with Lady Porter.

"The irony of the situation," he said regretfully, "is that it might have been otherwise."

"Otherwise?" queried Aunt Olive, immediately sensing some new possibilities.

"Yes, if your brother had not executed the second will."

"The second will?"

"Yes indeed, his former will executed on his return from Jamaica left everything to Mr. Bonaventure Preston, or in the case of his death, to his niece Miss Pamela Preston. Indeed I still have it amongst his papers."

Mr. Hamilton fussed around for a few minutes through a pile of documents. When he found it, he handed it to Lady Porter and then excused himself for a few minutes. Aunt Olive considered the relevant facts in succession. The latest will left everything to young Allen who was, however, as ignorant of this as of his relationship to Captain Preston. And the only living person, apart from herself, who knew these circumstances was Mr. Hamilton. But Aunt Olive was no fool. She had summed up Alexander Hamilton as soon as she walked into his office. Why had he appraised her of all this information when she was not even a beneficiary? Why had he not written directly to Stephen Allen at Murrisk? Why had he not told her immediately of the former will?

Aunt Olive did not know the answers to these questions, but her intuition (a characteristic which the late Judge had often admired) told her all she needed to know: namely, that Mr. Hamilton was up to no good. She took up the latest will, tore it clean in half and threw it in the wastepaper basket just as Mr. Hamilton was returning to his office.

"Lady Porter," he expostulated, "I am surprised at you…" And he bent down to retrieve the torn document. "How could you do such a thing?"

"Save your breath, Mr. Hamilton," replied Aunt Olive in a stern and righteous tone. "That will was an aberration in the first place, and should never have been drawn up. I cannot imagine how you ever permitted my poor brother to execute it. The unfortunate man was obviously unwell at the time. But you can now save us the trouble – and the expense – of contesting it. There are times, as indeed my dear husband the late judge often remarked, when the course of justice must needs divert from the strict letter of the law. And this is exactly one such occasion – as you must surely see. But if you don't recognise the valid claims of a near destitute member of this respectable and loyal Protestant family against the so-called right of some bastard stable-boy, then I have no doubt that a court of law will."

Mr. Hamilton was nodding his head and frowning as if the whole burden of the decision was a most difficult one for him.

"Of course I realise that your brother could never have foreseen these most unfortunate developments," he said. "And I do know that his niece had gained a very particular position in his affections. But I am not free to act as Captain Preston might have wished if he were here now, that is, if knowing the present circumstances, he was to make his decision here and now."

Aunt Olive was getting tired of all this shadow boxing. She decided to play her trump card.

"I would not be surprised," she said, "if we are dealing with an entirely theoretical situation. Half the young peasants in Mayo have been out fighting with the French and for all we know this young man may be amongst them. If he has joined the rebels he has forfeited his right to inherit any property at all. So let us find out, first, whether he be dead or alive before we make the final decision. Then we can proceed with confidence."

This line seemed to intrigue the canny solicitor and, always cautious, he agreed with the suggestion.

And so a few weeks later, after the last of the French invaders had been rounded up and a degree of normality restored to that troubled area, Mr. Hamilton arranged for a notice to be inserted in *The Mayo News*, requesting anyone who had knowledge of the present whereabouts of Mr. Stephen Allen of Murrisk, County Mayo, to contact his office.

The notice was seen by the O'Reillys and others in Westport and by Mrs. Barton out at Murrisk who was an avid reader of *The Mayo News*. She cut out the notice and put it in the back of her prayer book. But as no-one knew of Stephen's whereabouts, although a rumour that he had gone abroad to join the army had circulated for some time, no one replied to the notice in the paper. Mr. Hamilton carefully filed the relevant copy of *The Mayo News*, and after a decent period had elapsed, arranged a new appointment with Lady Porter.

⁓⁓⁓ • ⁓⁓⁓

"It now appears," he told her at their next meeting, "that Mr. Stephen Allen is either a fugitive or dead. Strictly speaking I should report this to the Court of Probate but, having regard to the very particular circumstances, and to the former will, and to my own close association with Captain Preston over many years,

I have decided to execute his wishes as I believe they would be at this moment. In effect I will act on the disposition stated in the first will, subject however to the following guarantees. Until Miss Preston attains the age of twenty one, I shall act as her guardian with full powers of attorney over the funds demised herewith. I will, of course, make full allowance in the meantime for the young lady's education and maintenance to a standard that an heiress is entitled to expect – something in the region of two thousand pounds per annum I would suggest. In this fashion, I believe, I can best honour the trust bestowed on me by your dear brother, the late Captain Preston."

Aunt Olive didn't argue, and anyhow it was not a bad bargain. Pamela would come into her fortune in a few years, and in the meantime the expense of keeping her niece would be well covered. In fact, she had every reason to be more than satisfied by her own part in the outcome. But she shuddered to think how close to disaster the whole business had come.

Of course, Pamela was told nothing of the will in favour of Stephen Allen. But she soon came to feel what it is to be an heiress and she was amazed how it affected the attitudes of almost everyone towards her.

Chapter X

STEPHEN IN JAMAICA

"THAT'S PORT ROYAL – or what is left of it," said Captain Powell to Stephen, indicating a little village to starboard. As the *Expedition* sailed gently into Kingston Bay, Stephen surveyed the small cluster of houses perched at the tip of the narrow neck of land that protected Kingston from the sea. Except for the coconut trees, it might have been Bartra Strand.

"It used to be Henry Morgan's hideout," the Captain added. "Now, most of it is at the bottom of the sea."

"How come?", asked Stephen, who had shifted his gaze ahead to the panorama of encircling mountains.

"Swallowed up in the earthquake of 1692. Simply sunk to the bottom. Just Morgan's luck that he wasn't there at the time. Bloody man had nine lives."

"What happened to him then?", asked Stephen.

"He became respectable. Was eventually made Governor of the Island. That is what can happen here. Even to a pirate. This is a land devoted entirely to making money. Morgan made more than anyone else, so finally they gave him a title. Sir Henry Morgan, no less."

Within hours of being dispatched by Aunt Olive from Merrion Square, Stephen had walked aboard the *Expedition* bound for Jamaica and had spent much of the voyage in the company of Captain Powell. But he was never quite sure when the old sea-dog was pulling his leg. He had heard so many fantastic stories of the sea, of storms, of vessels lost, of tragedies and near disasters, of strange sea monsters and, most of all, of pirates, that he no longer knew what to believe. But he enjoyed listening to the old man's tales and during the fifty-five long days and nights since they lost sight of the Irish coast, Stephen's acquaintance with Captain Powell had ripened into a real friendship.

Captain Powell also told Stephen of the early days in Jamaica under Spanish sway, during which the native Arawak Indians had been entirely obliterated. Then, how the British had seized control in 1655 and of the growth of the huge plantations and the importation of African slaves to work them. And he told him of the great sugar magnates like William Beckford and Simon Taylor and Charles Price and others whose wealth now dazzled London.

"As rich as a West Indian," is a common saying now in London," the Captain told Stephen. "But as you will see, most West Indians here have nothing at all."

Kingston at that time was a town of about thirty thousand souls – mostly black or coloured ones. The unpaved streets ran right down to the seashore and a few small wharves jutted out into the calm waters of the bay. But as the draft was not sufficient for the *Expedition* to draw alongside, both passengers and cargo had to be off-loaded onto smaller boats to reach the shore.

"Why don't you stay aboard until the unloading is complete?" Captain Powell said to Stephen. "Then I can show you something of Kingston," he added with a twinkle in his eye. "But if you want to take lodgings, Diana Cole's place on the Parade is the best of a bad lot."

Captain Powell had taken quite a liking to Stephen. He had lost his own son at sea some years before and there was something in Stephen's open expression which reminded the Captain of his own boy. Or so he imagined. So Stephen stayed aboard for the five days it took to unload the vessel, and despite the oppressive heat it was a useful period of acclimatisation. He enjoyed his first taste of papaya and mango fruits, and his ear began to attune itself to the native pidgin English.

"Remember three things in Jamaica," The Captain told Stephen one evening. "Keep your head covered at all times; keep in the shade when you can and drink plenty of liquids. You won't meet many old people on this island," he added. "If the heat doesn't kill them, the fever consigns them to an early grave."

The Captain never tired of advising Stephen about conditions on the island – the food, the climate, the slaves, the fever and the opportunities for employment.

"Overseers are paid about one hundred and fifty pounds per annum," he told Stephen, "bookkeepers only fifty to sixty pounds. A man of your experience and intelligence should get at least one hundred pounds. Believe me, you'll earn it, my boy. My advice would be to get yourself fitted out for the tropics at Dean & Atkinson's. A few of your sovereigns would be well spent there. Everyone is taken at face value in these parts."

Although he had often heard Captain Preston speak of Jamaica and was aware that Lord Altamont too had property here, Stephen decided against revealing these connections in the first instance. He wanted to make his own way and he put it about that he was a gentleman's son from the West of Ireland seeking his fortune in the colony. But Captain Powell directed him to the offices of Mr. Samuel Queenborough, who was the agent for several owners of large estates in Jamaica.

It was unusually hot and humid as Stephen was shown into Mr. Queenborough's office and the old man didn't attempt to get out of his chair. But he was happy to discuss several possibilities with Stephen in various parts of the island. The last of these was a position as assistant over-seer on the Cocoa Walk estate which paid £120 p.a.

"The estate belongs to Lord Altamont whom you may have heard of in Ireland," old Queenborough mentioned in passing.

Stephen signed up there and then without revealing any connection.

~~~~~~ • ~~~~~~

Cocoa Walk was not just a plantation. It was an entire valley locked in by sharp-edged and heavily-wooded hills – a self-contained community bound to a single purpose. A small stream meandered through the basin and the tall weaving sugar canes stretched from the river banks to both east and west and well up into the sloping hills. As he crested the only track leading into the valley, Stephen spotted the residence away to his left, standing high off the ground. In the centre of the valley, the sugar works and distillery were positioned close to the river, and not too far distant were the slave quarters, a village of small thatched huts, each with its own small plot for cultivation. The slaves, as Stephen was to learn, had to provide their own food and the law allowed for this as for every other particular affecting their existence. Every second Saturday was allowed to them for tending their own food plots where nature bountifully supplied the yams, breadfruit, plantain, coconuts, mangoes and other staples of their diet. In addition, owners were required by law to have one acre planted in ground provisions for every ten Negroes kept.

But the reality of the slave existence was still far from Stephen's mind. Looking down on the luxuriance of the cane fields, on the swaying crowns of the high coconut trees and on all sorts of evergreen foliage with which he was not yet familiar, Stephen could only think of the Garden of Eden. And he thought to himself what a lucky man Lord Altamont must be to have acquired such a paradise in this part of the world.

John Tallon, the overseer, was a dapper little Scotsman on whom seven years in the army had made an indelible impression. Army manners and mores epitomised for him the perfection of behaviour. He believed in discipline, including self-discipline. He ran the plantation strictly according to the book and was impatient of any deviation. He sent back to the Royal Bank of Scotland in Edinburgh practically his entire salary of one hundred and sixty pounds per annum and was determined to retire from Jamaica in his forty fifth year. Mr. Queenborough regarded him as the most efficient overseer in the several plantations for which he was responsible. The slaves both feared and hated him and Stephen instinctively disliked him too.

Stephen rode out with the overseer at six thirty on the morning after his arrival.

"You've come just in time for our busy season," said Tallon, while his eyes swept the vast expanse of tall swaying sugar canes. "Most of the crop is cut between January and April – but sometimes it runs into May and June. We try to have it finished before the rains come in May."

They rode for a half a mile before they came up to the first gang of slaves in the fields.

"During the cutting season, work starts at first light, or around 5 a.m.," said Tallon. "There is a half-hour break for breakfast between eight and eight thirty and a two-hour stop in the middle of the day. All work ceases at dusk or around 6.30 p.m. That's half an hour within the legal limit," he added.

Stephen looked down for the first time on a slave-gang at work. The men were spread out in a line across the field, each facing into his own furrow of canes. There were between thirty and forty men at work here and behind them two drivers, with long cart-whips curled over their shoulders, controlled the pace of the work.

"Cutting the canes is easy enough," Tallon told Stephen, who was already feeling the heat of the day. "What slows them down is what we call the trash – the accompanying long whiskers or leaves."

Stephen watched the rhythmic swipes of the machete to the base of the tall cane, the upward strokes with the back of the knife to clear the trash and the slicing off of the topmost foliage. Shorn of its bits, the long thick cane was thrown behind on the ground and the next one cut, trimmed and dropped again. It was a steady monotonous motion, unceasing, day in day out, from one month to the next.

Standing in his stirrups, Stephen saw the cane fields stretching away as far as the eye could see. When this field was finished, there was the next and the next after that. There would be no variety in the routine over the next five months.

Behind the men, the women were binding the canes in bundles and loading them into high-railed carts drawn by teams of oxen. And to his amazement, Stephen noticed several children collecting the trash and heaping it neatly together.

"Do the children work too?", asked Stephen in some surprise.

"Of course," replied Tallon. "What else would they be doing? But it is light work. They like being out here with their mothers. And while they're in the fields, they can eat as much sugar cane as they like. So can the men. That's what gives them the energy you know. Very good for them too. However, they are forbidden to sell, or even give away, the sugar cane. The statutory punishment for that is thirty-one lashes."

"Is there a lot of whipping then?", asked Stephen, who could hardly keep his eyes off the long cart-whips which the drivers occasionally whirled and cracked, but had not, while observed, brought down on any individual.

"The absolute minimum," replied Tallon emphatically. "I discourage it – except where absolutely necessary. It detracts from their value. A lot of merchants will not buy a marked slave, knowing that it indicates a malefactor. Most of these field-slaves are worth anything up to one hundred pounds a piece, you know.

They're an expensive commodity. You mustn't damage them unnecessarily – anymore than you would a horse. There are more effective corrections," he added without elaboration.

"And the drivers?", asked Stephen.

"There are twelve now on the combined estate. All Creole – that is native born here in Jamaica. Of course they despise the fresh imports – which makes them good drivers. These two are of Ashanti origin. You know – from the Gold Coast. They're a tough race. But we have all sorts of slaves on the plantation. Papaws from the Congo region are rather docile. They are better tradesmen than field workers. Ibo women are good in the fields – that was their tradition in Africa but they are prone to suicide. We have some Mandingas too – from Sierra Leone. They're good workers and neat and tidy. But you can't trust them. They'd steal the shirt off your back. My policy is to mix them. That way they can wear off their aggression against each other."

"But the drivers," repeated Stephen, "what exactly is their authority?"

"They're my field officers," replied Tallon, who had never held a rank higher than corporal in the army. "We never speak directly to the field-slaves. Never. It's a principle of mine. Note it well."

"So what is the extent of their authority?", Stephen persisted.

"The law is quite clear on that," replied the overseer. "No slave may be given more than ten lashes at a time for any one offence, except in the presence of the overseer or proprietor of a property. And no more than thirty nine lashes on any account can be administered on any one day. That's the law. But I limit the drivers to three lashes except in my presence. And as you'll see, they seldom use the whip."

"Now I'll show you the works."

They followed the ox-cart trail down to the sugar works and passed Dick Perkins, the English book-keeper, on his way out to the fields.

"Any word of Jupiter?", Tallon asked him.

"No, not a word."

"Today's the tenth day, isn't it?"

"That's right. It's official now. The little bastard."

"Well, prepare the advice for Mr. Queenborough. I'll send it off this evening."

They rode on in silence, walking their horses on a loose rein.

"Jupiter is a runaway," Tallon explained after a while. "He's been gone ten days now. So we'll post a reward for his return in the *Gazette*."

"Is this a regular occurrence?", asked Stephen as he wiped the sweat off his brow.

"Not with me, it's not," Tallon replied firmly. "I don't like runaways. The last one was over a year ago. But Jupiter will be back. He's not tough enough to survive in the hills. He's an Ibo."

Stephen's appearance at the sugar works caused quite a sensation. The arrival of any newcomer in this enclosed community was always the subject of great interest. But a new overseer was a thing of huge consequence and for a moment work almost came to a standstill. Everyone stopped to stare at the new white *buccra* and several little boys ran up to hold his horse.

Stephen had only a moment to take in the whole complex of buildings, the crushing mill, the boiling house below, the distillery and all the ancillary works before Tallon dismounted and strode quickly into the mill.

Here the cane was being crushed noisily between two great cylinders and the juice squeezed out into a gutter which sloped down to the boiler-house.

"Don't distract them here," Tallon said to Stephen in an admonishing tone. "It's too dangerous. We've had a few bad accidents recently. After the last one, I had this machete fixed to the wall. We only saved the fellow's life by chopping off his hand. Got it caught in the wheel."

For a moment Stephen thought the overseer was joking. But as he found out later, it was quite true.

Stephen followed him round the giant drums to where the spent canes were being thrown out on the other side

"We use these to fire the boilers," Tallon shouted above the noise, pointing to a line of furnaces underneath the adjoining boiler-house. Groups of Negroes, mostly women, were carrying down bundles of the trash while others stoked the blazing fires.

They moved into the boiler house.

"It's hot in here," the overseer remarked as he led the way. But despite the warning, Stephen was unprepared for the suffocating atmosphere of the sugar factory. Clouds of steam from the line of bubbling cauldrons rose to the rafters and a sickly smell of syrup permeated the whole building.

"Jock is the expert here," said Tallon. "He'll tell you all about this place. I'll see you back at the house."

Jock was the third white man on the estate. He knew sugar-making inside out but he hated Jamaica and everything about it. He was always talking about going home to Scotland but was destined to die in the tropics. He had already succumbed to the twin attractions of plantation life – free rum and free women. He was trapped for life.

"It's simple enough really," he told Stephen, with whom he had sat drinking the night before. "You just boil it, skim it, and cool it. The wonder is that these buggers can muck it up so often. You've got to watch them all the time. They're so bloody stupid. The juice flows in from the crushing mill directly into this big pot."

Jock indicated the highest cauldron in the shed on the wide rim of which a slave was balancing himself while he skimmed off the simmering scum.

"Pretty hot up there, I imagine?", said Stephen, who had difficulty breathing even where he stood.

"Hot as Hell," Jock confirmed.

"Then," he continued, "the purer liquid flows into the adjoining cistern where it boils and then into another, until it begins to granulate. The men continue to skim it and stir it with the long-handled ladles, but even the scum is not wasted. It flows along the other gully to the distillery. When the sugar has cooled we transfer it into the hogsheads – ready for shipment."

"How do they work in this heat?", asked Stephen, who was sweating profusely.

"Oh, they don't notice it," replied Jock dismissively. "They're used to it. Better than the steaming jungle, isn't it?", he laughed.

Stephen looked up again at the man on the rim of the high cauldron. He noticed that he was sweating from every pore.

"How often is he relieved?", he asked the Scotsman.

"He does the full day like everybody else," Jock replied in a disinterested tone. "Come on, I'll show you the distillery."

At least the distillery was cooler, and Stephen did his best to concentrate as Jock explained the various tubes through which the sugar scum and molasses were heated and cooled until their final distillation into rum.

"She yields about eighty barrels of rum in the year," said Jock cheerfully. "Plus a few drams for home consumption," he added, giving Stephen a dig with his elbow.

Stephen spent another hour or so inspecting the cooperage, the forge, the stables, the various store-houses, the slave hospital and the infant house. And then he rode slowly through the Negro quarters which at that hour were almost entirely deserted.

As he rode back to the residence, disturbing a flight of chattering parrots as he went, Stephen heard the conch blowing in the fields. It was time for the mid-day break.

They brought back Jupiter two weeks later. He was a wiry little fellow, not more than five feet five inches high, and it was obvious that he had suffered during his brief spell of freedom. He had been trapped by the Maroons, a semi-independent tribe in the central highlands to where the runaways often fled. But the Maroons were a treacherous lot and were more interested in collecting rewards than in harbouring strangers. Tallon paid them the five pound reward and sixpence for every mile they had travelled as the law required. Then he ordered Jupiter to be locked in the Hell Hole, a low metal-covered construction fully exposed to the sun.

"They hate being locked up more than anything else," Tallon explained. "Its so unnatural for them. It's an old army trick for the natives. The hut is neither high enough for them to stand up, nor long enough for them to stretch out on the ground. Jupiter'll be pretty stiff after three days. And he won't be in any hurry to run away again."

But that wasn't the end of Jupiter's punishment. An example had to be made of him before the others.

On the third day, just before sundown, he was dragged out of the Hell Hole and up to the front of the Main Residence. There the whole force of slaves had been assembled to witness the ultimate fate of the runaway.

They stood around in a big semi-circle facing the house. John Tallon, Jock, Stephen and Dick Perkins looked out at them from the steps of the Residence. In between, the drivers drawn up in a single line gave the impression of a guard.

"The punishment for the runaway according to law is thirty nine lashes," John Tallon called out. "Proceed with the punishment."

At the overseer's command, a Creole driver tore off Jupiter's smock and ordered him to lie flat on his belly. Then he pulled down his trousers exposing his buttocks. But Jupiter resented this humiliation most of all and twice tried to pull them up again until the Creole hit him with the stock of the whip on the side of the head.

Stephen looked out over the ring of slaves trying to gauge their reaction; but their faces were impassive. Not one of them raised the least semblance of protest.

Another driver now stepped forward, a long cart-whip in his hand. He was the one responsible for the gang from which Jupiter had absconded and John Tallon had already threatened to put him back in the fields. Towering over the prostrate form of his victim, this giant of a man now whirled the lash round his head before bringing it down with a crack onto Jupiter's back. After the third lash, the blood began to spurt with every stroke and Stephen felt his stomach heave in revulsion. The runaway was writhing like a worm in agony, but he didn't try to move or resist in any way. He just cried out pathetically, "Lord, Lord", every time the whip cut into his body. But the flogging continued at a steady pace and still there wasn't a word from the slaves opposite.

"Surely eighteen strokes is sufficient?", Stephen demanded of John Tallon who was standing at attention beside him as if participating in a military execution.

"Shut up," he ordered through the corner of his mouth. "This is the law."

"Well, no law says I have to watch it," said Stephen as he turned on his heel and retired into the house.

And so the flogging continued but as the count passed twenty four, some of the women began to count out loud in a sort of sing-song and others to call the Lord for mercy and a few children began to whimper. But the whipping continued to the bitter end as stipulated by the law of the land.

After it was all over, John Tallon stormed back into the house.

"How dare you break ranks like that in front of the natives," he shouted at Stephen.

"I wasn't employed in that rank and you'll never get me into it again," Stephen shot back.

"You will do as you are ordered under my command," Tallon replied while drawing himself up straight as he imagined some Colonel would.

"You nearly killed the poor devil," Stephen said.

"I acted according to the law."

"Thirty-nine lashes is the absolute maximum, as you told me yourself. You didn't have to go the whole hog. It was brutally excessive."

"I know the law and I know the conditions out here better than you ever will. I made my decision and acted accordingly. And I won't tolerate any questioning of my authority. If there is a similar breach of discipline in the future, I will have to report it to Mr. Queenborough in Kingston."

"That won't be necessary," Stephen cut in "I'll be writing to Lord Altamont myself."

John Tallon was astounded. Was Stephen bluffing? He couldn't be sure. Typical of most bullies, he was a coward at heart and suddenly he felt at risk in front of this enigmatic Irishman. He had found it impossible to pigeon-hole Stephen since the day he arrived. He was a skilled horseman, his clothes came from the best outfitters in Kingston and he appeared to have some knowledge of Lord Altamont. He wasn't a drunk like Jock or a contrary bastard like Dick Perkins, and he had already shown himself to be a very competent overseer. But what puzzled John Tallon most was the Irishman's self-confidence – a cool assurance in himself that conveyed itself to the natives and enhanced his authority over them.

" He's obviously officer class," Tallon had concluded to himself.

"It's been a tough day," he muttered in a different tone. "This heat gets to us all. Here, have a drink and let's forget about the whole bloody thing."

Stephen downed the rum and papaya juice and cooled down himself. But the incident had affected him irrevocably.

Lying in his hammock that night and gazing up at the brilliant starry sky while a Mocking-bird sang in the distance, Stephen's thoughts turned to Lord Altamont and that day he had stood in his study. He remembered coming into the great hall and the huge staircase straight ahead and the giant antlers hanging on the wall and Lord Altamont's library lined with books and his strange French table with legs that weren't straight. And all this grandeur, he thought, was built on the backs of African slaves. Poor devils like Jupiter. Lord Altamont had never been to Jamaica. He probably didn't know what really went on there. Or didn't want to know. But whatever it was, he was the beneficiary of it all.

And then his thoughts shifted to Pamela and Malcolm and Mrs. Barton. Why hadn't he written to them? He knew they'd be concerned for him. But something was holding him back. Why had he cut himself off like this? It was Lady Porter really. The humiliation of it all. Being tossed out on the street like that. And she a Preston too. Captain John would never have treated him like that.

"I must get out of this hell-hole," he thought to himself. "But I won't return to Murrisk to work as a groom. I won't return to Ireland until I can live there like Captain John. Or I won't return at all."

Later in the loneliness of the night he got up and wrote a long letter to Mrs. Barton. He told her everything that had happened since he rode out of Murrisk Abbey after the tragedy: of the journey to Dublin with Pamela; of the treatment accorded to him by Lady Porter and of his taking ship for Jamaica. He told her all about Cocoa Walk and the slaves toiling there for Lord Altamont, and of how much he missed Mayo and all his old friends in the West of Ireland. But of his future intentions he gave her no hint. Finally, he asked her to send all the news from home and particularly what news she had of Pamela to Mr. Stephen Allen, c/o Mr. Samuel Queenborough, Kingston, Jamaica.

In the morning, word spread around the estate that Jupiter had hanged himself from the huge cotton-tree that stood at the entrance to the slave quarters.

Stephen was so ashamed of his association with the slave business that he decided not to post the letter after all.

Chapter XI

BRENDAN AT THE DUBLIN EVENING POST

BRENDAN O'REILLY was delighted when the *Dublin Evening Post* published his account of the battle for Castlebar. But he was even more pleased to receive a letter from the editor, *Mr. John Magee, inviting him to forward any other contribution on the troubled conditions in the west of Ireland. This greatly encouraged Brendan in an idea that he had been pondering for some time – that of joining the Gentleman of the Press in the capital. Certainly he did not relish continuing in Westport in the bitter climate of recrimination which followed the defeat of the French.

Brendan was disgusted at the excesses of the High Sheriff and his lackeys in running the rebels to ground. Scores of peasants were incarcerated in the Castlebar and Ballinrobe jails awaiting the verdict of the courts martial. Many others were transported for life to Van Diemen's Land. Dozens were simply strung up by the neck from the nearest branch of a tree. 'Soap the Rope' Browne, they nicknamed the High Sheriff whose unrestrained ruthlessness in the absence in Dublin of his brother, Lord Altamont , badly damaged the family name in Mayo for generations to come.

Early in October, Brendan got an opportunity to travel to Dublin where he presented himself to Mr. Magee who, quickly recognising young O'Reilly as a young man more in need of an occupation than remuneration, decided to give him a trial.

John Magee was the most notorious editor in the capital and an outspoken critic of the establishment. The Magees were Presbyterian and their paper provided the main platform demanding the reform of parliament and the admission of Catholics and Dissenters to the fullest enjoyment of the Constitution. Far from reforming the parliament, however, the government was planning to abolish it altogether. John Magee had supported every move towards greater independence for the Irish administration. He was now fully committed in his opposition to the proposed Union between the British and Irish parliaments. Indeed he had become convinced that, ultimately, the connection with the British Crown must be terminated.

The offices of the Post were located in a side-alley off Brunswick Street where, upstairs in one large open room, the editorial office was dominated by Mr. Magee's enormous roll-topped mahogany desk which had been made in Calcutta for a director of the East India Company. How it got to Ireland, and eventually to the offices of the *Post*, was a story that Mr. Magee often repeated to visitors while initially taking their measure.

"You're joining us at a most interesting time, young man," the editor told Brendan on his first morning in the office. "A testing time for us all." "This Union proposal is the greatest threat to the country since Cromwell," the editor added.

"Since Cromwell?", Brendan questioned, although talk of a parliamentary Union between Dublin and Westminster was all over the town.

"Yes, since Cromwell," continued the editor who was not known for his understatement. "Even Cromwell left Connaught to the natives. But this is a complete take-over. An annexation. Call it what you will. But it is not a Union. A Union implies an equal partnership: a voluntary and willing coming together; as in marriage. But this is a shot-gun affair if ever there was one."

"Won't there be advantages to trade?", asked Brendan, anxious to display some interest in the subject.

"Commercial questions are a secondary consideration when the very survival of this parliament is at stake," Mr. Magee snorted. But it will be over my dead body," he added darkly. "You'll be covering the proceedings in the House and at the Law Courts. George Pollack here will show you the ropes," he said indicating a rather arrogant looking youth in the far corner of the room. "Make yourself at home. There's a lot of work ahead."

Although he knew the city intimately since his student days, Brendan was astonished at the changes that confronted him on all sides. The military were swaggering all over the town and the Courts Martial were sitting daily. There were constant rumours of another invasion by the French which set the tone for the hangings and imprisonment of anyone even vaguely suspected of sympathy with the erstwhile rebels. Theobold Wolfe Tone had been arrested, tried and convicted. Of course he was considered an extremist, but his lingering death, after he cut his own throat in prison, evoked widespread sympathy among the lower classes as had, among the professional classes, the hanging of the brothers, John and Henry Sheares, both respectable members of the Bar.

The new hard mood was evident even in his old college at Dublin University. The college authorities had expelled many young men of patriotic spirit and had even taken down the portrait of *Henry Grattan (who had temporarily retired from politics) from the Dining Hall. The temper was completely changed from

Brendan's days in residence there. Then it had been all good humoured, boisterous but well mannered. Now every dinner he took there seemed to end up in bitter debate and recrimination. Heading into the new century, Dublin was a very different place from the carefree days of his youth, and many of his favourite old haunts were being pulled down in an orgy of building and reconstruction.

Of course, Brendan arranged to call on Pamela soon after he arrived in the capital. But that courtesy call did not go as expected.

Lady Porter received him in the upstairs drawing room but regretted that her niece was indisposed.

"In fact she has not been at all well since her escape from the West," Lady Porter explained. "You can well imagine the shock of it all."

Lady Porter thanked him kindly for arranging the funerals of her brothers and for his other services for which "she was indeed indebted to him." Lady Porter was polite but distant and appeared interested only in "the deplorable state of the country." When the name of Stephen Allen strayed into the conversation, she feigned to know nothing of his whereabouts although she did recall her coachman mentioning that he had taken ship for foreign parts. And when Brendan took his leave, she refrained from inviting him to call again.

When Brendan mentioned all this to his sister Margaret, she replied simply: "Don't forget that we are not of her persuasion."

There was another side to Brendan's new career that he found strangely exciting. His work now brought him into contact with a part of society that previously was barely known to him. This was the world of the *demi-monde*, of gambling and duelling, of men with new money or no money and of woman with loose morals or no morals at all. The Rebellion and the war, of course, had flooded the capital with adventurers and opportunists all hoping to capitalise on the presence of the victorious military establishment. And Brendan was surprised to find in this circle, many young men of good birth, like *Richard Bingham, eldest son and heir to *Lord Lucan, who seemed set on gambling away the family fortune. There was a brashness in society which was new to the capital and a tension which entered every discussion on the political future. There was also a lot more money in circulation, with grand new buildings being created around Merrion and Fitzwilliam squares and stretching right out to the Grand Canal. To Brendan, Dublin seemed more cosmopolitan than it was in his student days but also more brash and a lot more expensive. Happily, his father had settled a generous allowance on him before he arrived in town.

Chapter XII

PAMELA AT
THE CASTLE BALL

"YOU'LL BE THE belle of the ball," said Aunt Olive, beaming with pleasure as Pamela gingerly descended the stairs to the stone-flagged hall in Merrion Square. Lady Porter had personally chosen the rose-pink cotton muslin for Pamela's gown which was trimmed with silk at the neck, sleeves and hem. This was to be Pamela's first introduction to Dublin society and Aunt Olive was determined to make an impression.

Pamela was excited but nervous in her new gown now that she was all dressed up for the Viceroy's Ball. The design was of the latest French fashion, high waisted and short sleeved. But the embroidered bodice was cut low and, with her hair swept up behind, only her aunt's strings of pearls protected her long neck.

The pre-Christmas Viceroy's ball was the most glittering occasion in the social calendar in Dublin. Traditionally, it was held on the third Wednesday in December when both the Bar and the College had recessed for Christmas, and this year it was billed as a special celebration after the suppression of the rebellion.

"You don't think it's too bare on top?", Pamela asked as her aunt prepared to leave.

"It's the height of fashion, my child," she replied, "and it suits you to perfection. But wrap yourself up well. It's very cold outside."

Pamela was still trying to adjust to her very changed circumstances. And the contrast between then, and now, could not have been more dramatic. She was only beginning to appreciate how isolated had been her life in Murrisk. Not that she had ever felt herself to be unhappy, but she recognised that she had lived mostly in a world of her own. On the other hand, she loved Murrisk and the country people with their fantastic tales of fairies and pishogues and holy saints and heroes of long ago. And she loved the country music. Sometimes, when the servants were playing their fiddles in the big kitchen at night, Pamela used to dance around in her room above. Now she was going to her first ball.

~~~~~~~ • ~~~~~~~

It had just passed nine when they arrived at the Castle but the approach was already crowded with carriages, the horses snorting white breath in the frosty air. The windows all round the courtyard were ablaze with light and the portico was hung with dozens of coloured lanterns. Liveried footmen were moving around everywhere, directing the carriages, helping the passengers to alight and dispatching the emptied conveyances to the lower yard.

Pamela stepped out under the flagged portico and followed her aunt into the crowded vestibule where they deposited their coats. She was struck by the boisterousness of the crowd and the exaggerated laughter from the many men in dress uniform. Her first impression was that everyone looked so old. It all added to her nervousness as they began to make their way up the wide staircase that led to the reception rooms upstairs. Flanking them on both sides were members of the Viceroy's personal bodyguard in full ceremonial. On the landing a huge looking-glass reflected all the sparkle of the candles and the colour of the guests as they mounted towards the receiving line. Pamela took a quick glance at herself and hoped that her hair would stay up.

The cream of Dublin society was packed into the long anteroom upstairs, which again was noisy and very crowded. Aunt Olive proceeded down the full length of the salon and, of course, Pamela was soon the subject of considerable comment as she passed through the distinguished gathering. Amongst this tight-knit elite every new face immediately engendered infinite speculation as to birth, background and fortune. Dublin society liked to pigeon-hole all newcomers before it decided to embrace or destroy them. And Pamela's adventures provided ample material for gossip. But what impressed the onlookers most were the stories of her huge inheritance, said by some to yield £5,000 a year. And the higher the estimates, the greater the wonder expressed that a girl of such fortune should appear so innocent, so unspoilt and so obviously unconscious of her own radiant beauty.

"It is a very political evening," Aunt Olive remarked having cast her experienced eye round the assembly.

"Who is that in the beautiful blue gown?", Pamela asked with an arch of her eye towards a group of ladies near the fireplace.

"That is Mrs. La Touche, the banker's wife."

"What magnificent jewels!"

"She can well afford them," said Aunt Olive caustically. "Her husband is said to have an income of ten thousand a year."

Pamela had never seen such style. She wondered again about her cotton muslin.

"That's Mrs. Myerscough, General Lake's sister," Aunt Olive whispered, indicating a distinguished-looking matron in black. She's talking with Mrs. John Foster, you know, wife of the Speaker."

Pamela was trying not to stare. She was listening to the loud clipped accents – so different from the soft tones of the West.

"They'll think me a country bumpkin," she thought to herself while Aunt Olive continued her commentary on the guests.

"I think I see Colonel O Donnell from Newport," said Pamela, indicating a tall whiskered gentleman in uniform standing under a huge portrait of the King. And at the same moment the colonel saw them too and made his way over with a broad smile.

"Well! well! and how different you are looking tonight," he laughed. "And how beautiful," he added with a bow. To the colonel, Pamela looked like a figure on a classical Grecian urn – which was exactly the effect that Lady Porter had striven to achieve.

"My niece has often mentioned your kindness to her in Athlone," said Aunt Olive after the introductions. "You must call on us while you are in town."

"That time will not be forgotten by any of us," the Colonel rejoined. "And yes, I'd be delighted to pay my respects at Number Ten. But now may I have the pleasure of escorting you inside?", he suggested as they heard the first strains of the orchestra from the ballroom.

And so they joined the line of guests passing into the gilded Throne Room where they curtsied before the Viceroy, *Lord Cornwallis, who was ensconced on an enormous red plush and gold throne trying not to look bored. Thence they passed through the long picture-gallery and finally into the ballroom itself.

For a moment Pamela paused to take in the beauty of it all: the gilded columns, the richly painted ceiling, the multicoloured flags of the Knights of St Patrick bedecking the walls. She had never seen such magnificence. The orchestra was assembled on the gallery above one end of the hall. The small gallery facing them, at the other end, was overcrowded with visitors, officials and gentlemen of the Press.

" The West is well represented here to night," said the colonel. "I see Lord Altamont ahead. You know him, of course, Lady Porter?"

Lord Altamont bowed as he was introduced to the ladies.

"I knew your brothers of course," he said to Lady Porter, "and I was greatly saddened by their tragic deaths."

Then, turning to Pamela, he smiled. "However your father would never forgive me if I failed to do the honours for his daughter at a Ball. So, let me see now. Who is there here who is worthy of such a beautiful *cailin* from Mayo?"

Pamela blushed at these attentions but Aunt Olive was flattered to be in the company of this Grandee from the West. Lord Altamont seemed to be enjoying himself, and he commandeered several young men who dutifully invited Pamela to join in cotillions and minuets which, fortunately, she had practised again and again in Miss Meredith's Academy in Westport. Later, Lord Altamont invited them to join him at supper, and he might have spent the whole evening in their company had not Lord Castlereagh requested his presence in the Bermingham Room where a discussion was in progress on the Union. But, just before he left, Lord Altamont introduced the Hon Richard Bingham, only son and heir to Lord Lucan. And from that moment the evening assumed an entirely different character for Pamela.

Richard Bingham was not yet thirty, very dark, and very tall. From his mother he had inherited an artistic touch which showed in his taste for extravagant clothes and, sometimes, in the turbulence of his temper. To his father's side must be attributed that distant air that seemed like arrogance on first acquaintance. Because of this he seemed older than his years, and there was a certain harshness in his blue eyes. Heir to an ancient title and connected at the very highest level in London society, the honourable Richard Bingham was considered to be the most eligible bachelor in Dublin. That he was also a gambler was known only to a small circle of sycophants who helped him to squander his fortune. Lord Altamont was entirely unaware of this side to young Bingham's character, as was Lady Porter. Pamela only saw the most handsome man in the room.

Although she loved dancing, Pamela at first was nervous on the floor. But Bingham seemed to inspire her. She never put a foot wrong and even the complicated quadrille came to her as if she had been at every ball of the season. And when they danced the Polka, Bingham literally swept her off her feet. She was enchanted.

～～～～ ● ～～～～

Officially, the Gentlemen of the Press were there to report on the success of the evening, the sumptuousness of the appointments and the graciousness of the host. The precise details of what was worn by Lady Kilwarden, the Duchess of Fingal, Lady Telverton and many others would appear in the pages of the *Post*, *Faulkners Journal* and *The Hibernian Magazine*, in the course of the subsequent week. But the conversation amongst the gentlemen of the press had nothing to do with fashion or frolic. It was confined almost exclusively to politics and to that game of counting votes for and against the Union which had now become the most popular past-time in Dublin.

"There are three men here tonight who could decide the issue," said Arthur Noonan, the veteran scribbler for the *Journal*.

"Oh?", queried Brendan, whom Mr. Magee had sent to cover the ball.

"Lords Shannon, Ely and Downshire between them control twenty borough seats. If they stand behind the Union, it cannot fail. The question, is will they? Shannon's brother-in-law is George Ponsonby, whom you know is a principal in the Opposition, and Downshire has hated Castlereagh since the '90 election. I wouldn't count on them if I were in Castlereagh's shoes."

"Do you really think it can get through then?", asked Brendan, consciously picking the brains of his more experienced colleague.

"There's your answer," replied Noonan, indicating two men who had just entered the ballroom. "My Lords Clare and Castlereagh. That's some combination. Tougher than all the rest of them put together. Castlereagh will find the means and Clare will provide the persuasion. It is hard to stand up to them. They will have their way at the end of the day – mark my word."

But Brendan's attention had been diverted to something entirely different. Although he had noticed Pamela earlier in the evening as one of the more glamorous young ladies present, he had not at first recognised her as the Pamela Preston he knew from Murrisk Abbey. Only when he had seen her with Lord Altamont and Colonel O'Donnell did the penny drop. Now, to his horror, he saw her not just dancing with that Bingham cad, but smiling innocently straight into his eyes.

Brendan knew all about the darker side of Bingham's character. He had seen him in action at some of the less salubrious gaming-houses in the town . He also had heard about his debts. As his eye followed the couple dancing and laughing below him, he knew exactly what Bingham was up to.

It was almost two o'clock when Aunt Olive finally insisted that they must be going home.

"We mustn't be the last to leave," she chided her niece who was obviously reluctant to depart.

"Please don't go yet," said Pamela, flushed with the excitement of the evening. "Couldn't we have just one more dance?", she pleaded.

"Well, just one more then," Aunt Olive conceded as the orchestra broke into yet another lively polka.

Aunt Olive watched the young couple swirling and hopping to the strains of the gay music. At this hour of the night they had plenty of room on the floor to do justice to the energetic polka and they didn't miss a beat.

"What a lovely couple they make," mused Aunt Olive whose mind was already researching the pedigree and suitability of young Mr. Bingham. "I must invite him to call," she thought.

They were waiting in the vestibule for their carriage when Pamela saw Brendan O'Reilly approach. At first she could hardly believe her eyes. Brendan was not in evening dress and Aunt Olive had never mentioned that he had come to town and called on them.

"Good evening, Miss Preston," he said with a broad smile. "I have been watching you dance all night."

"The carriage is waiting, my dear," Lady Porter announced as she headed for the door.

"How lovely to see you," Pamela said, "but I have to rush now. Do please call on us in Merrion Square. I would love to see you – and Margaret. I have to go now. But you will call, won't you?", she repeated as she followed Lady Porter into the night.

Pamela never said a word the whole way home. She was gazing out the window of the carriage as it swayed down Dame Street, past the imposing House of Parliament and the front of Trinity College. Her knees covered with a heavy wool rug and with her feet on an oven-warm brick, Aunt Olive was almost asleep beside her. A hard frost had made the ground slippery and the groom was handling the mare with care. But Pamela was unaware of anything but the stunning beauty of the Christmas sky and a sense of excitement inside her that was a completely novel feeling. The whole night had been like a dream. She remembered precisely the first moment Mr. Bingham had been introduced. She recalled his mannered bow and the faint smile that never left the corner of his mouth. She would never forget that first formal minuet, while it seemed to her that everyone in Dublin was looking at them, and just the touch of his fingers seemed to command her every pirouette. Everything had been so perfect. She wished it could have gone on for ever.

Of course, she had never seen such splendour before: the magnificent setting, the evening gowns, the jewels and the music. But it wasn't all of these that had her enthralled. It was Mr. Bingham. He was so charming and graceful and attentive. In a word, noble. Yes, that was it. Noble. And he had devoted the entire evening to her. Pamela was not just flattered. She was smitten. Is it love, she asked herself, as she gazed up at the full moon in the cold night sky? And she thought back to that conversation with Margaret at the picnic. She had asked Margaret, "How do you know when you are in love?" Margaret, typically, had replied, "I haven't the slightest idea." Then Pamela had said, "I thought you felt it in every fibre of your body." Now she herself had that tingling feeling running through her veins, but she was also apprehensive. It was all too good to be true. She was afraid to wake from her dream. As the carriage turned into Merrion Square, she prayed that Mr. Bingham would call on her the very next day.

Chapter XIII

LORD ALTAMONT
WITH JOHN FOSTER

LORD ALTAMONT was fortunate to have been in Dublin when the French landed in Mayo. At least he was spared the danger to his person, if not the apprehension concerning his property. After it was all over, he was pleased to learn that the damage to Westport House had been slight, but he was most unhappy with the treachery of some of his tenants. To think that even his own steward, John Gibbons, had joined the insurgents. Lord Altamont could hardly credit it.

While his brother was restoring a wholesome respect for law and order in Mayo, Lord Altamont continued his residence in Dublin at his house on Sackville Street. The whole town was abuzz with talk of a legislative Union with Great Britain and His Lordship was determined to play his part in that most important development.

Lord Altamont had taken an early opportunity to advise Lord Castlereagh of his support for the Union proposal, and he was gratified to receive a request from the Chief Secretary to wait on him. The two men met in the Chief Secretary's office in Dublin Castle in the early part of October.

"I need your help to get this measure through," said Lord Castlereagh, referring to the Union proposal after they had finished with the subject of the French. (Lord Altamont was none too happy with the repatriation of the French soldiers. He felt at least some of them should be shot, or hanged like the rebels.)

"We intend introducing the Bill immediately after Christmas," Lord Castlereagh continued.

"Yes, so I understand," replied Lord Altamont. "But I wonder if the public mind is prepared for it? Aren't you rushing things a little?"

"I think not," said Lord Castlereagh. "The rebellion has changed a lot of feelings. The British connection is now seen for what it is worth. Now is the time to cement the relationship."

"Have you spoken to many of the country gentlemen?", Lord Altamont asked.

"We are just starting on that process," the First Secretary replied. "And we know it will be tight. Every vote will count."

At first Lord Altamont had been none too keen on the idea of a Union with Britain – but the French and the Mayo mobs had changed his mind. The Papists could never be trusted, he felt. They were increasing in numbers and wealth all the time. Sooner or later they would gain entry to the Irish Parliament and that day would be the beginning of the end for the Protestant Ascendancy. He would prefer to abolish the parliament than to admit Papists to it.

"We need your help on a matter of the highest importance," Castlereagh confided in an intimate tone, and Lord Altamont was all ears now as he sensed, correctly, that he was about to learn the real purpose of this meeting.

"We are worried about *John Foster," said Lord Castlereagh in a tone that only hinted at the enormity of the problem he was now raising. "His influence is immense; his opposition to the Union proposal is implacable; and his power in the House, as Speaker, is a huge disadvantage to our strategy in Parliament. Will you talk to him?"

Lord Altamont was surprised. This was no small request. It was a call on his personal connection and reputation. Foster's opposition to the Union was indeed well known.

"I know it will not be easy," continued Lord Castlereagh. "But you are a personal friend of his. You've been on the Linen Board with him for years. You know how his mind works. He might listen to you."

Lord Altamont took it all in while he pondered the audacity of the young Chief Secretary. Lord Castlereagh was only twenty-nine, and his rise to power had been meteoric. Although he was both intelligent and assiduous, there was no denying that he owed his youthful advancement to his uncle, Lord Camden, who had been appointed Lord Lieutenant of Ireland three years previously and whom Lord Cornwallis had succeeded. During that time young Castlereagh's career had advanced in leaps and bounds over other, more mature, heads. Last year, when only twenty-eight, he had been sworn in as a Privy Councillor. Such nepotism had caused a lot of comment at the time. Yes, this was the right man for the job, Lord Altamont considered. He is calculating, he is daring and he is totally unprincipled. When he went up to Cambridge hadn't he turned his back on the family's Presbyterianism and conformed to the Church of England? Hadn't he been elected with Whig support in '90, and thrown in his lot with the Tories soon afterwards? Yes, this was the man who would stop at nothing to get his way. "I'd rather be with him than opposing him," Lord Altamont thought dourly.

"Of course I'll do what I can," he assured the First Secretary, "but I don't hold out much hope of changing the Speaker's mind."

"Try to find out what he wants," said Castlereagh. "Every man has his price, as I am continuously reminded these days," Castlereagh concluded.

Lord Altamont was stung by this vulgar remark, especially in relation to a man of Foster's integrity. The man lacks breeding, he thought, and he recalled how recently the Stewart family had been advanced in the peerage.

"That may not be the best approach with Foster," he replied coolly. "But leave it to me. I'll try to get his mind at least. I'll see what I can do."

"I knew we could count on your support," said Lord Castlereagh, rising now from behind the huge flat-topped desk. "And be assured that it will not go unnoticed."

This parting hint was not lost on Lord Altamont. His only son, Howe Peter, was now at school at Eton. Thanks to the boy's mother's connections at court, he was confident that a great future lay ahead of his only child whose entry into the established church had been sponsored by the Prince Regent himself, who had graciously consented to act as the boy's Godfather. Lord Altamont hoped to see the apple of his eye advanced further in the peerage. For that reason only, he was desirous of some advancement for himself. Best of all, he considered, would be an appointment in the English peerage.

But the timing was not yet right to mention this matter to the Chief Secretary. Better to earn the young man's confidence and perhaps his gratitude. Lord Altamont knew that so controversial a measure as the Union would never be passed without considerable persuasion – even pressure. He intended his name to be amongst those to whom recognition would be given in the course of time.

⁓⁓⁓⁓ • ⁓⁓⁓⁓

It was late in the month before Lord Altamont was able to have a private word with the Speaker John Foster. And the meeting did not go well. Or rather it did not go as Lord Castlereagh would have wished.

Lord Altamont stayed on after the monthly meeting of the Linen Board and the two men disputed the Union proposal all afternoon while the short day gave way to the early winter darkness.

"Our objective is the same," the Speaker concluded. "We both want to preserve the Protestant supremacy. We only differ on the means to that end. But I am convinced that the abolition of the Parliament will undermine our whole position. It is the source of our power and the means of our patronage. Without it, we are finished."

"Of course we're not finished, but we have to adjust to the changing times," Altamont replied. He had run out of arguments over the past hour and he knew he was getting nowhere with the Speaker of the House. "We can't close our eyes to what is happening all round us, in the American colonies and in France."

"That's the damned trouble," replied Foster testily. "We've conceded too much already. Now there's no stopping the Papists."

"Which proves my point," countered Altamont. "Even if they do gain representation in the British Parliament, their numbers in Westminster will be small . But here! Once they gain access here, we will be swamped. Don't you see it would be just a question of time?"

"We've held the line for a long time," answered Foster slowly and deliberately, "and enjoyed a hundred years of peace and prosperity thanks to our firmness and determination. No man will convince me that we cannot continue in that vein. Why should we follow every latest fashion in Europe? Our task is to ride out this passing storm. We must never surrender."

Altamont watched the Speaker as he lit the glass oil lamp on the large partner's desk which occupied one corner of the room. Old Foster was not an aristocrat but he was a man of property whose life had been spent in public affairs. He controlled the county of Louth as effectively as Altamont himself controlled Mayo – and in this, most of all, the two men were alike. But there was no man living who could boast a greater experience in Parliament and a greater understanding of the affairs of the Nation. Foster was respected for his authority, his deep knowledge of economic affairs and his unswerving loyalty to the Protestant cause. He had opposed the concessions to Papists in '93 – particularly the enfranchisement of the 40-shilling freeholders. And now all the weight of his position and connection was being thrown against the Union proposal.

"Most of our life in politics is spent on minor matters," the Speaker said, standing now with his back to the fire and warming his hands behind him. "When I think of all the hours I have spent on the financial estimates over the years, it really depresses me. But in every generation some great issue arises that will establish the character of society for a long time to come. The proposed Union is such an issue and because of that it deserves a lot of thought. We should not be stampeded into it in this fashion. I blame young Castlereagh for this unseemly haste."

"I agree he is rushing his fences," replied Lord Altamont. "But you can't blame him for that! He knows the unsettled state of the country is working in his favour. Many of the country gentlemen now see the Union as the best hope of preserving their security."

"I wouldn't count on the country gentlemen to support you," said Foster. "Don't forget that most of them will lose a place in Parliament. Nor will the Union tranquillise the country or raise the tone of its civilisation. If a resident Parliament and a resident gentry cannot soften manners, amend habits and promote social intercourse, do you suppose that no local Parliament here and fewer resident gentry will?" he asked. "Take your own case. Has not the town and district of Westport benefited from your constant attention and residence? Can you persuade me that it will, in future, be the same? If you are to attend the British House of Lords, will you not have to purchase a residence in London? Of course you will. And so will all the others. Not only will this unfortunate country suffer the blight of absentee landlords but of absentee legislators as well."

He moved over to the window and for a moment gazed into the twilight. "And tell me this," he said, turning again to Lord Altamont like a prosecutor, "is it credible that a parliament in London, unacquainted with the local circumstances of a kingdom which it never sees, at too great a distance to receive communication or information for administering in time to the wants and wishes of the people, or to guard against the excesses of discontents, can be more capable of acting beneficially than the one which being on the spot is acquainted with the habits, prejudices and dispositions of the people? No, it won't work! It won't work from any point of view."

"I think you are diverting – if I may say so," said Lord Altamont in a chiding tone. "We mustn't confuse the efficiency of any parliament with the rationale for it. It's the latter point which is the most vital to us. Our only security is the powerful and commanding protection of Great Britain. If that ever fails, we are at the mercy of the old inhabitants of the island. I heard my *Lord Clare put it rather bluntly the other day: 'Confiscation is our common title,' he said, 'and only Great Britain is strong enough to protect our position against the masses'."

"I don't believe it for one moment," replied Foster with vehemence, "Wasn't it our own militia and yeomanry that confronted the late rebellion before the arrival of any English troops? And if I had my way, the situation would never have got as far out of hand as it did! Firm, even harsh measures, back in '96 and '97 could have nipped all that agitation in the bud and prevented all the recent bloodshed."

"Lord Clare says…"

"Never mind Lord Clare," Foster cut in, "You know I have the greatest respect for him – but always remember he is not one of us. One should never forget that his grandfather was a papist peasant. I don't hold it against him. Certainly not. But that background influences his judgement. He lacks our roots; our confidence. That is why he is so anglophile. He feels the need for their support. But I know we can stand alone."

Lord Altamont allowed himself a wry smile. Foster's own roots in this country were planted with Cromwell – a mere century and a half ago. Bitter plants in an unwelcoming soil. Of all the immigrants to Ireland, the Cromwellians alone never acclimatised to the native habitat: never mingled their blood with the conquered race. They remained apart, brown-eyed, knock-kneed and unloved. They came like avenging angels and stayed, like all their less righteous predecessors, to have and to hold. They were do-or-die men. Uncompromising to the end. In the West it was different. A place of moving sands and shifting loyalties and much longer memories.

"Is there nothing that would persuade you to support the Union?", he asked finally and almost desperately – but, even as he said it, he feared it might be taken up wrongly.

"I declare from the bottom of my soul," replied the Speaker, "that if England were to give us all her revenues, I could not barter for them the free constitution of my country."

And suddenly Lord Altamont felt a tinge of admiration for this incorruptible old man. There is something uplifting in the mere association with such integrity, Lord Altamont felt. He still didn't agree with the Speaker but that did not matter. In fact it rather pleased him. John Foster's character was infinitely superior to young Castlereagh's and Lord Altamont felt honoured to be counted among his friends.

The two men parted with expressions of very sincerely-felt admiration and Lord Altamont reported to Lord Castlereagh on the failure of his mission. But he did so with such a light heart that Lord Castlereagh barely thanked him for his trouble.

"I sent the wrong man on that job," Castlereagh concluded to himself. "Every man has his price. I'll have to see Foster myself."

Chapter XIV

THE UNION REJECTED

"THIS IS AN historic day, gentlemen," the editor announced, "and we must miss no part of it."

It was January 22nd, 1799, the day Parliament reconvened after the Christmas recess.

"It's not everyday a Parliament is asked to abolish itself," the editor hissed. "Bring note-books and record everything you hear and see. You will be writing history today."

"Any wager on the outcome?", Brendan teased Mr. Magee who had been speculating about the Union vote since before Christmas.

"The Castle cannot be underestimated," the editor replied. "So many members are totally dependent on the grace and favour of government that it is hard to imagine any measure can be defeated. Yet I hope and pray that something of the spirit of '82 may resurface today. What a pity Mr. Grattan is not here to give the lead again."

The editor headed out of the office and strode down towards the House flanked by his two assistants.

"I presume you both know the history of our Parliament building," he asked expansively and continued without waiting for a reply. "The first Parliament convened in Ireland after the Restoration was opened in 1661 in Chichester House, a large edifice on this site which dated back to the sixteenth century when it was used as a hospital. But Chichester House was replaced in 1728 by the magnificent building you see in front of you now."

"Where did the Parliament of James II sit?", Brendan prompted the old man on his favourite topic.

"Ah, that was an unusual Parliament," the editor replied." Predominantly Catholic, it survived but one session. It was convened by that well meaning but ineffectual monarch, James II, in May 1690 and was held in the old law building across the river. Before that again, the infamous "Poynings" Parliament of 1494 was held in Drogheda, the principal purpose of which was to annul the famous statute of the 1460 Parliament in Dublin declaring that "the land of Ireland is, and at all times has been, corporate of itself by the ancient laws and customs used in the same...etc." That was the first statutory declaration of the legislative and legal independence of this country. Never forget it. Indeed, even as far back as 1320, the Irish Parliament enacted legislation "by the common assent of ...the archbishops, bishops, earls, barons and the entire commonalty of the land of Ireland." This is a very ancient tradition gentlemen – a parliament that goes back for hundreds of years."

They had reached College Green and the press of people on all sides disturbed the editor's dissertation.

"I shall join you later in the gallery," he said as he pushed his way into the House and headed in the direction of the refreshment rooms.

Just as he was about to enter the House, Brendan noticed the arrival of a large coach bearing Lord Lucan's livery. Mr. Bingham was the first to alight, followed by Lady Porter, and they proceeded into the House with their heads in the air. Pamela was about to alight when Brendan stepped forward and offered her his hand.

"How nice to see you, Brendan," she greeted him enthusiastically. "How are you and how is Margaret? I've been expecting you to call on us in Merrion Square?"

"My apologies," he replied. "I certainly will soon. I've been working very hard at the *Post*."

"Yes, I know. I read you all the time. I always said you were so clever."

Brendan was pleased with the compliment.

"Perhaps you'd come to supper some evening at Margaret's?" he asked.

"Yes, I'd be delighted," Pamela smiled as she moved ahead to catch up with her aunt.

The crowds were now pressing on all sides but Brendan thought he recognised one face in the crowd. He could have been mistaken, of course. He got only a fleeting glimpse before the crush carried him into the House. But he could have sworn that he had seen the red head of Hugh O'Malley, the fisherman from Murrisk.

Brendan never entered the House without responding within himself to its noble proportions. It had been designed by a young Irishman, Edward Pearce, who had travelled in Italy and was obviously influenced by Andrea Palladio's revival of the classical style there. It was later extended both to the east and to the west as the growing importance of Parliament required. The centrepiece of the noble structure was the Commons chamber itself – a perfect rotunda with Ionic pilasters enclosing a corridor which ran round the interior. The cupola, of immense height, bestowed a magnificence on the setting while providing uncommon acoustic perfection. And a gallery, supported by columns divided into compartments, and accommodating up to seven hundred spectators, commanded an uninterrupted view of the Chamber. A small part of the gallery was reserved for the Gentlemen of the Press and Brendan took his place there with George Pollack, looking down over the heads of the government benches to the Opposition facing them from the other side. To his left below was the Speaker's chair. To his right the main entrance to the Chamber.

Brendan watched the gallery filling up much earlier than usual. Some ladies of the very highest rank had taken their seats and he noticed Lady Lucan talking to Lady Porter. Members arriving to take their places, bowed gravely in the direction of this or that distinguished personage. Everyone was enjoying the spectacle on this day.

"I have never seen the House so crowded," said Arthur Noonan who was sitting just behind Brendan.

"Who is that sitting alone?", Brendan asked him, indicating a forlorn figure opposite.

"That is Lord Charles FitzGerald," replied Noonan, who knew every face in the House. "Brother to poor Lord Edward, you know," he added by way of explanation.

Just after 1 p.m. the clerk called the House to order and everyone rose as Mr. Foster, preceded by the Sergeant at Arms bearing the Speaker's mace, emerged from the vaulted side-entrance, bowed gravely to the assembly, and took his seat on the ornate Speaker's chair. The most fateful-ever session of the Irish Parliament was about to begin, and Mr. Magee slipped into a seat beside Brendan just in time to witness the start of that historic event. Brendan could smell the whiskey off his breath.

Brendan didn't have to take notes on the Viceroy's speech because copies were immediately made available to the Gentlemen of the Press. But he marked the one significant passage. It spoke of His Majesty's "anxious hope" that the new session of Parliament would provide "the most effectual means of maintaining and improving a connection essential to the common security of both kingdoms and of consolidating as far as possible, into one firm and lasting fabric, the strength, the power, the resources of the British Empire." And lest anyone was left in doubt of what His Majesty had in mind, Lord Castlereagh spelt it out when he rose to support the Viceroy's address. He thought "the only means of settling this unhappy country in permanent tranquillity and in connection with Britain incorporated, were to be found in a legislative Union." And after that the debate took off.

The regular business of Parliament, such as the tedious discussions on money bills, can indeed be very dull. But in the Irish House of Commons on this and the subsequent day, every man was aware that he was participating in a great occasion. The fate of the Parliament itself was in the balance. The subject had been the principal topic of conversation in the country over the past several months and the papers were full of it. Almost one hundred pamphlets had been published concerning it. Families were divided over it – as was the nation itself. And the speakers who now rose from this or that side of the House were supremely sensitive to the importance of their contributions. Many of them had devoted long hours of their Christmas recess to preparing and polishing their points of view. So, that day and night, the House heard some of the finest flights of oratory that had ever risen to the towering dome above them. Most of the talent – and certainly most of the passion – belonged to the Opposition. But there were over three score speakers in all, and Brendan noted the highlights of the best among them.

Mr. James FitzGerald, the late Prime Sergeant, made the point that "A King may abdicate for his own person, but he cannot abdicate the monarchy. And by as strong or stronger a reason, the House of Commons cannot renounce its share of authority."

Colonel Vereeker – he who had clashed with General Humbert outside Colooney – opposed the Union because it would drain away the men of property from the country.

*Mr. Jonah Barrington delivered such a spirited oration that the Speaker had to call him to order. But his reasoning was unanswerable. "Nothing," he said," can control or counteract Parliament within its constitutional bounds, but nothing can warrant it to exceed them. The very instant the delegated representatives in Parliament grant away the constitution which they were appointed to protect, the compact between them and their constituents becomes a nullity; their law of relinquishment is a nullity, and the Constitution is virtually and instantly dissolved."

And, of course, the government was not without its supporters, among whom was Mr. Bingham whose contribution however was more notable for its vitriol than its logic.

"Call me if there is anything of interest," the editor whispered to Brendan as he headed off for some more refreshment.

And so the debate swung back and forth into the evening. The galleries gradually thinned out and Brendan noticed when Lady Porter and Pamela took their leave. Members wandered in and out of the Chamber in the most casual fashion, as did Brendan himself after the first few hours, but he kept an eye cocked for the principal speakers and hurried back into the Chamber when any star performer took the floor.

The climax came in the early hours of the morning when Mr. William Conygham Plunkett raised both the temper of the House and the spirit of the Opposition by the uncompromising tone of his delivery. He first accused the government of outright corruption.

"During the Viceroyalty of Lord Cornwallis", he charged, "and during the administration of this unassuming stripling," (a reference to Lord Castlereagh), "within the last six weeks a system of black corruption has been carried on within the walls of the Castle, which would disgrace the annals of the worst period of the history of either country."

"George, slip down and alert the old man," Brendan asked his colleague. The editor's absences had become more frequent as the night wore on. "Tell him Mr. Plunkett is in capital form."

A few minutes later Mr. Magee returned looking rather flushed but in good time to catch the main part of Mr. Plunkett's speech.

"Sir," Mr. Plunkett continued, facing directly across to Lord Castlereagh, "in the most express terms I deny the competency of Parliament to do this Act of Union. I tell you that if, circumstanced as you are, you pass this act, it will be a mere nullity and that no man in Ireland will be bound to obey it. I make the assertion deliberately, I repeat it and I call on any man who hears me to take down my words. You have not been elected for this purpose, you are appointed to act under the constitution and not to alter it; you are appointed to exercise the functions of legislators and not to transfer them; and if you do so, your act is a dissolution of the government; you resolve society into its original elements and no man in the land is bound to obey you."

"Magnificent," exclaimed Mr. Magee, as Mr. Plunkett concluded to sustained applause from the gallery.

"If oratory can ever influence the cold hearts of public men, then surely that performance will swing some support," the editor remarked to Arthur Noonan who remained professionally dispassionate.

"It should, but it won't," he replied dryly.

Lord Castlereagh then decided to go on the offensive, and that night displayed powers far beyond what he was commonly supposed to possess but which indicated the eminence of his future career. There was no assertion he did not risk and no aspersion he did not cast. To the Bar he applied the term "pettifoggers" : to the Opposition "cabal", "combinators", "desperate faction", and to the nation itself "barbarism, ignorance and insensibility to the protection and paternal regards she had ever experienced from the British nation."

By the time Lord Castlereagh had finished, he had certainly fired many of his supporters to more lively contributions. But he had also fully excited the Opposition. The discussion afterwards proceeded with ever-increasing asperity and ever-less restraint until Colonel O'Donnell of Newport, in a maiden speech, caused the final sensation by the audacity of his language. Brendan noticed that the whiskered Colonel – whom he had often seen in Westport – looked very flushed as he rose to speak. But whether this was due to his indignation or to a more usual stimulant, he could not be sure. What the Colonel said was short and to the point, but it afterwards was the cause of his being deprived of his colonelcy of the Newport Militia.

"There is no person in or out of this house," he said, "who can be more anxious to support the closest connection between England and Ireland than I have been and ever shall. I have fought to preserve it from being interrupted by external and internal foes. But should the legislative independence of Ireland be voted away by Parliament which is not competent thereto, I shall hold myself discharged from my allegiance."

At this point there were noisy interruptions, and the Speaker had to call for order.

"I say, Mr. Speaker," the colonel continued undismayed, "the Constitution will be violated. I will join the people in preserving their rights. I will oppose the rebels in rich clothes with as much energy as I ever have done the rebels in rags."

As he sat down there was uproar in the gallery, many people cheering and waving while others shouted "shame" and "withdraw" until the Speaker, on whose nerves the long hours of debate were beginning to tell, threatened to clear the gallery entirely if order was not maintained. After that there was quiet. One did not meddle with Mr. Foster.

"I never thought I'd hear such sentiments in this house," said Mr. Magee to whom every word of the Colonel's speech had been sheer music.

"And you may not again," put in Arthur Noonan. "When members start to talk like that you can understand why the government wants to shut up the shop."

"When members talk like that, let the whole country sit up and listen," said the editor triumphantly. "It is the spirit of '82 again." And there was a gleam in his eye that Brendan had never seen before.

"That spirit is dead and gone," said Arthur Noonan, "which is why Mr. Grattan is not here tonight."

"My God I wish he was," said Mr. Magee. "He should not have missed this night."

Finally a division was called for by the Opposition. Over seventy members had spoken during the debate. The subject was exhausted and all parties seemed equally impatient for the resolution. The house divided as the rising sun was sending its first rays into the great dome over the Chamber. Everyone knew the result would be close. But the outcome was still wide open.

The members filed in past the Bar of the House to the Court of Requests, counted by the tellers as they passed. Then the tellers passed their count to the Chair and Mr. Foster rose to announce the historic result.

> For the Address to His Majesty 105
> For omitting the Union clause 111
> Abstentions 84
> Majority against the government 6

At the announcement, loud applause broke out all over the House and spread to the corridors and to the streets outside, and the Speaker, for once, showed a rare indulgence for such demonstrations. Brendan, too, jumped out of his seat and started clapping and cheering with the rest and he even threw his arms around Arthur Noonan.

For a while the editor sat slumped in his chair as if stunned by the result. John Magee had grown cynical with the years and few events in public life surprised him, much less moved him. But this night was different. For a moment he was overcome by a sense of awe, conscious that the impossible had become possible in his own time.

"It's a miracle," he exclaimed. "Nothing less than a miracle. I just cannot believe it. I really find it hard to believe." Then rising wearily he announced with gusto, "Gentlemen, there will be champagne for breakfast."

A few weeks later, Lord Castlereagh, the Chief Secretary, arranged a series of very private dinners at his official residence in Mornington House on Merrion Street, which had been leased from Lord Cloncurry. He had had time to reflect on the setback of the Union proposal in the House of Commons, and to receive the reaction from London. The British cabinet was absolutely determined to press ahead with its proposals and the Chief Secretary wanted to map out a new plan of campaign.

"I thought we would dine in the study to-night," he said to Lord Altamont, who was his guest that night. "It is more intimate and more conducive to business," he added with a sly smile.

"Yes, and we can be warm there," said Lord Altamont, rubbing his hands. It was a bitterly cold night in February, 1799.

The serious business of the evening did not commence until after the servants had withdrawn and the port was in circulation. Then, at a favourable moment, Lord Castlereagh introduced the real worry that was on his mind.

"I was really disappointed with the county members," Lord Castlereagh said. Thirty six of them voted against the Union. Nineteen were in favour, and nine did not vote at all. In other words it was two to one against."

"And who would blame them?", Lord Altamont replied. "They still don't know how many of them are to be admitted to the Imperial Parliament. Until that simple question is settled, why should they offer themselves like sacrificial lambs?"

"I can understand that," said Lord Castlereagh, "and I have given it a lot of thought. But there can only be two members from each Irish county elected to the Parliament in London. The real problem, of course, is the Borough members. The cabinet is adamant that not more than one hundred Irish members in total may join the Imperial Parliament. So what do we do with all the borough holders?"

"Buy them out," said Lord Altamont emphatically. "There is no other way. They must be compensated."

"Compensated?" queried Lord Castlereagh.

"Yes, compensated for their former expense. If you are to abolish their property, then compensation must be paid."

"I can see the Opposition making a meal out of that," continued Lord Castlereagh. "The rights of the representation of the people being treated as property – and the people then taxed to buy out that property."

"Let them say as they will," cut in Lord Altamont again. "If you want the boroughs – you'll have to pay for them."

"I suppose means might be found", put in Lord Castlereagh, "to satisfy the private interests of a sufficient number of individuals affected without resorting to the embarrassing principle of avowed compensation."

"It won't do," repeated Lord Altamont emphatically. "You must get down to details. Where were we disappointed? I can think of two Peers who between them control eighteen borough members and whose influence was lost to us. Instead of my Lords Downshire and Ely bringing forward eighteen members as these noble lords might have done, only five appeared, and one of Lord Downshire's men actually voted against us. How are we to win over these votes and others like them? In my opinion, they must be bought out – and a great reform it would be too."

"There is another category we must consider," said Lord Castlereagh, leaving aside the question of compensation for the borough members for the moment. "I mean the unpledged. On the critical vote in the House on January 24th, there were no less than eighty-four uncast votes in the House of three hundred. I believe there is great potential here for winning over to our side many of those who are still undecided."

"Great potential, yes," said Lord Altamont with a note of sarcasm. "It just depends on your price."

"Perhaps we should allow the subject to rest for a while. Let the Opposition revel in its victory. That way it will get complacent. I'm inclined to leave things until the Summer recess. We don't want the Opposition stirring up the country with public meetings."

At the mention of public meetings, Lord Altamont shifted himself in his chair.

"Damned if I'd let them call a single meeting," he snorted. "We can't have them encouraging the lawless element in the country. Things are bad enough as they are. Cattle being houghed. Houses burned. Arms stolen. What we need is another spell of martial law. That would put paid to your meetings."

"I wish we could do more to persuade the public of the real benefits of the Union," Lord Altamont added. "You know there is a great fear in the country of higher taxation. The rumour has been circulated that Irish taxation will be brought up to British levels. Why not get the Viceroy out into the country? Cornwallis is the man to talk to the men of property in the country. He is the man to win over the country members."

"A damned good idea," said Castlereagh "And we could produce demonstrations of support from every town he visits. Yes, we must stir up manifestations of support from the town Corporations, from the Sheriffs, from the Grand Juries and the men of property in every county in Ireland."

And so the discussion continued into the early hours of the morning. Lord Castlereagh had jotted down a few points here and there. At the end of the evening he felt greatly encouraged.

"It is obviously a question of the price," he concluded to himself later, "although the payment may be in kind as much as specie. As long as the Catholics are quiet, and I think we can count on the bishops for that, we can deal with the rest. It will cost a couple of million – but this cost is spurious. It will all come out of Irish taxation. In fact it will be only be a matter of re-distribution."

A few days later, Lord Castlereagh met with the Under Secretary Cooke and drafted out his plan of campaign. The private meetings had been extremely useful. It now remained to activate the new strategy during the long summer recess.

Chapter XV

PAMELA'S MISFORTUNE

EVEN BEFORE he called that first afternoon, Aunt Olive had decided that the Hon. Richard Bingham was the perfect match for Pamela. He was heir to a fortune and connected not only with the very cream of London society but through his sister Lavinia, Countess Spencer, with the core of the Whig party as well. Aunt Olive had visions of Pamela captivating Dublin society as Lavinia Bingham had done in her day. And why not? The Prestons were every bit as old a family as the Binghams – if not so celebrated in terms of fashion. As for beauty, Pamela, if anything, had the advantage.

During the subsequent few months, they saw a lot of young Bingham at Number Ten. He often escorted the ladies on their morning walk in the Square or, weather permitting, drove them out in his chaise to Blackrock for a breath of sea air. Towards the middle of February, there was an exceptionally hard frost and the lakes everywhere were frozen over. Ice skating briefly burst into fashion and Mr. Bingham, who had perfected the art while in Switzerland, introduced Pamela to the thrills and spills of this exciting recreation, at first coaching her slowly and with great patience, then improving both her style and confidence and finally quickening the tempo until their elegance on the ice was commented upon favourably in *The Hibernian Magazine*. Pamela delighted in this new sport which combined the several pleasures of an exhilarating exercise, the acquisition of a whole range of fur muffs, collars and caps, and the intimate proximity of Mr. Richard Bingham.

Pamela's life was now a constant round of entertainments, of supper parties and balls, of fittings for new dresses and of flattery on all sides. She was flattered most of all by the attention of young Bingham and was influenced by the universal opinion, continuously asserted, that he would make a most suitable husband.

Aunt Olive, of course, was foremost in the expression of this opinion. The more she saw of Mr. Bingham, the more she liked him, and her only fear was that he might slip through her fingers. Nevertheless, she was beginning to feel that it was high time for the young man to declare his intentions when, at last, the Great Day arrived. They had driven out to Ranelagh Gardens earlier in the day to watch Mr. Crosbie make one of his celebrated ascents in an elegant balloon. It was a bright, crisp and sunny Spring day, and they all felt the exhilaration of the special occasion. Mr. Bingham had joined them for tea afterwards in the drawing-room upstairs in Number Ten.

Although she had been looking forward to his declaration and had been hoping, indeed praying, for it, Aunt Olive was rather embarrassed once Mr. Bingham began to broach the delicate topic. She missed her late husband at times like this. He would have been better able to deal with the business side of the affair. Nevertheless, she braced herself as required; listened carefully to his proposal and was able to confirm to Mr. Bingham that her niece's fortune exceeded one hundred thousand pounds in the funds, apart from her property in Mayo. Lady Porter looked forward to meeting the Earl of Lucan at an early date and to finalising the details. And when Bingham later repeated his proposal personally to Pamela, the cup of joy was overflowing at Number Ten Merrion Square.

～～～～～～ ● ～～～～～～

To Lady Porter's great surprise, however, Captain John's solicitor, Mr. Alexander Hamilton, was strongly opposed to the arrangement once he had been fully informed.

"Miss Preston is much too young to contemplate marriage," he asserted, " It would be extremely imprudent to attach any lien to her estate before she attains her majority. And her father is not yet cold in his grave," the solicitor complained in a shocked tone that for a while quite astonished Aunt Olive. But she was determined that nothing and nobody was going to stand in the way of this excellent match – and least of all Mr. Hamilton.

"I think I am the person best qualified to decide such matters," she said archly, "and I have given the couple my blessing. All that remains is for you to draw up the terms of the settlement."

"You seem to forget, Lady Porter," the canny solicitor replied "that I am Miss Preston's guardian and that I hold full powers of attorney over her funds until she reaches the age of twenty-one."

Aunt Olive was taken aback and all her old suspicions came rushing back to her. But she controlled her feelings while she tried to discover what the old fellow was really after. Obviously, he had some quid-pro-quo in mind before agreeing to the proposal. But, to her surprise, it turned out that the solicitor was beyond persuasion. He had no intention whatever of handing over control of the estate, and the best Aunt Olive could do was to get his agreement to the formula of a transfer that would become effective on Pamela's twenty-first birthday.

Mr. Bingham, of course, was even less happy. He had been looking forward to the availability of cash to meet his debts and was not at all pleased to learn of such complications. But the very rumour of his intended marriage to Miss Preston had greatly improved his credit in the town, and he found the expectation of one hundred thousand pounds in even two years time to be eminently discountable. Nevertheless, he took the precaution of sending his own solicitor, Mr. Gerald Beauchamp, to see Mr. Hamilton and to copper-fasten the settlement.

Mr. Beauchamp was a pedantic and pernickety little man who had acted for the Bingham family for years, and he took great care in working out a very long agreement with Mr. Hamilton covering every imaginable eventuality. The date of transfer for the funds was agreed as 17th May 1801, Pamela's twenty-first birthday – but they allowed for the possible death of either party before that date; they allowed for the possibility of children and they allowed for the possible death of the children. Every clause of the agreement was drafted and redrafted to the eventual satisfaction of both solicitors and, in the end, Mr. Beauchamp came to feel a certain admiration for his colleague. Mr. Hamilton had not been at all obstructive. He had simply insisted on the exercise of his rights and responsibilities as guardian until the girl's maturity. Mr. Beauchamp was forced to acknowledge that in similar circumstances he would have acted in exactly the same way.

He was about to leave Mr. Hamilton's office with the final draft when his meticulous mind remembered one last point.

"And now, if you don't mind," he said to Mr. Hamilton, "I would like to examine the certificates of the funds held in Miss Preston's name. A mere formality, of course," he added deprecatingly.

Old Hamilton never blinked an eyelid.

"Of course, Mr. Beauchamp," he replied, "I'll be happy to make them available for inspection. But I don't hold them in this office. For safe keeping they are deposited in Mr. La Touche's bank. I'll make arrangements for you to examine them there."

But no examination ever took place. At first it slipped Mr. Beauchamp's mind, but a note on his file reminded him well after the agreement had received the final approbation of both parties. Once again, Mr. Hamilton promised to make arrangements for inspection, but once again some other business intervened on the appointed day. A third time, Mr. Beauchamp applied to him but, most unfortunately, Mr. Hamilton was then confined to bed and could attend to no business. And there the matter might have rested but for Mr. Beauchamp's casual mention of the difficulty to Mr. La Touche after a meeting of the Dublin Society in May. And when Mr. La Touche denied that Mr. Hamilton held any securities at all at his bank, imagine the wonder, increasing to consternation, that suddenly took a grip of Mr. Beauchamp. For the first time, the awful truth began to dawn on that honest man. He immediately dispatched a note to Mr. Hamilton at his residence, demanding that the certificates be produced within twenty-four hours.

The note came as no surprise to Mr. Hamilton. In a way he had been expecting something like it for years. He knew inwardly that sooner or later it would catch up with him and strangely he felt a certain relief. For years he had been gambling with clients' funds, first on quite a small scale, but cumulatively mounting into tens of thousands of pounds. Not that he ever intended to defraud any one of them. He confidently expected to pay every last client when the time came. But in the meantime he drew on one client's resources to finance a deficiency in another. The control of the Preston funds had saved him from a serious embarrassment the previous October and, in an effort to recoup the situation, he had plunged heavily in the December lottery. But when he lost badly in that, he knew it was only a question of time. And he knew exactly what to do.

The morning after he received the note from Mr. Beauchamp, he walked down to the South Wall, which runs into the sea near the fishing village of Ringsend, and having very deliberately filled all his coat pockets with stones, he waded into the sea. Mr. Hamilton had followed in every detail the precedent set by his good friend, Mr. Richard Power, the former Usher of the Court of Chancery. Mr. Hamilton's body was fished out of the sea a week later but the unraveling of his affairs required several months, and what was left of his clients funds after the deficiency had been worked out to the last shilling was hardly worth mentioning.

<hr />

When Lord Lucan was announced at Number Ten soon thereafter, Aunt Olive knew exactly what to expect; and the Earl came to the point almost as soon as he was shown into Lady Porter's drawing-room upstairs,

"I have taken it upon myself to react to this terrible business as I know any uncertainty must be intolerable to dear Miss Preston," he said. "So distressed is my son at this unfortunate development that he begs to be excused from attending to any affairs. But he asked me to convey his compliments and best wishes to Miss Preston and to your good self. As you are no doubt aware, his heart is entirely committed to Miss Preston and he is more distressed on her behalf than you can imagine."

Aunt Olive was watching Lord Lucan closely. In her heart she knew the purpose of his visit and what he was about to say. But she hated him for it and all her former admiration for the Binghams now soured inside her. She despised the bewigged and ingratiating aristocrat now rolling his hands as he trotted out his excuses before her. Certainly she had no intention of letting him off lightly.

"My unpleasant duty must be faced," Lord Lucan continued, and if he had been looking at her he would have seen Lady Porter stiffen in her high-backed chair.

Aunt Olive didn't attempt to disguise the look of contempt that clouded her countenance as he continued his exculpation. Of course she had known it would be this way. But to think that young Bingham had not the courage, nay the decency, to face his fiancée. "Distressed, indeed," she thought to herself as the Earl droned on about the family's commitments, responsibilities and regrets. "And what of the distress to my poor, sweet Pamela," she thought.

"I am absolutely amazed at what you have to say, Lord Lucan," she cut in "Has your son no sense of honour? Has he no thought for Miss Preston's reputation?"

Lord Lucan moved himself in his chair. He resented having to iron out his son's difficulties and was hoping the interview could be concluded without acrimony. But he had underestimated Lady Porter.

"You will own the circumstances have altered fundamentally, Lady Porter," he countered defensively.

"Through no fault of Miss Preston," Aunt Olive shot back.

"Then where does the fault lie?", asked Lord Lucan and there was a stiffer tone in the question.

"Mr. Hamilton deceived us and defrauded us as you well know, Sir," Aunt Olive answered with some heat.

"But why was he given absolute control of the funds?"

"He had been my dear brother's solicitor."

"But surely it is normal to have at least two trustees, if not three? Surely it was imprudent not to protect your niece's funds in this fashion?"

Aunt Olive coloured deeply. Whether by instinct or by accident, the canny aristocrat had got to the core of the tragedy and Aunt Olive felt distinctly uncomfortable. The tables were being turned on her and Lord Lucan was converting an apology into an inquisition.

"I am not experienced in money matters, my Lord," she said rather grandly. "If only my dear husband, Lord Porter, were alive, he would have seen to all these affairs. This terrible business would never have happened."

Lord Lucan knew that he had scored a point and he drove home his advantage.

"I don't wish to appear critical in any way," he said in a more confident tone. "It is a difficult time for all concerned. I merely want you to understand why, most regrettably, the marriage cannot go ahead. Of course, if there is anything that...."

Aunt Olive rose abruptly and cut him off in mid sentence.

"I understand entirely," she said coldly. "Please do not trouble yourself further, Lord Lucan. Of course this will be a grave disappointment to my niece and, coming after the tragedies of the past year, is a double blow to one so young. But I will look after her and care for her as no husband would. Good Morning, Lord Lucan."

The scandal of Mr. Hamilton's ill-use of his client's funds and of his subsequent suicide was soon the talk of the town. And when Richard Bingham broke off his engagement to the unfortunate Miss Preston, even *The Hibernian Magazine* found space to mention it

Immediately he heard the news, Brendan decided to call again to Number Ten Merrion Square and this time his reception by Lady Porter was of a very different character.

"How kind of you to call, Mr. O'Reilly," she said. "I know Pamela will greatly appreciate your concern and support in these most difficult circumstances. In the course of a year she has lost her father and now her fortune, but the cruelest blow of all was the dastardly behaviour of Mr. Bingham who had declared – in my hearing – his undying love for my poor niece. The situation is well nigh unbearable."

"If there is anything I can do to alleviate her distress, please be assured that it would be an honour for me to do so. Perhaps I can help in Murrisk?" Brendan proffered.

"You are very kind," Lady Porter replied, and for once she appeared genuinely appreciative, "but I think I can cope with the practical problems. My real concern is the psychological blow to one so young."

"On that score, may I offer an opinion, with the greatest respect. I believe Miss Preston is most fortunate to have avoided any contract of marriage with that man."

"Whatever can you mean?"

"Principally that Bingham is unworthy of her and would certainly have made her very unhappy."

Lady Porter frowned but was eager to hear more.

"Richard Bingham is a gambler and keeps very bad company in this town. I believe his principal motivation in seeking Pamela's hand was to get control of her fortune."

"That is a most serious allegation."

"But I believe it to be the truth – however painful it may be to accept at this time. I believe Pamela is very lucky to have escaped his clutches."

Lady Porter was intrigued with this information, which evidently she wanted to believe. Brendan knew that she would investigate it further. But it didn't really help Pamela very much. However, Lady Porter was happy to discuss the situation with Brendan for half an hour while they took tea. Then she accompanied Brendan to the door and repeatedly invited him to call again.

Chapter XVI

STEPHEN QUITS COCOA WALK

THE LAST SUNDAY in August was traditionally a day of celebration in Cocoa Walk. It marked the end of the season. From the beginning of September a new season of planting was begun and September was the busy month for shipping the finished hogsheads of sugar and puncheons of rum.

The four men had been drinking since sundown, but the evening had turned sour early on with Tallon hinting that Jock Reid was siphoning off rum from the distillery and Reid in turn accusing the overseer of falsifying the accounts from the sugar-mill. It was that time of the year when Jock Reid knew that he should be heading home to Scotland and equally knew that he never would. And to add to the bad mood, another slave had gone missing.

"So what's the word on Angelo?", Jock asked just to annoy John Tallon.

"No word yet."

" So he's in for the Jupiter treatment, is he?"

"He'll get what he deserves. But it's none of your business."

"Well it is my business if he has taken Celina with him."

"Celina?", Stephen asked

"Yes, the plump one in the kitchen. Tallon's tart in fact," Jock threw in maliciously.

"Shut your mouth," the overseer barked.

"Well, has she gone or hasn't she?", Jock continued.

"Yes, she's missing too. But we don't know if she went with Angelo."

"She nearly went with Jupiter didn't she?", Jock asked slyly.

Tallon turned white with rage at this remark and jumped out of his chair. For a moment it looked as if he was about to launch himself onto the drunken Scotsman but, instead, he turned on his heel and strode out onto the veranda.

"What was all that about?", Stephen asked.

"Celina? Well, you know Tallon used to fancy her. But her mother was an Ibo and she had set her eye on Jupiter. Essentially, that's why Jupiter ran away in the end."

"And that's why Tallon beat him so badly when he was brought back?"

"Well of course. Why else?"

Stephen was dumfounded and threw back another measure of rum. And then and there he determined to quit Cocoa Walk before the week was out.

Just as the sun was dipping below the horizon, Cocoa sounded the gong for dinner – a nightly touch of ceremony on which Tallon insisted. It was meant to be reminiscent of "the old country" or something like that. The overseer returned inside and took his place at the head of the table. Not another word was said about Angelo or Jupiter or Celina.

As the meal progressed, Stephen noticed that Jock was paying a lot of attention to Cocoa, running his hand up her thigh when she served the turtle soup and patting her bottom whenever she came within reach again. But Stephen pretended to ignore it.

Cocoa's mother was a mulatto and obviously her father had been white – though who he was nobody now remembered. Cocoa herself had a beautiful body, slender and elegant in form, sparkling teeth, light brown skin and jet black straight hair. But her most attractive feature was her large soft brown eyes that seemed to follow Stephen wherever he went. From the first moment of his arrival, Cocoa had attached herself to him and jealously attended to his every want. And although Stephen felt nothing whatever for her, he appropriated her as his property as one would a stray dog – and allowed her to act as his personal servant.

There was a long tradition in Jamaica that the coloured slaves – the progeny of former white masters – enjoyed a special status on the plantations. The Mulatto men were trained as craftsmen rather than sent for field work. And the women worked as domestics, cooking, cleaning, washing, sewing and serving the licentious demands of the white men as required. Although they had their own quarters close to the house, in practice they occupied the main residence as informally and as regularly as the domestic pets. The houses, of course, were designed to avail of the least breeze from any direction. They had slatted shutters instead of solid walls and doors were seldom closed. No one looked for or expected any privacy whatever. The white man ate, conversed, slept, dressed, bathed, even fornicated within view of all. Assured of his absolute superiority, he lived a life open to uncritical observation by the slaves.

"When are you going to make Cocoa happy?", Jock drawled across the table to Stephen, who ignored him.

"Will you answer me?", demanded Jock truculently. "When is the happy event to take place?"

"You're drunk," Stephen replied with contempt. The heat was oppressive.

"I'm only asking a question," Jock mocked again.

"Well, mind your own business," said Stephen, who had had enough of Jock's ribaldry for one night.

The meal went on; a whole roast kid followed by jerked pork and ring-tailed pigeon. The men ate and drank to excess and the conversation became more acerbic and ever more lewd. Dick Perkins replayed his repertoire of dirty jokes and John Tallon – who thought it beneath him when sober to display any sense of humour – actually laughed out loud. But Jock persisted in trying to tease Stephen.

"I think I'll have to oblige her myself," he announced, as Cocoa was serving cassava cakes with syrup.

"What's that?", asked Tallon from the top of the table.

"I said, I think I'll have to show the way."

"What the hell are you talking about?", demanded Dick Perkins.

"Cocoa, of course. What else, you fool?"

Perkins looked across to Stephen who pretended not to notice. He refused to be provoked by this drunken Scot. Jock pushed back his chair noisily.

"Cocoa, my little one," he called loudly, grabbing for the girl. "You come with me."

"Take your hands off her," Stephen spat across the table and suddenly the air was electric.

"Cut it out, Jock," the overseer ordered. The last thing he wanted was a bust-up of the furniture.

"Cut what out, damn you? If Stephen doesn't want her, she mustn't go to waste."

Stephen looked at Cocoa and saw the terror in her eyes. And for the first time, he actually felt for her as a human being. Jock was holding her tightly by the wrist, hurting her, and her whole body was pulling at an angle to escape from his clutches. And her very vulnerability incensed Stephen. He got up slowly but menacingly and rounded the table towards the sodden Scotsman. But Jock didn't have to be persuaded. With a deft manoeuvre, he twisted his grip on Cocoa and positioned her between himself and the oncoming Stephen. Stephen, without a word, scooped her up easily in his arms and strode into his bedroom. And as he kicked the door shut, the others let out a loud cheer.

Stephen hardly knew what he was doing. He had brought her into his room for her own protection. But he was drunk and confused.

"Are you alright?", he asked the girl lying splayed-legged on his bed.

Cocoa smiled up at him. She had recovered herself completely.

She twisted her body as she spoke as if to make room for him on the bed and her short shift moved even higher up her thigh.

"Don't leave me, Master," she implored, those huge brown eyes looking straight up at him.

Stephen looked down at her again and his gaze lingered on her as it had never done before. His hand brushed against her thigh and he felt her whole body twitch suddenly like a nervous filly.

She smiled up at him again, welcoming and wanting. But he still stood by the bed undecided. She lifted one hand to him and almost unconsciously he took it. He had never touched her before but now yielded involuntarily to the soft coaxing palm of the warm hand that gently enticed him down towards her.

But at that moment a great roar of laughter went up from the dinner table at yet another lewd joke from Jock Reid's collection. Stephen drew back suddenly and got a grip of himself. My God, he thought, I'm no better than the rest of them.

"Off with you now," he said to Cocoa, but in a kind voice and he slipped her a coin as she disappeared into the night.

~~~~~~ • ~~~~~~

Stephen awoke before dawn. His head was buzzing and he walked out onto the veranda in his bare feet to breathe in the morning air. The sun had not yet come up over the horizon but its rays had started to brighten the sky away to the east. Everywhere was so quiet and so calm. And it was cool. Stephen remembered the first day he had arrived and he recalled how he thought of the valley as the Garden of Eden. And then he remembered the night before. He knew it was time to go.

He dressed quickly and scribbled a note to John Tallon which read "I'll leave the mare with Mr. Queenborough." Then he walked over to the stables and saddled up "Sunny" and set off for Kingston. He had a meal in Spanish Point and then rode on till he arrived at Diana Cole's celebrated boarding house on the Parade in Kingston. He was tired and dusty and very hot and was glad to find Miss Cole herself sitting out on the veranda.

"Welcome to Kingston," she announced as Stephen walked up the wooden stairs.

Stephen noticed a look of surprise on Miss Cole's face as he drew level with her and held out his hand, his ring flashing in the sun.

"My name is Allen," he said. "Mr. Stephen Allen"

"And where do you come from?"

"From Cocoa Walk."

"Yes, but before that. Are you English?"

"No. I come from Ireland. From Mayo in the west of Ireland."

"Glory be to God," Diana exclaimed, as she turned on her heel and led him into the house.

Chapter XVII

THE DEATH OF AUNT OLIVE

FOR SEVERAL DAYS after Aunt Olive told her the terrible news, Pamela refused to leave her room. Most of the time she just lay in bed with the shutters closed tight and the heavy curtains pulled over. She locked out the world physically but she could not rid her mind of the humiliation.

Pamela wasn't worried about the loss of her fortune but she felt betrayed. Was it possible that Mr. Bingham had wanted only her money? She knew that was what the gossips would be saying all over town, but she refused to believe it herself. Nevertheless, she dreaded facing out into society again.

"Lucky to learn his real character before it was too late," Aunt Olive comforted her.

"No proper gentleman would behave in such a fashion. I often thought the Binghams lacked breeding."

"It wasn't Richard's fault," Pamela replied. "I'm sure it was Lord Lucan's doing."

Aunt Olive didn't bother to contradict her. And what good would it do anyway? Her real worry was that Pamela was so depressed and eating practically nothing. Finally she decided to consult her good friend and neighbour Dr Walter Wilkinson.

"Unfortunately she is making no effort to recover," Dr. Wilkinson complained to Lady Porter after his series of calls to the patient. "She will not listen to my advice."

"She needs to be taken out of herself completely," Aunt Olive replied. "Surely a change would do her good.?"

Aunt Olive herself had travelled very little during her own life but she always imagined that travel, somehow, must be good for others. "What about a visit to London?", she suggested.

"I don't believe she is well enough for that," Dr. Wilkinson replied. "But perhaps a visit to Bath might prove beneficial."

The pros and cons of a sojourn in that Spa were discussed over several days and had almost been decided upon when a letter was delivered to Number Ten from Mr. Brendan O'Reilly.

"I have to travel to Westport in the near future," Brendan wrote to Lady Porter "and I wonder if I could have the honour of escorting Miss Preston for a visit to the West?"

For the first time since Lord Lucan's fateful call, Pamela showed a spark of interest. A hundred times over she had anticipated the veiled sneers of the very same people who previously had flattered and fawned on her. An escape to the West, to see Murrisk again and Croagh Patrick and Clew Bay, suddenly seemed a wonderful idea.

⁓⁓⁓⁓ • ⁓⁓⁓⁓

They left for the West about two weeks later on the post-chaise from Islandbridge. There were six people inside the carriage and Brendan positioned Pamela beside a window with, opposite her, Lady Porter's maid who had been sent to look after Pamela while she was in the West. Brendan sat beside Pamela, thus protecting her on that side from any disturbance from the other passengers.

On the first day, Pamela hardly spoke at all while Brendan read through the July edition of Walker's *Hibernian Magazine*. But Pamela was not asleep. She had retreated into a sort of daze while her thoughts went back to the last time she was on this very road coming from Athlone almost a year ago. So much had happened since. Of course she thought a lot about Richard Bingham, of his charm and his manners and of all the wonderful, sweet endearments he had whispered in her ear. She blamed him for nothing at all. He was an aristocrat and aristocrats are different. It wasn't that he didn't love her. Of course he did. Lord Lucan was to blame. Money was everything to aristocrats. It had to be. Richard was just a victim of the unfortunate circumstances. Just like herself.

The horses were changed at Kinegad and again at Kilbeggan and then they headed through the long summer evening to Athlone. And now Pamela's thoughts turned to Stephen Allen and she remembered how they had both arrived in Athlone a year ago, exhausted and wet through and through and how they had been rescued by Colonel O'Donnell. But how strange that Stephen had simply disappeared. Something extraordinary must have driven him out of Dublin. And how odd that no-one had heard a word from him. He could have gone to India and the East India Company or to the Americas. But why hadn't he written? There might be word of him in Murrisk. She had never properly thanked him for getting her safely to Dublin. She had always taken him for granted – every since she was a small girl. And he had always been around when she needed him. Could he have joined the army and been killed or died of fever? It was awful not to know. How selfishly distracted she had been not to get to the bottom of this question before now.

It wasn't until they had left Athlone behind them and crossed the Shannon that they had the carriage to themselves and Brendan was able to sit at the window opposite to Pamela. He was browsing through the *Hibernian Magazine* again when his eye fell on the death notices.

"Good Lord, did you know that? Lord Lucan has died."

Pamela looked up with interest.

I'll read what it says. "Aged 69, the Rt. Hon. Charles Bingham, Earl of Lucan, baron Bingham of Castlebar and baronet of Nova Scotia: he is succeeded in titles and estate by his only son Richard, now Earl of Lucan."

But Pamela made no comment and gazed out the window again.

"I can't help thinking how lucky you are to be free of that man," Brendan said.

"Lucky?", Pamela replied nervously.

"Yes, lucky to be saved a lot of unhappiness."

"Please, I'd rather not discuss that subject," Pamela replied. "I've been trying to shut it out of my mind."

"I still say you had a narrow escape. You must know that Bingham was a cad and completely unworthy of you."

"How can you say such a thing?", Pamela protested.

"Bingham is a gambler and a cheat and he was deceiving you from the start. I told Lady Porter all about him."

Pamela recoiled.

"How could you say such horrid things about Richard," she cried. "It's not his fault at all. It was that dreadful Mr. Hamilton who deceived us all. Anyhow I don't want to talk about it. Please don't mention Mr. Bingham to me again."

They continued on in silence for some time.

"I'm sorry," Brendan said, "I really must apologise. I didn't mean to upset you."

"I know," she said and in a sudden change of mood she lowered the glass and put her head out the window. There was a strong gust of warm air and the smell of new-mown hay pervaded the carriage. Brendan saw her breathe in the country air like an elixir while the wind blew straight into her face. But suddenly the wind caught her bonnet and whipped it right off her head.

"Stop the carriage," Brendan cried and knocked hard on the roof of the cabin. The horses were gradually pulled up and Brendan walked back the road to retrieve the bonnet and Pamela came running behind him.

"Oh, it's good to be back in the West," she said and she took Brendan's arm while they walked back to the chaise. "You're such a good friend."

~~~~~~~ • ~~~~~~~

"I always read your pieces in the *Post*," Pamela said as they resumed their journey. "But you sound so serious about politics now."

"Well, of course, I am. It's a serious business."

"Aunt Olive is for the Union. She says it will prevent the French making any more trouble."

"It may well do, but that's not the point."

"So what is the point?"

"The whole point is to keep the Catholics out of Parliament. It's as simple as that. They would rather abolish Parliament altogether than allow representation to the Catholics."

"Oh, it will probably never happen," she concluded. Politics bored her. Her mind was already running ahead to Murrisk. But as the day wore on she relaxed more and more and gradually slipped into a light sleep.

Brendan could now let his eyes rest on this picture of innocence whose limp form he was almost touching. Before him was a young woman he barely knew. He had never been alone with her before except for that dance at Margaret's wedding. Never had a real conversation. Their paths had crossed over the past year but in a casual fashion only. And yet he had grown to feel a compassion for her. Or was it more than that?

As the carriage rolled into the West, Brendan began to examine his own feelings. He recognised he felt something special for Pamela. Why else had he called on her in Dublin and why else had he suggested this visit home to Murrisk? But there was no evidence that she returned his feelings although to be counted a "friend" was better than nothing. She was an only child and had been brought up surrounded by love. Everybody loved her and her own personality seemed to reflect this reservoir of warm affection. She had even survived the past year without the blemish of bitterness.

Brendan leant back on his seat and stretched out his legs before him. He was looking forward to his first return home in almost a year. But much more than that, he was looking forward to spending more time in the company of Miss Pamela Preston.

~~~~~~ • ~~~~~~

In some ways Pamela had dreaded this return to her home. But after the initial shock of seeing the house still in ruins and after the first embarrassed greetings from the staff, she felt her old strength returning. Pamela found herself drawn into all sorts of decisions concerning the house, the estate, and the servants. The decision to rebuild the house on the same site but to a more modern design had been taken several months ago and plans had been drawn up. Malcolm, too, had decisions for her to face, rents to be reviewed, stock to be replenished and some men to be replaced. Pamela relished all this activity and the very demands on her time and authority stimulated her both mentally and physically. She considered that she was doing something useful for the first time in many months. The discharge of these responsibilities gave her more pleasure than all the balls and parties of the Dublin season. Gradually the hurt inflicted by young Bingham receded from her consciousness. In fact, she began to admit to herself that she may well have been fortunate to have avoided a life-long entanglement with that gentleman.

<center>~~~~~~ • ~~~~~~</center>

Pamela had expected to find word of Stephen in Murrisk but nobody had heard from him since the day he had left with her for Dublin.

"Not even a short note," complained Mrs. Barton, who was convinced he had joined the army in England.

"I hope he came to no harm," Malcolm added, "but he was well able to look after himself. I'd wager he is in the army all right and probably in India or some place foreign. We'll hear from him no doubt one of these fine days. And probably when we least expect it."

One day she went up to Stephen's old room in the stable-yard. It was exactly as he had left it, neat but very masculine and smelling of leather and tackle and boots.

"I must ask Aunt Olive about him again," she thought. But the very next day she received a letter from Dr. Wilkinson which put all other considerations entirely out of her head. Aunt Olive was seriously ill and Dr. Wilkinson requested that Pamela should return to Dublin as soon as possible.

<center>~~~~~~ • ~~~~~~</center>

It was early in September before she got back to Dublin and Pamela was alarmed at the deterioration in Aunt Olive's condition.

"I am afraid she is not at all well," Dr. Wilkinson admitted.

"May I know the real situation, Dr. Wilkinson?" Pamela asked him. "It is better that I know the truth now."

Reluctantly Dr. Wilkinson gave his opinion that Lady Porter had only a few months to live.

"And that if she is lucky," he added. "In fact she could go at any time."

Six or seven months ago this news would have been enough to plunge Pamela into a severe depression. But not any more. Having been through her measure of suffering, she was now more capable of dealing with it. Now she thought only of making the remaining months of her aunt's life as tolerable and as comfortable as possible, and she settled into a routine of looking after her every whim and want.

Pamela often sat up half the night with her aunt, sometimes playing cards with her, sometimes sewing or reading or just chatting and quite often dozing off in the big comfortable chair near the fireplace. She knew she couldn't really do anything for her aunt except keep her company. But this was what pleased Aunt Olive most of all. She dreaded being left alone.

It was during this time that Pamela learnt whole chapters of the family history that she had never heard before. Aunt Olive seemed to have powers of almost total recall – especially events of forty, fifty, and even sixty years ago. Often she rambled on with stories of the old days, of Dublin society in the sixties, and seventies, and the exciting times of the Volunteers, of course. She blamed the revolution in France for all the deterioration of manners in society – and the decline of standards.

"Nobody cares anymore," she used to complain with more sadness than rancour. "And I don't know where it will all end."

"You are well rid of that Bingham fellow," Aunt Olive said one night apropos of nothing in particular. "Well rid of him. I often bless the day that you were free of him."

Pamela smiled without looking up from her *petit point* frame. She had often heard this line from Aunt Olive, and she recognised it for what it was – an attempt at consolation.

"There couldn't be any luck with that money," Aunt Olive added enigmatically but with sufficient emphasis to alert Pamela's attention.

"What do you mean by that?", she asked casually.

"Just that it was never meant to be," said Aunt Olive, closing her eyes and lapsing back into an apparent stupor.

But Pamela's interest was now aroused.

"What do you mean, it was never meant to be?", she asked.

"Never what?", asked Aunt Olive, starting up again.

"Never meant to be. What did you mean by that?"

"The money."

"Yes."

"Your uncle John's money."

"Yes. What about it?"

"It was never meant for you. It was meant for that young stable boy – Stephen Allen."

For a moment Pamela thought her aunt must be raving. This was something entirely different from the usual stream of anecdotes and reminiscences. She put down her needlework and moved closer to the bed.

"Aunt Olive," she said in some agitation, "you must explain. How could Uncle John's fortune be meant for Stephen Allen? And why have you never mentioned this before?"

Aunt Olive had said more than she intended to. But it wasn't entirely unpremeditated. It had been at the back of her mind to tell Pamela the whole story one of these days. She didn't want her niece to find out from some other source and she knew that time was no longer on her side. So, while the candles burnt low in her bedroom, Aunt Olive finally told Pamela the story of Uncle John's will – or rather part of the story.

She exaggerated old Hamilton's attempts to trace young Allen and the importance of the original will which left everything to the family. She repeated her own utter conviction that the young man was a victim of the turmoil following the French invasion and the terrible slaughter at the time. There was not a doubt in her mind that he was dead, she said. But she withheld one vital piece of information that she knew could only distress her niece. She made no reference at all to Mr. Allen being her brother's natural son.

But she said enough to alarm Pamela, who heard the whole saga with ever increasing horror. Stephen Allen had been done out of his lawful inheritance.

"But why were not the funds put into a trust for Mr. Allen, at least until his whereabouts had been definitely established?", Pamela asked.

"I know, my dear, that might have been a better course to adopt. But think of the legal complications. Setting up a trust for a person whose very fate is unknown. And then possibly having to unravel it again years later. The lawyers would have had a field day. Indeed I doubt if there would have been much left for any beneficiary."

"Still, it was the correct thing to have done," Pamela admonished.

"Perhaps, perhaps," said Aunt Olive weakly. "I really don't know. I suppose I am to blame. But I only did what I thought poor John would have wished in the circumstances."

Pamela felt deeply ashamed and disturbed. She tried to get more out of Aunt Olive – but without success. Whenever she raised the subject again she drew a total blank. Her aunt obviously had said all she intended and that was that. And Pamela was left to mull over the wrong that had been done to Stephen Allen and the terrible position into which she herself had now been cast.

All during the autumn, Aunt Olive continued to weaken, and as her strength declined Pamela felt an increasing draw on her own energy – not just in the physical sense but in the very exertion of her will. Sometimes she felt that only her energy was sustaining her aunt's will to live. And she wondered how long it could go on.

Lady Porter finally expired on November 28th at about four o'clock in the afternoon on a dark drizzly day, and all the blinds at Number Ten were drawn down to their full length. She was buried beside her husband in a little graveyard just above Rathfarnham.

Pamela drove home from the funeral in Brendan's carriage. He helped with all the arrangements, settled the funeral details, and even instructed the staff. He could not have been more kind and more efficient in his own quiet way.

"You know, I didn't feel at all sad at the graveside," Pamela said. "I didn't feel it was Aunt Olive we were burying. Just an old and very tired body that was being laid to rest."

Brendan let her talk on.

"Her spirit was somewhere else," Pamela continued. "I mean it wasn't with that corpse so it must be somewhere else, mustn't it?"

"I suppose so," said Brendan without conviction.

Brendan stayed for supper at Number Ten and they talked into the night about Aunt Olive and the Prestons and Murrisk and everything else that came to mind. Pamela was very tired which might explain why she took more wine than usual.

"You're my very best friend," she said to Brendan as he was leaving "and I don't know how I can ever thank you enough."

And with that she threw her arms around him and quite innocently gave him a warm hug at the door.

Brendan was first elated and then a little deflated. He didn't really want to be just her friend any more. He knew now that he wanted more than that.

Chapter XVIII

THE UNION IS PASSED

"HOW IS THAT list coming along?", the editor called over to Brendan as he came bustling into the office later than usual.

It was January 16th, 1800, the first month of the new century and the first day on which the House was to reconvene and debate again the question of the Union.

"I've got some more surprises," replied Brendan, who had been working on the list of promotions, patronage and downright bribes connected with the Government's determination to reverse the decision of last year.

"Good," said Mr. Magee as he slumped down behind his desk piled high with letters, papers, books and galley-proofs. "This is what posterity will want to know about. How many pieces of silver? What price their birthright? Mr. Barrington will be joining us shortly. He too has some interesting information," he added.

Mr. Jonah Barrington was one of the most colourful members of the Bar and a great source of information for the editor. He also contributed editorial opinions when the editor was absent.

"Well, I think I've nailed down all the elevations in the Peerage," Brendan said as they settled into their daily editorial meeting. "I make it twenty new creations to the Irish Peerage, twenty promotions within the Irish peerage and six elevations to the English Peerage."

"Incredible," gasped the editor "are you sure?"

"I have cross-checked the lists with three good sources."

"Why, that's most of the House of Lords in their pocket. Which peers are to be elevated into the English Peerage?"

"The Marquess of Drogheda is to be Lord Moore in the English Peerage.

The Marquess of Ely to be Lord Loftus.

The Earl of Ormonde to be Lord Butler .

The Earl of Carysfort to be Lord Carysfort.

And the Marquess of Thomond is to be Lord Thomond. All in the English Peerage."

"What about Castlereagh?"

"There is no word yet of his promotion in the peerage."

"And Lord Altamont?"

"Yes, he is getting a Marquessate. He will be the Marquess of Sligo, in the Irish peerage.

Mr. Barrington arrived and took a seat at the big editorial table.

"They've certainly bought the Bar," he announced, "My colleagues have performed true to form. I've noted down everything I could find," he said, passing a long list to Mr. Magee who read it out slowly.

"Mr. St George Daly is to be appointed Prime Sergeant, worth three thousand five hundred pounds a year.

Mr. William Smith, who so ably defended the Union proposal in the House, is to be Solicitor General, also at three thousand five hundred pounds a year.

Both Mr. Robert Johnson MP and his brother, Mr. William Johnson are to be appointed Judges of the Common Pleas worth three thousands pounds per annum.

And Mr. James McClelland is promised the succession as Solicitor General to be followed as Baron of the Exchequer.

County Judgeships, worth six hundred annually, are held out to fourteen barristers, each of whom had voted in favour of the Union at the celebrated meeting of the Bar last December.

And County Chairmanships, also worth six hundred pounds per annum, are offered to several others."

"Lord Clare did a remarkable job of conversion on the recalcitrant members of the legal profession," Mr. Barrington added wryly.

"Will there not be uproar when this becomes known?", Brendan exclaimed.

"Don't be naive," Mr. Barrington replied. "Lord Castlereagh has paid the price and you will see the result in the House today."

"And is it certain that every member of the House is to get £15,000 compensation?", the editor asked.

"Yes, that is confirmed," Brendan replied.

" But why should they be compensated at all?", George Pollack asked.

"Compensation is just the euphemism, my boy," Mr. Barrington replied. "£15,000 each is simply the price for their vote. It matters not that the members are selling something that doesn't belong to them, i.e. the representation of the people. They are being paid to vote the way Lord Castlereagh wants them to vote."

"Do you know of any precedent for such compensation"?, the editor asked.

"The answer is no," Mr. Barrington replied.

"Now George, give us the details on the Church of Ireland," the editor asked.

"The support of the Church of Ireland has been secured in different ways," George Pollack replied.

"The influential Archbishop Agar of Cashel is promised the succession to the See of Dublin. His case was supported by Lord Clifden, who had influence over seven votes; by Lord Callan who had two close friends in the House of Commons, and by Mr. Preston, MP for Navan who is a relation.

The Rev Mr. Trench, a brother of the Hon Richard Trench MP, was assured an appointment to the Bench of Bishops.

Lord Castlereagh promised the Rev Mr. Cleland, his erstwhile tutor, the rectorship of Armagh, and Lord Kilwarden's nephew, the Rev Mr. Richard Wolfe, better preferment. To please Mr. Robert Cope, the MP for Armagh, Lord Castlereagh promised a living to his cousin the Rev Mr. Bisset. A similar pledge was given to the Rev Joseph Palmer to gain the support of Mr. David La Touche, the member for Newcastle. In all, the First Secretary has promised about two dozen preferments in the Church of Ireland directly related to the Union vote."

"Good Lord, is there no end to this?", the editor exclaimed. "And what of the Roman Catholic Church?".

"I thought you understood how their support had been secured?", Brendan replied. "The Catholic curates are to be paid a stipend from public funds but Parish Priests must take the Oath of Allegiance. The Church of Ireland tithes are to be commuted and Catholics may be voted into the Imperial parliament in London once the King has approved the Bill.

"So is the whole country bought?" the editor demanded.

"Well, that certainly applies to the commercial names I have here," Mr. Barrington put in. "I am reliably informed that Mr. Rutledge MP was promised a seat on the Navigation Board, worth five hundred pounds per annum.

Mr. Cotter, MP, Lord Shandon's friend, is to be appointed to the Tontine Office at four hundred pounds per annum.

Major Creighton, MP, Lord Erne's son, was promised the Barrack Board worth eight hundred pounds per annum. A pension for Sir Boyle Roche, MP, is to be four hundred pounds per annum for his life, and for Mr. Faithful Fortescue, three hundred pounds per annum.

The Weighmastership of Cork, worth five hundred pounds per annum, was held out to Sir Vere Hunt, MP, and Mr. Brooke, the member for Donegal, was promised the place of Judge Advocate at three hundred pounds per annum for his friend Mr. Leslie. And this was just the tip of the iceberg."

"Was there ever such rank corruption of the soul of a nation," the editor exploded as he rose from the table.

"Well, let's see if it is sufficient for Lord Castlereagh to finally get his way," he said as he exited from the office and led the way down the street to the House of Commons.

Once again on that day and right through the night, the Irish House of Parliament witnessed a most exceptional debate; and this is how Brendan described the most dramatic part of it, namely, the surprise appearance of Mr. Henry Grattan, in his account which appeared in the *Dublin Evening Post*.

"The House had nearly exhausted itself and the subject, when, about seven o'clock in the morning, an incident the most affecting and unexpected occurred. A vacancy having occurred for the close borough of Wicklow, it was tendered by Mr. Tighe to Mr. Henry Grattan. But it was not until the day of the meeting of Parliament that the writ was delivered to the returning officer. By extraordinary exertions, the election was held immediately on the arrival of the writ and a sufficient number of voters were collected to return Mr. Grattan before midnight. By one o'clock the return was on its road to Dublin; it arrived by five. A whisper ran through every party that Mr. Grattan was elected and would immediately take his seat. The Ministerialists smiled with incredulous derision, and the Opposition thought the news too good to be true.

Mr. Egan was speaking strongly against the measure when Mr. George Ponsonby and Mr. Arthur Moore (now Judge of the Common Pleas) walked out and immediately returned leading, or rather helping into the body of the House, Mr. Grattan, in a state of total feebleness and debility. The effect was electric. Mr. Grattan's illness and deep chagrin had reduced a form, never symmetrical, and a visage at all times thin, nearly to the appearance of a spectre now clad once again in his old Volunteer uniform. As he feebly tottered into the House, every Member simultaneously rose from his seat. He moved slowly to the table; his languid countenance seemed to revive as he took those oaths that restored him to his pre-eminent station; the smile of inward satisfaction obviously illuminated his features and reanimation and energy seemed to kindle by the labour of his mind. The House was silent – Mr. Egan did not resume his speech – Mr. Grattan, almost breathless, as if by instinct, attempted to rise, but was unable to stand – he paused, and with difficulty requested permission of the House to deliver his sentiments without moving from his seat. This was acceded to by acclamation, and he who had left his bed of sickness to record, as he thought, his last words in the Parliament of his country, kindled gradually till his language glowed with an energy and feeling which he had seldom surpassed. After nearly two hours of the most powerful eloquence, he concluded with an undiminished vigour, miraculous to those who were unacquainted with his intellect.

Never did a speech make a more affecting impression, but it came too late. Fate had decreed the fall of Ireland, and her patriot came only to witness her overthrow. At length the impatience of the House rendered a division necessary and in half an hour the fate of Ireland was decided. The numbers were –

For the government motion (in favour of Union) 138
Against the Motion 96
Majority for the government 42

When it was all over, Brendan mingled in the refreshment rooms with some members of the government party who appeared more relieved than exuberant. Of course they were satisfied with the result but they had nothing to be proud of. And not one of them could deny a feeling of nostalgia for an era, and an institution, on which they had brought down the shutters. But Brendan had no appetite for the prolonged post-mortem and was glad enough to go home for a rest before the party that his sister Margaret had planned for that evening to mark the Union vote – whatever the result.

Later that day, Mr. Magee sat alone in his office composing an editorial worthy of the occasion. As always he had to force himself to the task. As usual he sketched out a few main points beforehand.

"In origin," he noted," the measure was an English one and not demanded by any section of Irish opinion…"

"It was forced through without a dissolution of the Parliament and by means of gross corruption…"

"It was carried in open opposition to the great preponderance of the unbribed intellect of the country…"

"And the Parliament lacked the constitutional competence to effect it…"

Then he filleted a few good quotations from speeches in the debates, drawing particularly on Mr. Grattan and Mr. Plunkett. Mr. Magee worked for several hours on his composition, going over it again and again, balancing his sentences and honing them down until he was fully satisfied. It was early evening before he left his office, walking in the cool air to clear his head. He was very tired and deeply depressed but at the same time well satisfied with his own editorial on the historic day.

"My editorial will be there long after these pygmies are forgotten," he consoled himself as he headed home.

Chapter IXX

MARGARET'S PARTY

SOON AFTER HE was called to the Bar, Charles Bourke, Margaret's husband, began to get briefs from the Catholic Hierarchy, thanks to a family connection with the Archbishop of Dublin, Dr Troy. These briefs were usually on cases connected with property and disputed bequests, but recently his advice had also been sought on the all-important issue of the Union and its likely effects on the position of the Catholic Church. He was a member of the Catholic Association which advised the Hierarchy and from which emanated the decision NOT to oppose the Union – provided certain conditions were met. After that Charles openly joined the pro-Union lobby at the Bar and was soon receiving briefs from an even better source – the Solicitor General's office. It was commonly remarked that Charles was "doing very well" at the Bar – and that a great future lay ahead of him.

On the domestic front, however, matters were very different. Margaret had recognised from the very first night that her marriage to Charles was a disastrous mistake, but typically had determined to make her own life and enjoy herself in the capital as best she could. Thus she soon became well known for the entertainment in her new house on Harcourt Street.

As she remarked to Brendan one evening, "The surest way to other's people's houses in Dublin is through entertainment in your own." And working on this principle, she had started holding Open House on the second Sunday of every month. Of course she entertained also at other times, but her Second Sundays soon became something of an institution in the capital.

Their success was mostly due to Margaret's skill as a hostess. She had a capacity for easy repartee and an informal, almost intimate directness that men found flattering or at least intriguing. She believed in entertaining on a generous scale. No expense was spared and no one could ever complain that they had lacked for anything at the Bourkes. Margaret had no hesitation in inviting to her parties artists, musicians or writers with whom she had little or no formal acquaintance. That they came into public attention was sufficient reason for her to invite them, and they invariably responded positively to her delicately phrased invitations. These intellectuals and persons of prominence Margaret used as bait for bigger social fish – and again she was seldom disappointed. After some months the reputation of her "Second Sundays" had become so well established that some younger members of even the first families began to be seen there.

The evidence of her good taste was everywhere to be seen in the two large reception rooms on the first floor, separated by folding doors but decorated and furnished by Margaret as one room. The total impression was one of informal elegance, such as Margaret associated in her own mind with the houses of the oldest families. Nothing brash, nothing too new, but everything falling into place as if it had been there for decades. The niches on either side of the two fireplaces were replete with old leather-bound volumes, including the works of such Irish favourites as Jonathan Swift, Oliver Goldsmith and William Congreve. One whole wall – that facing the high windows in the front room – was covered with an assortment of paintings in different styles and sizes, but all adding up to a visual impact that was unusual in Dublin. And in the return room, the presence of both a pianoforte and a harpsichord indicated Margaret's real pleasure in music.

Her party on 16th January, 1800 had been planned to coincide with the conclusion of the Union debate. She calculated, correctly, that the excitement of the debates would enliven her supper party – and she was not disappointed.

First to arrive were two old friends, Mr. Wesley Doyle and Mr. Billy Warren, who had promised to render some musical entertainment. Mr. Doyle's father was a professor of music and Mr. Warren gave music lessons at the Academy. They were followed by many others and by eight o'clock the two big rooms were resounding with talk and laughter and gaiety.

Margaret had decided to serve supper in the dining room, and it was just as she was leading her guests down to supper that Charles arrived with a group of his Unionist friends from the House of Commons.

"I hear Mr. Grattan was magnificent," she mischievously called out from the stairs. But Charles did not rise to the bait.

"May I introduce to you Mr. St George Daly, Mr. Jameson, and Mr. William Smith," he said, indicating each of his companions "and this is Richard Bingham, Lord Lucan."

Margaret had never met Bingham but, of course, she had heard all the gossip about his behaviour with Pamela and took an instant dislike to him. But she was too shrewd to show her real feelings

"You are just in time for supper," she said gaily. "Do come in and warm yourselves. Charles will do the introductions."

And so they all crowded into the crimson dining-room, which was already overflowing with guests helping themselves to the buffet and wines set out on the long sideboard.

~~~~~~~ • ~~~~~~

Upstairs, after supper, Mr. Doyle was the first to commence the music with two of Dibdin's songs, which were in high vogue that season, and he accompanied himself on the pianoforte. He was followed by Mr. Warren, whose handsome face assured his success with the ladies even more than the sweetness of his voice. Mr. Armitage then gave a spirited rendering of 'The Lass of Richmond Hill', to the chorus of which several young men added their lusty contribution. And so the singing and the playing continued into the evening.

Brendan was late to arrive and Margaret went out to meet him.

"Let me see what we can scrape together for you," she said as she ushered Brendan into the dining room and sent Patsy to the kitchen for a fresh platter of meats.

Brendan slumped down in a high-backed wing chair beside the fire, a large glass of whiskey in his hand. He was still tired after the long series of debates in the House, and taking a quick look around the room, was none too pleased to find such a collection of Unionists in this house. He had expected to find more of his own persuasion.

Margaret perched for a moment beside him to hear the latest news.

"It was a disastrous night," said Brendan told her. "But it was almost worth it all to hear Mr. Grattan again."

"But by what stratagem is he back in Parliament?"

"He was returned only this morning. It was really sensational. As you know, he has been absent since '97 and was heartily sickened with all politics. But a vacancy having arisen in Wicklow, he was persuaded by his friends to accept the borough. The debate, of course, had been proceeding all night and was still in progress when Mr. Grattan made his entrance at about seven o'clock."

"How dramatic!"

"Yes, and he looked dramatic too. He had donned his old Volunteer uniform, blue with red cuffs and collar, like a ghost from the past. And he was ghostly frail."

"And what of his speech then?", she asked.

"It was the finest oration ever heard in that House – in my opinion. But the poor man was so weak that he had to remain seated, although he held the House enthralled for a full two hours. But it is all too late. If only he had been active over the past twelve months. He is the only man who could have roused the country as he did twenty years ago. Now all is lost."

Brendan swallowed down half a tumbler of whiskey in one gulp.

"How exactly did the House divide?", asked Margaret.

"One hundred and thirty eight for the government; ninety six for the Opposition; a majority of forty two," Brendan read from his notebook.

"Which proves that every man – or at least every member of Parliament – has a price," said Brendan loudly.

Bingham, who overheard the remark, turned to face Brendan.

"I can assure you, Sir, that there was no price on my vote," he said. "It was given freely, voluntarily, indeed enthusiastically."

"Am I to understand then that you will refuse the fifteen thousand for the borough you represent?", Brendan asked, looking him straight in the eye.

"Certainly not! That is a compensation for loss of office. It cost me dearly to get elected, and if the borough is now to be abolished I will certainly accept some compensation."

"Then we differ only in semantics," said Brendan over the top of his glass. "You call it compensation. I call it a price. I had thought the representation of the people to be a privilege, not a property. But if it be a property does it not belong to the people rather than to their representative pro-tem? Surely you are selling something which does not belong to you?"

Bingham was clearly stung. In truth he would have supported the Union without any financial inducement, but as even members who opposed to the Union were accepting the fifteen thousand, why should he turn his back on it?

"I hear Lord Shannon will be compensated to the tune of forty-five thousand for the three boroughs he controls," Brendan continued. "The passing of the Union will require so-called compensation of at least two million. A little more than thirty pieces of silver, you might say."

"That's a dastardly remark, Sir," Bingham shot back.

"The judgment is no harsher than posterity will pass on you and your like," said Brendan, now thoroughly aroused.

"Please gentlemen, please," Margaret interposed, fearful that things were getting out of hand.

But the heated exchange had been noticed at the other end of the room and Charles with a few of his friends now crossed over to join the exchange.

"You are here to relax, Brendan," said Charles in a patronising tone that made Margaret cringe. "Vent your feelings tomorrow in the *Post*."

Brendan felt the deepest contempt for his brother-in-law with his Castle accent, but he restrained himself.

"I fear," he said, "that you, most of all, will rue this day."

"Me?", asked Charles, genuinely surprised.

"Yes, you and the faction you represent. This is a bad day for the Catholic people."

"That is not the opinion of the Catholic bishops," Charles replied in a rather pompous tone. "As you know, they have supported the Union enthusiastically."

"I did not mention bishops. I spoke of the people. The Catholic clergy too have been bought. I hear that they are to be paid. But there is not a word in the Act of Union about enfranchising the Catholics."

"We have been given assurances on that from the highest authority."

"Assurances?"

"Yes, from the Prime Minister himself."

"But nothing in writing."

"Are you suggesting that Mr. Pitt is not a man of his word?"

"I am saying that the Church has supported the Union without securing the *quid pro quo* of enfranchisement for their flock."

"That will follow for certain."

"And what about the King, the head of the Church of England? He has given no assurance at all. I thought you were a clever lawyer, Charles, but it seems to me that you have been sold a pup!"

"A rather jaundiced view, if I may say so," said Charles. "One has to expect a certain scepticism in journalists, but such cynicism is as sterile as it is stupid."

Brendan felt he could take no more. He had indeed come to the party to relax. He had expected to find some good companions to help drown his sorrows. Instead he felt irritated by these stooges of the administration.

"Well, I must be going," he said rising from his chair.

But just at that moment a new group of guests arrived in the hall and Brendan heard the name of Pamela Preston being announced.

"You didn't tell me that Pamela was expected," Brendan said to his sister.

"They have been at the theatre. She wasn't sure they could come on."

Immediately she saw Brendan, Pamela crossed the room to greet him warmly; but suddenly, to her horror, she saw the flushed face of Richard Bingham over his shoulder. It was a year since she had last seen him but still it was a shock. It was a nasty surprise too for Bingham, who immediately turned on his heel and disappeared.

Margaret was fit to be tied and took Charles aside.

"How dare you bring that dreadful Bingham man to this house," she chided her husband."

"I had no idea Miss Preston was coming."

"That's by the way. You had no right to ask him in the first place. You have ruined my evening. Don't ever dare to bring that man to my house again."

"Your house. So that's it. Am I to be reminded every day that I am your father's guest here?"

"Why not. He paid for the house, didn't he?"

"My God, you're so common. Well, you can have your party. I'll take my entertainment elsewhere."

And with that he stalked out into the night, followed by his rather startled drinking companions.

Happily the party continued apace upstairs where the guests were oblivious to the drama in the dining room. But Pamela had lost any appetite for further revelry.

"I think it's time to go," she told Brendan, who immediately offered to escort her home.

"I'm really sorry for that embarrassment," Brendan said to her as they jogged along in the cab. "I wouldn't be surprised if Charles set it up on purpose."

"Yes, it was a surprise – but perhaps it was just as well. It had to happen sooner or later and I think I've got him out of my system now. He looks much older, doesn't he?"

Brendan slipped his hand into hers. It was an involuntary movement intended to comfort her and she took it as such and gave his hand a little squeeze.

"I have been thinking of returning to Murrisk soon," she said out of the blue and much to Brendan's delight.

He helped her to alight from the cab at Number Ten and, before the door was opened, he kissed her hand. He fell into bed a happy man.

Chapter XX

THE HOUSE OF PEERS

IT WAS THE month of July, 1800 when Brendan, once again, and for the very last time, stood inside the House of Parliament. Brendan, with Mr. Magee, had arrived soon after noon and noticed Lord Altamont arriving at the House accompanied by his son, Howe Peter, and a young companion from Eton, Mr. *Thomas de Quincey. The two young gentlemen were on holidays from their college and were due to set out for Mayo the following day.

Now that the battle was over, Lord Altamont seemed to have lost the bounce in his stride. Not that he regretted his own part in the protracted negotiations and debates, but he couldn't repress a nostalgia for the institution with which he had been personally associated for over twenty years. It was the best club in town.

Lord Altamont almost bumped into Mr. Foster in the great hall and hastened to introduced his two young companions. The bitterness of the past few months had damaged their relationship and Lord Altamont genuinely regretted this estrangement from such an old friend.

"My congratulations on the Riband," said Mr. Foster with a wry smile and Lord Altamont, who had been invested as a Knight of St Patrick the previous week, thought he detected a touch of sarcasm. But he had to press on.

They were running behind time and Lord Altamont had barely taken his seat in the House of Lords – hung around with huge tapestries celebrating the glories of William III – when the noise outside indicated the arrival of the Viceroy.

Lord Cornwallis entered the chamber to the fanfare of trumpets. Leading the procession was Thomas Lindsay, Esq, Usher of the Black Rod, followed immediately by the Sergeant at Arms. Walking ahead of the Viceroy was the Earl of Clare, Lord Chancellor and Speaker of the House of Lords.

Lord Cornwallis, who was followed by a long train of pages, ushers and lesser notables, looked rather bored and certainly bereft of that energy on which his reputation had been founded. In fact, his thoughts were elsewhere as he first paid deep homage to the Throne and then mounted the crimson steps. Two years of cajoling, bullying, threatening and bargaining with this Irish plantocracy was more than enough for him.

After prayers, the Yeoman Usher of the Black Rod was dispatched to the Commons to convey the traditional summons: "It is His Excellency, the Lord Lieutenant's pleasure that the House do forthwith attend him in the House of Peers"; and within minutes he returned, followed now by the whole assembly of the Lower House. Leading this procession was Mr. John Foster, the Speaker, immediately followed by Lord Castlereagh and, behind him, Sir John Blaquiere and Mr. John Beresford. But conspicuous by their absence were such leading members of the Opposition as Mr. Ponsonby, Mr. Grattan, Mr. Saurin, Mr. Bushe, Mr. Plunkett and many others who had followed the example of Mr. Charles Ball in quitting the House after the last vote, never again to set foot therein.

Then the Viceroy, holding the text quite close to his troubled eyes, read the last speech from the throne. In it he communicated to the assembly, by His Majesty's express command, 'the warmest acknowledgments for that ardent zeal and unshaken perseverance which you have so conspicuously manifested in maturing and completing the great measure of a legislative union between this Kingdom and Great Britain."

Brendan already had a copy of the short speech and his eye ran ahead on the text as the Viceroy came to the conclusion.

"I cannot conclude without offering to you and to the nation at large, my personal congratulations on the accomplishment of this great work which has received the sanction and concurrence of our Sovereign on the anniversary of that auspicious day which placed his illustrious family on the throne of these realms. The Empire is now through your exertions so completely united, and by union so strengthened, that it can hit defiance to the efforts its enemies may make, either to weaken it by division, or to overthrow it by force. Under the protection of the Divine Providence the United Kingdom of Great Britain and Ireland will, I trust, remain in all future ages, the fairest monument of His Majesty's reign, already distinguished by so many and such various blessings conferred upon every class and description of his subjects."

Lord Clare then began a recitation of all the Acts passed during the most recent – and final – session of the Irish Parliament. And to each, like the response in a litany, Lord Cornwallis exclaimed, "*Le Roi le veut.*"

But the Union Bill was not the very last on the list. The ultimate enactment of the Irish Parliament was the Compensation Bill – by which the outgoing legislators approved the raising of one and a half million pounds additional taxation. These funds were to be shared amongst themselves, as compensation for their lost representation.

"*Le Roi le veut*," intoned the Viceroy for the very last time and then it was all over.

Of course as the Irish Houses of Parliament were being abolished, all the functionaries of that ancient institution also had to be compensated. In the House of Lords, there were forty-four such people to be considered, and generous annuities were arranged for each one of them. Lord Clare, as Speaker of the House of Lords, was to get an annuity of three thousand nine hundred and seventy eight pounds. John, Earl of Mayo, Chairman of the Committees, one thousand four hundred and forty three pounds. William Meeks Esq, Clerk of the Parliaments, two thousand seven hundred and five pounds and his deputy John Gregg Esq, seven hundred and eighty pounds. Thomas Lindsay Esq, Usher of the Black Rod, was to get nine hundred and sixty four pounds, and Mrs. Taylor, Keeper of the Parliament House, eight hundred and seventy seven pounds.

For the House of Commons it was the same story. The Speaker, Mr. John Foster, whose opposition to the Union was well known, accepted the enormous annuity of five thousand and thirty eight pounds. Sir George FitzGerald Hill, Clerk of the House, was to get two thousand two hundred and sixty five pounds. The two Masters at Arms were to get one thousand two hundred pounds each, and so on. Altogether, annuities had to be arranged for fifty two retainers in the House of Commons. The total annual cost for both Houses was approximately thirty two thousand pounds per annum.

<hr />

Brendan gazed down on the splendidly attired assembly in their robes and ribands and decorations and imagined another one and a half million sovereigns raining down on top of them.

"Why don't we feel sad for them?", he asked the editor.

"Because they don't deserve our sympathy," he replied.

"Well, sad for what they represent?"

"They represent only themselves."

"The Irish Aristocracy?"

"Aristocracy, be damned!" said Mr. Magee." Sons of adventurers, land grabbers and usurpers. Upstart Cromwellians! The Wild Geese have flown. These are but vultures, hawks and scarecrows my boy. Look down the list for yourself. Beresford, Bingham, Butler and Boyle. Castlereagh, Cavendish, Coote and Cotter. Henniker, Holmes, Hutchinson, Howard. Take them one by one. There is hardly a real Irishman amongst the lot of them."

Brendan was surprised but delighted at the vehemence of this outburst, but suddenly his eye fell on Lord Altamont. In his antecedents were Kellys and Gores and Dalys and the hot blood of the Bourkes mixed with the calculating coolness of the Brownes. Was he any less an Irishman?

"You can't say that of Lord Altamont," Brendan said.

"Of course, there are exceptions," the editor replied. "Altamont should have known better."

⁓⁓⁓ • ⁓⁓⁓

That night, Lord Altamont attended a gala dinner in St Patricks Hall in Dublin Castle, while at his home in Sackville Street, young de Quincey completed his journal for the day.

"How is it," Thomas de Quincey wrote, "and by what unaccountable magic that William Pitt can have prevailed on all these hereditary legislators and heads of patrician houses to renounce so easily, with nothing worth the name of a struggle, and no reward worth the name of an indemnification, the very highest jewel in their coronets? This morning they all rose from their couches, Peers of Parliament, individual pillars of the realm, indispensable parties to every law that could pass. Tomorrow they will be nobody – men of straw – *terrae filii*. What madness had persuaded them to part with this birthright and to cashier themselves and their children forever into mere titular lords?"

After it was all over and Brendan had completed his report for the *Post*, he went to drown his sorrows with George Pollack. They went first to the *Cock and Bull* on Dame Street – a favourite haunt for the Gentlemen of the Press. Then they trawled their way slowly and unsteadily to several other taverns in the area, including that favoured by the Defenders called *An Beal Bocht*. But to Brendan's surprise, the place was so boisterous that there seemed to be a general celebration in progress.

"Nobody here gives a damn about the Union," said George.

"And why should they?", interrupted a red-headed peasant who was passing.

Brendan turned to see none other than Hugh O'Malley, the fisherman from Murrisk.

"Do you want a pint?", he asked Brendan. "I suppose I owe you that much."

Brendan demurred. He had hoped never to see O'Malley again. But he was caught.

"So you care nothing for this Union?", Brendan said.

"Not a tuppeny bit," said O'Malley. "They are all the same to us. It won't put food in our mouths one way or the other."

"Are you saying that the abolition of the Irish Parliament means nothing at all to you?"

"Yes I am. And why shouldn't I? We never got anything from that lot anyway. Here, come over to the snug and I'll tell you a few home truths."

They moved over to the snug which at least was a little quieter and Brendan called for another round of drinks.

"Forget about the Union," O'Malley almost gasped after a very long draught

146

of ale. "It won't last long anyhow. We're in a new century for God's sake. Everything is changing and the people want their say. It's as simple as that."

Brendan looked at him with a puzzled expression.

"If we had control of our own affairs, everything would be different," he countered.

"My arse, it would," O'Malley spat back. "The whole system is rotten and it's got to be blown away. Like in France. We need a proper revolution here. And mark my word, it won't be long in coming."

"You mean the blood of '98 flowing again?"

"Nobody wants that – but that's how it will have to be. Them that has everything here hold onto it to the bitter end. They grabbed it in the first place and they'll never give an inch."

They drank on for some time but the conversation was getting more and more desultory as one pint followed another. Finally, Brendan tired of listening to this peasant who had already caused him so much trouble and he looked around for George Pollack. But Pollack had already left and Brendan, too, staggered out into the street. Without really thinking about it, his steps directed him to Dr Achmet's celebrated Turkish baths near the College. He knocked three times on the heavy Georgian door and was received with a warm welcome into this gentlemen's home from home.

Chapter XXI

STEPHEN QUITS JAMAICA

WHEN DIANA FIRST saw Stephen walk up her steps she thought for a moment she was looking at Captain John. Stephen's features, his colouring, even his walk reminded her immediately of her former lover. And when she saw the ring – the Captain's Claddagh ring – she was left in no further doubt. But she soon realised that Stephen was blissfully unaware of his true relationship to her former lover. And while she considered it none of her business to enlighten him, she nevertheless assumed an almost proprietorial interest in his welfare.

When Captain John Preston was leaving Jamaica in 1792, he gave his coloured woman, Diana Cole, her freedom and, as required by law, this manumission was recorded in the Montego Bay parish vestry. Furthermore, he secured for her an annuity of five pounds per annum during her lifetime. This too was required by law as a precaution against former slaves becoming a burden on the community. Also, as the law required, a certificate was issued by the church wardens and sent for signature to the Commander in Chief in Spanish Town. Unfortunately, this certificate had not been returned to Captain Preston by the time he sailed from Jamaica. In fact, it had been mislaid somewhere between Montego Bay and Spanish Town and never was delivered or signed. Even Diana forgot about the certificate in the excitement of Captain John's departure – a traumatic experience which was, however, greatly ameliorated by his generosity. On the eve of his sailing, Captain Preston gave into her hands a parting gift of five hundred gold guineas, and no sooner had his ship dipped below the horizon than Diana turned her back on Montego Bay and her years of slavery and headed for a new life in Kingston.

At first she rented a small house on Princess Street, close to the waterfront, where she accommodated mostly sailors; but after only two years she was able to acquire a bigger house on Orange Street in which her business prospered considerably. However, it was her move to the large house on the corner of West

Queen Street and the Parade which really put her on the map in Kingston. Since that time, Miss Cole's boarding house had become recognised as one of the most fashionable in the town and, on the strength of this success, she was able to acquire several other properties in Kingston.

Diana had soon coaxed out of Stephen the whole story of his coming to Jamaica, the long crossing with Captain Powell on the *Expedition* and his mixed experience on the plantation at Cocoa Walk. And, of course, she learnt of Captain John's demise in Murrisk.

"Well, I can't imagine why Captain Powell allowed you to go to Cocoa Walk," she said to Stephen. "There are much better opportunities here in Kingston. You should follow Captain Preston's example and get into the shipping trade. That's where he made his fortune and I've no doubt you could do likewise."

And, so thanks to Diana's connections in the town, Stephen was soon admitted as a junior partner with the shipping agents Ritchie and Fitch, who specialised in the American trade. Then he secured rooms in nearby Beckford Street, and settled into the routine of a young man of affairs in this booming colonial outpost.

～～～～ • ～～～～

Among the more distinguished members of Kingston society at this time was a certain Judge Patrick Delap, a small, fat, bespectacled man with a tight mouth who was very conscious of his own importance. He was a pillar of Kingston society and several members of his family occupied influential positions in the town. The judge was accorded special attention at Diana's, and in some respects he came to feel more relaxed there than he did in his own home. Diana valued his patronage as she knew it added a certain respectability to her establishment. And she used him for other purposes too. The previous year he had managed to quash an objection which had arisen against her being granted a renewal of her boarding-house licence, and more recently he had promised to arrange for her manumission of '92 to be regularised. Diana was exceedingly grateful to him and, as a mark of her appreciation, arranged a little party for him and some legal colleagues on the last day of the Hilary term. It was the last week before Easter .

Judge Delap was not the only one to get very drunk that evening. Diana was more than liberal in her hospitality, but the party deteriorated into such raucousness that Diana decided to slip away quietly not long after midnight. She heard afterwards that Mr. Barber, the King's Counsel, had drunk himself footless and that Mr. Burrows, another barrister, had to be lifted into his carriage. But she learnt all this long after the events of that night had become the topic of scandalous comment throughout the town.

It was a hot, humid night and Diana lay on top of her bed fitfully tossing in a light sleep until awakened by a clammy hand on her breast. Her first inclination was to scream but, even as she drew her breath, a sticky hand clamped down over her mouth. Diana reacted instinctively and her sharp nails lacerated the face that was slobbering close to her own. In the darkness she could only make out the outline of the head but her nails soon drew blood and a howl of protest from the form above her. It backed off just as Diana found her voice and her screams must have been heard halfway to Spanish Town. But she was too terrified to move from her bed. She heard a rough shuffling of feet down the front steps as the general commotion woke the whole house and candles began to flicker in every room. Then people were rushing in all directions, some crying thief, others murder, and all calling out for the watchman.

Diana huddled in her bed too terrified to move, and it wasn't till her maid came running in, a flickering lamp in one hand, that she collapsed into a fit of hysterical sobbing. It was the following morning before she learnt the identity of her attacker and by that time the scandal was all over town.

<center>~~~~~~ • ~~~~~~</center>

"What can I do?", Diana asked desperately of Stephen when he arrived the next day, having heard the wild rumours. "The wretch has made a fool of himself and he'll take it out on me. I know he will. I know him."

"The whole thing will blow over in a few days," Stephen assured her.

"You don't know Kingston," said Diana bitterly. "He's a judge. And a white man. Do you know a slave can be hanged for 'offering violence' to a white? And for a coloured it won't be much less. No, they'll never forgive me for marking him – the drunken lecher."

"But what can they do?"

"The whispering campaign has started already. There wasn't a soul here today. But I know them. They're vindictive. They'll drive me out of town. That's what they'll do."

"Ridiculous," said Stephen emphatically. "You're overwrought. Understandably, of course. I think he'd be well advised to keep his mouth shut."

"Oh no. He'll twist it somehow. Say I attacked him or something. And the others will support him. Mark my word, he'll have his revenge."

"You could sue him for assault?", Stephen suggested.

"Don't be ridiculous," she answered. "I have no witnesses. And his friends will swear to anything. The juries are all white. And who could ever win against a judge in court? No, he has all the cards. The only question now is how he intends to play them."

Diana had not too long to wait to find out. A few days later she received a letter from the Office of Manumissions requesting her attendance and ordering her to bring her Certificate of Freedom with her.

"Oh the bastard, the bastard!", she cried to herself in the emptiness of her house, "the low, mean, rotten scum of the earth." And she collapsed onto her bed, sobbing and beating the lace counterpane in her frustration.

She lay there for a long time thinking and rethinking on her predicament. But she could find no easy solution.

~~~~~~~ ● ~~~~~~~

"I told you they would get me," she said to Stephen, when she showed him the letter. "And what a dirty trick."

"But you can fight this," he said. "Isn't your freedom registered in Montego Bay vestry?"

"It was. But they will have seen to that too. I can't produce my Certificate and they know it."

"But surely you cannot be enslaved again?"

"Why not? It's entirely possible," she said "Then they could confiscate my property."

"What do you mean?"

"No slave can own property over the value of one hundred pounds, nor any horse, mare, mule or gelding. It's the law. That's what Delap has in mind. To dispossess me. He probably has his eye on this house himself. Oh may he burn in hell!"

Stephen looked around the empty house. The wooden floors were as highly polished as ever and the great jardinière just inside the door was as full of exotic flowers as on the first day he had arrived from Cocoa Walk. But there was not a soul to be seen. The word had obviously gone out that the place was to be boycotted. And for the first time Stephen felt really sorry for Diana. She had always appeared so confident, so self assured, surrounded by her clients who were more like courtiers. Now she was like any other coloured woman – a threatened female at the mercy of a man's world and a white man's world at that.

"That solicitor, Jackson's our man," Stephen said confidently. "He'll know a way out of this. Why don't we go down to see him?"

"The law is on their side," Diana replied despondently "as it always is. That's what they'll use to destroy me."

"There is always one law to beat another," said Stephen. "I'm sure Mr. Jackson will have the answer."

And so he did, although it was a little unorthodox.

~~~~~~~ ● ~~~~~~~

"It doesn't surprise me at all," said Mr. Jackson when he heard the whole story. "I always suspected that sanctimonious little man. But we'll have to act fast if we are to thwart him. Miss Cole, you will have to leave town until all this has blown over. If you can leave the island, so much the better. But you must lie low somewhere, at least until I can check into the whole record of your manumission; and that may take some time. But in the meantime all your property is at risk. It could be confiscated when you fail to appear at the manumission's office. It must be put outside the reach of the law immediately.

"How is that possible?", she asked.

"It is possible by transferring the titles into another name."

"Another name?", she asked "What name?"

"The name of anyone you can trust."

"You mean of any white person?"

"Of any Freeman."

"Can they be put into your name?"

"No! If I am acting as your solicitor that is not possible. But I can hold the deeds in safe keeping. And the rentals can be forwarded to you."

Mr. Jackson looked across at Stephen.

"No, I wouldn't risk it," said Diana reading his thoughts. "They would take it out on him in some way."

"It's a perfectly legal transaction," said Mr. Jackson. "Once it is completed there is no danger of it being overturned."

"Use my name if it will solve the problem," Stephen volunteered. "It's all the same to me."

And so, after much deliberation, Mr. Jackson finally transferred all the properties held in the name of Miss Diana Cole of No.1, West Queen Street, Kingston, Jamaica, into that of Mr. Stephen Allen, 24, Beckford Street, Kingston, Jamaica, the consideration being one shilling on each transaction. Diana scribbled her name on a whole bundle of documents which Mr. Jackson took into safe-keeping, and the same day Diana removed her things from West Queen Street, closed up the house and left town.

Thus Diana Cole dropped out of Stephen's life as suddenly as she had come into it. The scandal was soon forgotten and the scratches on Judge Delap's fat face healed up before the month was out. The only reminder of the whole affair was the boarded up facade of No 1, West Queen Street. But Diana was taking no chances. She stayed well away from Kingston, although Stephen heard from her occasionally, first from Montego Bay, then from Port Maria, and finally from Port au Prince in San Domingo. And it was from Port au Prince that, more than two years later, Mr. Jackson was advised that his client had been seized of the yellow fever and had expired within three days.

～～～～ • ～～～～

In Mr. Jackson's safe-keeping Diana had left two short notes to be opened in case of her demise. The one addressed to Mr. Jackson was a statement more than a will. It said simply that she wished to leave all her possessions to Stephen Allen, but that as the transfers had already been executed, it remained only for Mr. Jackson to release the deeds. The note to Stephen was equally short. It contained some fond references to Captain John in whose memory she was bequeathing him her property and she asked only that Stephen should leave the island as soon as possible. "Jamaica," she said, "is a corrupt and corrupting society." She asked him to quit it before "it was too late."

"Do you realise the value of these properties?", Mr. Jackson asked Stephen a few weeks later, pointing to a heap of documents on his desk.

"I have no idea," answered Stephen truthfully.

"I would say about fifty thousand sterling, at a modest estimate," the attorney answered, his great bushy eyebrows raised in respect for such a figure.

"Fifty thousand? My God I had no idea Diana had so much property," said Stephen. He was completely overcome by this sudden windfall. Fifty thousand pounds was a fortune which he found hard to even imagine.

"Fortunately, they're already in your name, so there are no complications," said Mr. Jackson. "It's really only a question of what you want to do with them."

"Well, I'll do exactly as Dianna wished. Sell them all," answered Stephen firmly. "I'll be leaving Jamaica as soon as you have made all the arrangements."

"Are you really decided about that?", asked Mr. Jackson.

"Yes, I had made up my mind about that some time ago. I've learnt a lot about shipping here in Kingston and I'll put that to good use at home."

"Do you think it's a good time to sell?", asked the attorney cautiously. He was really covering his tracks for the future – an automatic precaution.

"Yes, I do," said Stephen, whose business acumen had been considerably sharpened over the past two years. "Prices always collapse after a war and it looks as if Bonaparte wants peace."

"Perhaps you're right," said Mr. Jackson, who was thinking of some other properties in his care. "I'll have to dispose of them bit by bit, but we should have you pretty liquid in a few months."

~~~~~~ • ~~~~~~

Stephen's first thought had been to return to Mayo as soon as he could book a passage. But, slowly, different ideas began to germinate in his mind. Now that he was a man of means, the world was his oyster. Why rush back to Ireland before he had seen something more than a slave colony in Jamaica? He thought of proceeding to new America or even to South America. But the arrival in Kingston Bay of his old friend, Captain Powell, aboard the *Expedition* made up his mind for him. After resting and refitting, Captain Powell was due to return across the Atlantic and call first on the French coast at Brest. Why not see the new Republic in France, Stephen thought? The whole world was talking about

General Bonaparte. Why not see for himself this new wonder of the Western world before heading back to Ireland … and Murrisk … and Pamela?

Stephen set sail for Brest in the Summer of '02 and quit Jamaica with not a single regret. But before he left, he arranged, through Mr. Jackson's office in Kingston, for the manumission of Cocoa in Cocoa Walk and for a personal gift to her of five hundred guineas, and secured for her an annuity of five pounds per annum during her lifetime. He knew Captain John would have approved.

BOOK III

Chapter XXII

DUBLIN AFTER THE
ACT OF UNION

MR. MAGEE had aged since the Union. Or at least the old fire seemed to have gone out of him. The House of Commons had been the centre of his life. Now it was all gone; the great building itself shut up and empty and all his old associates and adversaries scattered to the country or to London. He simply didn't know what to do with himself and seemed to have lost interest even in his own paper. His friends encouraged him to write his memoirs. Instead it was noticeable that he was drinking more heavily than before and that he was becoming even more eccentric.

One consequence of all this was that much more work fell onto Brendan's plate. He was now reporting regularly, subbing other copy and standing in generally for Mr. Magee. In effect he was acting as the deputy editor, although he was never designated as such. But he didn't mind the extra work, indeed he welcomed it as a diversion from the sense of lethargy, indeed boredom, that had enveloped the city since the Union.

"More disturbances are expected today," the editor grumbled as Brendan came into the office. "Get over to Sackville Street and see what's going on. But keep out of trouble. The military will be on the streets today."

The trouble had started earlier in the week after a few urchins had snatched some loaves from a baker's van in Sackville Street Pursued by the irate van man, they fled into Marlborough Street where, as luck would have it, they ran straight into the arms of the Parish Watch and were beaten and kicked to the ground. But such were the screams and howls of the *gasúns*, that an angry crowd appeared from nowhere and both the Watch and the van man had to beat a hasty retreat. The crowd then swarmed back onto Sackville Street and helped themselves to all the bread and anything else that they could lay their hands on before the police were seen approaching over Carlisle bridge.

The cause of the unrest, of course, had been the soaring price of flour and bread. The price of potatoes too had doubled in recent months. Some people blamed the price rises on the poor harvest, others on the export of grain and others again on the Union. The latter was now blamed for almost every ill in society, as there was no denying that it had resulted in a great loss of employment particularly in the Liberties.

When Brendan got across Carlisle Bridge he could see a confrontation half way down Sackville Street. Immediately ahead of him a line of police with batons drawn was facing a noisy crowd well armed with sticks and cobble-stones and protected by some upturned vehicles. What the crowd could not see, however, was a detachment of cavalry drawn up around the corner on the Quayside, close to where Brendan was standing.

Brendan slipped down along the river quay and then swung back north, emerging finally onto Sackville Street, again just in time to witness the start of the riot. A charge by the police was met with a hail of stones and bricks and anything else that came to hand until the police were forced to retreat. But they fell back in orderly fashion, opening a path in the centre which was soon filled by the advancing cavalry – with sabers drawn. The riot then quickly turned into a rout, with the mob scattering under the horses' hooves and scrambling for shelter in all directions.

Brendan huddled in a doorway with a few wretched specimens from the slums, but he was soon rounded up with the others and dragged off in a police wagon to some warehouse that was obviously under military control. Facing the wall and with his hands over his head, he was left in the stench of this crowded shelter, without food or water, for several hours. All those arrested had to take off their boots – the first humiliation. Much later they were taken, one by one, to be questioned. The authorities were determined to weed out the ring-leaders.

Brendan wanted to protest that he was just a bystander: that he had taken no part in the disturbance and that he was a gentleman. But an inner voice warned him to keep quiet.

"Don't open your mouth," it said. "Just get out of here in one piece."

Standing beside him facing the wall was an old man. He must have been at least sixty and in his yellowed eyes Brendan saw the signs of jaundice. But he still had his pride,

"You bastards have no right to keep me here," he protested. "I done nothing."

With that, one of the soldiers, who was not in uniform, stamped on the poor man's bare foot with the heel of his boot. And when the old man lifted that foot in agony, the soldier moved behind him and stamped on the other one. The old man was reduced to sobbing uncontrollably.

Brendan thought back to Hugh O'Malley's evidence in Castlebar – about how he had been kicked and beaten unconscious.

"The bastards can do what they like within these walls," Brendan thought. "Note everything but say nothing."

More hours passed before a young officer in uniform appeared out of nowhere and enquired of Brendan: "And how does a gentleman like you get mixed up in a business like this?"

Several smart rejoinders came to Brendan's mind but he swallowed them all.

"I work with the *Dublin Evening Post*," he answered simply.

"No need to detain you then," the officer continued. "You are free to go." No explanation. No apology. No regrets. Just a sardonic grin on his tight mouth.

Brendan collected his shoes and was escorted out of the building.

By the time he had reached the offices of *The Post*, Brendan had worked himself into a white fury.

"How dare they hold a journalist and a member of the Bar in such a fashion," he almost roared at Mr. Magee.

"I'll send a protest to the Castle," the editor promised, "but you shouldn't be surprised. I told you to watch out. The military are now a power unto themselves. They do what they like and to whomever they choose – all with impunity. Without our own parliament, we are powerless – exactly as I had anticipated."

That night Brendan met *William Dowdall, an old friend from college days, in *The Wig*, a popular watering hole for members of the legal profession, and told him of his experience at the hands of the military.

"You were lucky to get off as lightly as you did. Must have been those expensive shoes you wear," Dowdall laughed. "I could tell you a few stories that would make you hair stand on end. These upstarts in the military have been getting away with murder."

William Dowdall was the natural son of Mr. Walter Hussey Burg, Mr. Henry Grattan's great ally in the stormy parliamentary debates of 1779-82. As a mark of his displeasure with the government, Mr. Burg had resigned the office of Prime Sergeant but he died soon thereafter at the early age of forty one. Mr. Grattan then generously had provided for young Dowdall's education, and Brendan had first met him when they were both studying law at the Inns. Afterwards, Mr. Grattan secured a modest employment for him in the House of Parliament under Mr. John Foster, but Dowdall's ever more overt Republican sympathies in '98 deprived him both of Mr. Grattan's patronage and his meagre employment. After the '98 Rebellion Dowdall was one of those who were rounded up and imprisoned for four years in Fort George in Scotland – an experience which greatly strengthened his Republican inclinations. Now, thanks to his old connections, he had renewed some work at the Bar and was proving a great source of information for Brendan.

William Dowdall seemed to be on intimate terms with half the town and, as a confirmed bachelor, he was in constant demand by the more entertaining hostesses in the city. And, of course, he was to be seen regularly at Margaret's Second Sundays. Despite his various misfortunes, Dowdall was one of those good-humoured souls who never failed to lift the spirits of his companions. He was a big man, showing a hint of corpulence thanks to his taste for good food and the best of wine. But he had a fine head, distinguished by what appeared to be permanently amused pale blue eyes which were protected by unusually bushy eyebrows. It was universally acknowledged that Bill Dowdall was "great company".

One evening early in 1803, Bill Dowdall brought Brendan to an old farm-house in Butterfield-lane near Rathfarnham, where they dined with a group of men including *Robert Emmet, about whom Brendan had heard only rumours, and *Thomas Russell, who was well known since 1798. The Emmets, of course, were a very well known family in Dublin society, although Brendan had never met any of them. Robert's father, Dr Robert Emmet, was unusual in his profession in that he had gone abroad to study medicine in the University of Montpelier in France – before the Revolution of course. Before that again, he had been a school-mate of Henry Grattan and, like Grattan, had taken an interest in public affairs all his life. But he also fancied himself as a poet and was regarded as a bit eccentric. Grattan famously quipped of him that "Emmet has his pills and his plans and he mixes so much politics with his prescriptions that he would kill the patient who took the one and ruin the country that listened to the other". But Dr Emmet was no fool. Far from it. Thanks to some influential family connections he had been appointed to the lucrative position of State Physician in 1770, and now practised from an impressive residence at 129 St Stephen's Green, close to Grafton Street. The family also enjoyed a substantial country residence in Milltown, about three miles outside the city.

Of the younger generation (Mrs. Emmet had given birth to seventeen children but only four survived), Robert's older brother, *Thomas Addis Emmet, was almost as well known as his father. He had first studied medicine in Edinburgh but later switched to the Bar, where he became involved in some celebrated cases against the government. He was one of the first to join the Society of United Irishmen in the early 1790s and soon became deeply involved. After the Rebellion he, too, had been imprisoned in Scotland for four years and then, on release in June 1802, had taken up residence in Paris.

It was a lively evening and the wine flowed while the political talk was mostly about Pitt and Bonaparte and the Irish ex-prisoners in Paris. But Brendan got the feeling that they were taking his measure. Or perhaps this group of friends with radical views were just being cautious in the presence of "the Press"? Still, he enjoyed the evening and was stimulated by the French flavour of the conversation. But he couldn't quite make out young Emmet. He was around the same age as Brendan yet was said to have had a meeting with Bonaparte in Paris the previous year. Emmet was known to have been a student in Trinity College for five years before being censured by the authorities for his political opinions. A warrant had been issued for his arrest in 1798, but he disappeared to the continent and, for the next few years, travelled extensively until meeting up again with his brother, Thomas Addis, after the latter's release from Fort George. Robert Emmet was small and wiry with a pallid face that was slightly pock-marked. He had a prominent nose which was straight and thin and ended in a sharp point. Strangely, in a man so young, he exuded an impression of intense gravity but with no suggestion of vanity or self conceit. If he had a sense of humour, he showed little evidence of it during dinner. He seemed to be entirely absorbed by politics or, as he called it, the state of the country.

"He takes himself very seriously, don't you think?", Brendan opined as he shared a carriage back to town with Bill Dowdall.

"Oh, that's his father's influence," Dowdall rejoined. "You'll find he's more relaxed on a one to one. Of course he is intense – but that's also his strength. Unlike me, he's a man of strong convictions."

" Has he any interests outside politics?"

"I'm not aware of any – except of course for Miss Curran!"

"Miss Curran?"

"Yes, Sarah Curran. You know, she's the daughter of John Philpot Curran, the barrister."

"Are they engaged?"

"I don't think so. That would be a real test of Emmet's courage – to ask for her hand. Personally I'd be terrified to ask Curran for sixpence!"

They both laughed.

"But what is he really up to?" Brendan asked.

"Oh, I think he wants to interest young men of opinion like yourself. Everybody can see that, since the Union, the country has gone to hell. Like his brother, Emmet is one of those people who feels compelled to do something about the society he lives in."

And after that night Brendan found himself drawn deeper into Robert Emmet's circle of friends and his particular brand of "politics".

Chapter XXIII

STEPHEN AND BRENDAN
IN PARIS

THE FRENCH COAST was already in sight when one of Stephen's many conversations with Captain Powell hit on a topic that was to have far-reaching consequences. They had been talking about the war with Bonaparte and the peace declared at Amiens in May '02 and whether the truce would hold.

"I reckon old Bony needs a breathing space," said the Captain. "But I'll tell you this. That so-called invasion fleet of his is a disaster. It will never cross the channel. It was the craziest idea he ever concocted."

"How come?", asked Stephen.

"Flat bottoms in the channel? The man must be mad. Signs on it, he's no sailor. That fleet could only cross the channel under perfect conditions. They're designed to run onto the beach and so draw not more than six or seven feet of water when fully laden – and half that when empty. They are flat underneath and heavy in the masts, they are extremely cranky in moving water, liable to keel over, or even capsize if caught in a sudden gust of wind. They are also liable to drift with the current, particularly so in the Straits of Dover where there are two strong and contrary currents every tide."

"So what are they good for?"

"They're fine for river work, and most of them have been built upriver on the Gironde and the Rhine and the Seine – even the Scheldt. I'm told there are hundreds of them."

"You mean they'd work as coal barges or lighters in rivers and estuaries?"

"Exactly. That's all they're good for," laughed the Captain.

While the Captain was talking on about Bonaparte, an idea had begun to germinate in Stephen's mind, born of his experience with the shipping agents in Jamaica. If Bonaparte really meant peace, he would have no further use for those barges. The brigs and cutters and coasters could be put to a thousand uses. But the barges were really a liability. If he managed to get his hands on a batch of them, could he not re-sell them for barge-work in England?

"Are they the same design as the Thames barges then?", he asked the Captain.

"More or less," the Captain answered, "except of course that they are more modern and in new condition. Most of the Thames barges are falling apart. Every shipyard on the river has been producing for the navy these past six years."

This information pleased Stephen greatly.

~~~~~~ • ~~~~~~

Stephen spent more than a month in Paris, waiting for an appointment to be received by M Forfait, the *Ministre de la Marine*. In the meantime he was able, through the most discreet enquiries, to find out more details on the invasion flotilla. To his amazement, he learnt that it numbered between 2,000 and 3,000 vessels in all. There were said to be no less than 1,400 boats of all descriptions in the newly-constructed harbour at Boulogne, about 500 up the coast at Ambleteuse and perhaps a further 400 down at Etaples. In addition to these main parts of the flotilla, two other expeditions were said to have been fitted out, one at Brest, and another in the Texel. The scale of the build-up was quite awe-inspiring. The cost must have been astronomical.

With time on his hands, Stephen also enjoyed some of the pleasures of Paris, and one day he got a chance view of the First Consul, clad simply in the blue uniform of the Chasseur Guards, with generals and Mameluke orderlies in his train, reviewing his troops on the Place du Carrousel. And, of course, he soon met some of the Irish community in the city. Many of the Irish prisoners released from Fort George in Scotland, following the Amiens Treaty in March had been exiled to France where they were being widely fêted.

But his meeting with Monsieur Forfait, when it finally took place, was most disappointing. The Minister almost laughed at the very idea of selling off any part of the flotilla, but he showed a keen interest in the West of Ireland once he established that Stephen hailed from that part. He called for maps and maritime charts and questioned Stephen closely on the navigation in Clew Bay.

"So you were close to where General Humbert landed in '98?", he asked Stephen.

"As the crow flies, less than thirty miles," Stephen replied.

"And did you witness any of the action?"

"No. The General marched to the East after Castlebar. We live to the West."

"But how interesting," the Minister added, "and you know, of course, that General Humbert is now in the West Indies?"

"No. I had no idea."

"Yes. In San Domingo – not far from Jamaica. But it seems that your paths are not destined to cross," he laughed. "However, I am sorry that I cannot hold out any hope for your proposal, but I will, of course, mention it to the First Consul."

On his way out of the meeting, Stephen heard some conversation in English and glanced in the direction of a small group standing near the window of the antechamber. To his surprise, one of the faces struck him as familiar, but he couldn't place it. He's not from Jamaica, he thought, so he must be Irish. But he walked straight ahead. He had no wish to disclose the nature of his business to any Irish émigrés.

—·—·—·—·— • —·—·—·—·—

A few weeks later, Stephen was dining alone in the Hotel d'Etrangers when he noticed the same party in the corner of the restaurant. They were more boisterous than the other diners and he soon heard their Irish accents and he saw again the face he had noticed at the Department of the Marine. Then the penny dropped. It was Brendan O'Reilly, the son of William O'Reilly of Westport.

Stephen's first instinct was to make himself known, as he was anxious to get news from home. However, he hesitated to intrude on the company. But later, as they were leaving, Stephen caught O'Reilly's eye and could not resist the impulse to address him.

"Mr. O'Reilly, I believe," he said as he rose from the table.

Brendan stopped in his tracks. He was not just surprised but apparently startled to be recognised at all.

"I... do I know you?", Brendan queried cautiously.

"Stephen Allen from Murrisk."

"From Murrisk? Murrisk Abbey? The Preston's place?"

"Yes indeed. You may remember I was in the employ of Captain John Preston some years ago," Stephen said.

"My God, I can't believe it. I heard you were dead. Everyone said so."

"Not a bit of it. As you can see, I am very much alive," Stephen laughed.

"And living in Paris?"

"No, I am just here on a matter of business."

"What a surprise! I really can't get over it. And the world has been good to you, I see," said Brendan as he admired Stephen's expensive attire.

"Yes, fortune has smiled on me," Stephen replied vaguely. "Won't you join me for a glass of claret?"

"Unfortunately, we are just leaving," Brendan replied. " This is Mr. Thomas Addis Emmet and Mr. William Dowdall, " he explained.

"I'm sorry we cannot stay," Mr. Emmet said after the introductions. "I hope we meet again."

But Brendan decided to stay behind and Stephen ordered another bottle of wine and the two Mayo men set to re-acquainting themselves with the news since they last met.

"Dublin is like a ghost town now," Brendan said. "The loss of the Parliament was a death blow to the capital. All the best society has moved to London."

"Has business suffered too?"

"Oh yes, even property prices have collapsed. A friend of mine quoted the example of *Lord Cloncurry the other evening. His father acquired Mornington House on Merrion Street in 1791 for £8,000 and it was sold recently for only £2,500. That will give you some idea."

"But what brings you to Paris?"

"I am here to interview some of the '98 prisoners for my paper. I am working with the Dublin Evening Post now," Brendan lied.

"Didn't I see you at the Ministry for the Marine a little while ago?"

Brendan looked surprised.

"Yes. I was able to arrange an appointment for my friend, Mr. Emmet. And how about you?", Brendan asked, anxious to change the subject. "I can see that you have been living in sunny climes."

"I was in Jamaica for some time."

"My word! How exciting! Margaret will be fascinated to hear all this."

"Your sister?"

"Yes. You remember her, of course?"

"Yes indeed. And what word of Miss Preston?", Stephen asked in a nonchalant fashion.

"Miss Preston? Oh yes. I can say she is much better now."

"Better?"

"Well, you heard about the Bingham business I suppose?"

"No, not a word."

Brendan then told Stephen the whole saga of Pamela losing her fortune and of subsequently being jilted by Richard Bingham.

"What a scoundrel," Stephen said.

"Exactly, but I am glad she has now recovered."

"Has she married someone else?", Stephen asked as casually as he could.

"No," Brendan replied abruptly. It was a subject on which he had no intention of elaborating.

Chatting on like this, the two men consumed another bottle of claret before they parted company well after midnight. Brendan had relaxed completely and dropped his earlier caution.

"We must dine some evening," Stephen proposed as they were leaving.

"Unfortunately, I leave for Ireland in a few days," Brendan replied. "But I do hope we will see you again in Dublin. Here is my card. It would be a pleasure to renew your acquaintance there."

Barely a week later, and much to his surprise, Stephen received a summons from the Ministre de la Marine, where he was presented with a draft agreement for the sale of fifty flat-bottomed barges, now lying at Ambleteuse, with detailed specifications and at a price, payable in Sterling, that was actually under his own estimate. One acquaintance in Paris explained that only as he came from Ireland would the French have considered doing business at all with him. But another had a more intriguing explanation.

"This is a very minor part of the invasion fleet and this decision has obviously come from the highest level. It is therefore politically motivated. It is probably meant as a ploy to deceive the English about Bony's real intentions."

Stephen had no reason to worry about the motivation. But he was delighted to have concluded the business. It would require time and trouble to organise the gradual transfer of the barges across the channel, as weather conditions permitted. But Stephen was confident that he could do so and that he would double his fortune in the process.

Chapter XXIV

STEPHEN AND PAMELA

"THANK YOU for asking Stephen Allen," said Brendan, as he admired the blazing fires in his sister's drawing room on Harcourt Street. Margaret was having another of her *soirées* and, Brendan noticed, she was looking particularly elegant this evening. Her hair was swept up at the back and held in place by little combs crowned with miniature pearls. And from her neck hung an antique emerald mounted in a simple gold setting. It subtly complemented the colour of her own eyes.

"He will certainly be the surprise of the evening," Brendan laughed as his sister rearranged the flowers in a huge jardinière.

"What an amazing story," Margaret commented "How did he make his fortune, do you think?"

"He mentioned shipping or something like that."

"Well, I hope he's not in the slave trade," Margaret scoffed. "But we'll find out before the night is over."

Immediately she saw Stephen, Margaret was taken by him. It was an instinctive reaction – but then she always said her first impressions were best. She was first struck by his bearing – a calm detachment and a laconic suggestion around the mouth that bespoke an experience far from the drawing-rooms of Dublin. And she liked his weathered face and the ink-blue eyes that surveyed her drawing-room with a sceptical air. His dress was unostentatious but noticeably from a first-class tailor. He was obviously his own man.

"My God, he's come a long way," Margaret reflected as she crossed the room to welcome him.

"I hope you remember me from Westport?", she said just a little grandly.

"How could I forget?", Stephen replied with a slight bow and such an enigmatic smile that Margaret was taken aback.

Fundamentally, Margaret felt a deep insecurity in Dublin society. She knew she was considered a *parvenu* by the older establishment which she both courted and despised at the same time. And she lacked that rock of security which a successful marriage and a burgeoning family should have provided. She was thus more at home with other slightly flawed characters with whom she felt less need to keep up appearances.

"Brendan tells me you have been abroad for some time," she said, more agreeably now.

"I have just returned," he replied simply.

"Well, you'll have a lot of catching up to do," Margaret added as she led him across the room. "I've seated you at Brendan's table for supper. Pamela Preston is there too."

Stephen felt his heart miss a beat. Since his return to Dublin, he had been pondering how best to contact Pamela. He saw her one evening at the Theatre Royal in Crow Street with some friends, but he hesitated to present himself. Instead, he observed her in her box all through the performance. He had thought of calling on her in Merrion Square, but hoped instead for a chance encounter at first. Most of all he feared a rebuff. He hadn't forgotten Lady Porter.

~~~~~~ • ~~~~~~

Pamela saw Stephen the moment she entered the drawing-room and her first inclination was to flee. She felt all flushed and fanned herself vigorously. Of course she had heard that Stephen had reappeared in Dublin, but it was still a shock to come face to face again. And when she found herself placed beside him for supper, she simply wanted to die.

How could she possibly tell him that he had been done out of his inheritance? This question had haunted Pamela ever since Aunt Olive had divulged the terrible truth on her death-bed .But what could Pamela do now? The money was gone, through no fault of hers. And yet she felt this burden of guilt. Stephen Allen had to be compensated, but how?

These questions and many more had been going round and round in Pamela's mind, but while Stephen was absent, and even presumed dead, she had been able to set them aside or at least to worry less about them as time went by. But the moment she learnt that Stephen Allen had returned to Dublin she knew the awful truth had to be faced.

But Stephen was all charm. He never mentioned Richard Bingham but steered the conversation to Murrisk and the West of Ireland.

Pamela told him all about rebuilding the house and about Malcolm and Mrs Barton, who had been ill, and about the horses and the mussels which were better than ever.

"But I want to hear more about Jamaica," she diverted, and kept Stephen on this subject until Colonel Jameson, on her left, interrupted and complained that she was ignoring him!

But, later in the evening, Stephen managed to get a chance for another quiet word.

"We must meet again," he ventured in a low tone.

"Yes, it's so difficult to talk here," she countered.

"May I call on you then? At Number Ten?"

Pamela felt her stomach turn. A thousand conjectures raced through her head at the same moment, and every one of them terrified her. But she knew there was no way out. Better to face up to it. The present situation was intolerable.

"Yes please do," she replied as calmly as she could muster.

"May I call on you to-morrow?", he asked eagerly.

"Why yes," she replied with as much enthusiasm as she could muster. "Call at eleven to-morrow morning."

~~~~~~ ● ~~~~~~

Stephen arrived promptly at 11.00 am the next day and was shown into the drawing-room upstairs. Pamela was standing by the window and the morning sun was lighting up her hair, which fell loose to her shoulders.

To Stephen she appeared older but more beautiful than ever.

"I remember this room very well," he said casually. "In fact you are standing exactly where Lady Porter was on the day she sent me packing – albeit with fifty gold sovereigns in my pocket."

But even as he spoke he felt he had said the wrong thing, and Pamela cringed inwardly.

"She really did you an injustice," she said. Then she blurted out. "I suppose that's what you wanted to talk about?"

"Well, not really," Stephen answered. "Although Captain John often spoke of her."

"Really?"

"Yes. But, strangely, he was quite in awe of her. For instance, he was always afraid she would learn about his passion for gambling. He even went through his solicitor to place his stakes in the Lottery. A fellow by the name of Hamilton, I think."

Pamela stole a quick glance at Stephen.

"Obviously he knows everything," she thought. "Isn't that what he's hinting at?"

She slumped down onto the chair and Stephen, after some hesitation, took a chair too. He noticed her distress and chided himself for having talked of Lady Porter at all. What a fool he was to have messed up their first meeting. So he hastened to mend his fences.

"I don't blame her at all for dismissing me at that time," he said lightly.

"And, in fact, she did me a favour. I have to thank her for setting me on the road to success."

But every word of this statement wounded Pamela to the quick. There was no longer any doubt that he knew all about Uncle John's will. So with an effort she blurted out:

"There is something I have wanted to tell you…"

But before she could proceed, Dr Wilkinson was announced and joined them for tea.

Stephen cursed his luck and excused himself as soon as he politely could do so.

After their first meeting, Margaret contrived to see Stephen as often as possible. She invited him to her house regularly and arranged for him to be invited to other parties to which she was going. Stephen became a regular guest at her Second Sundays and found himself included in a whole variety of theatre outings, supper parties and dinners. But to most of these he went with only one thought uppermost in his mind – the chance of meeting Pamela.

Margaret, meanwhile, was getting ever more interested in him. They were seen so often together that their association gave rise to considerable gossip. But for once the gossip was ill-founded. To Margaret's surprise, Stephen was quite happy for their relationship to remain entirely platonic. With anyone else, this would have suited Margaret admirably. With Stephen, however, she found it disappointing. And she began to realise that, for the first time in her life, she was falling in love.

Brendan, too, began to see quite a lot of Stephen. The two bachelors suited each other admirably. Brendan knew the best places to enjoy oneself in Dublin and Stephen had the resources to pay for them. But Stephen was alarmed at the virulence of Brendan's views. Since the Union, Brendan seemed to have lost all faith in constitutional politics.

"You sound ever more like a rebel," Stephen chided him one night after they had been on the town together.

"It may come to that."

"You can't be serious?".

"I hate violence," said Brendan. "Personally I couldn't kill a fly. So I pray to God that I will never find myself with a musket in my hand. But that doesn't mean that I have no pride in being an Irishman."

"Emotive language again, and dangerous too. Are you any less an Irishman because two governments are joined in one? Governments come and go all the time. But why should it excite you to treasonable talk?"

"Treasonable, did you say? How can you speak of treason? This government has no moral authority over me. I owe it no allegiance whatsoever."

"Sounds like a quote from one of Mr. Magee's editorials."

"He is one of the few who still speaks the truth in this country."

"What a pity not to look on the positive side – on the advantages to be gained from the Union."

"The Union was created by the British for their own interests."

"Without the British influence, this country would tear itself apart. Peasant against landlord; Protestant against Roman Catholic. We've seen it all before."

"There is only one form of government that has not been seen on this island for over six hundred years: an administration entirely under Irish control."

"I'm afraid you have more faith in them than I have."

"That's exactly where we differ. I believe we have the right to decide our own constitution and to live under it on this island. You obviously think otherwise."

"You're wrong there. I am no less an Irishman. And I long for the day when peace and harmony will prevail for everyone living here. But I believe the progress to that day must be reasoned and civilised if it is to endure. One has only to look to France to see the results of violent revolution. Deep down I don't believe that any political system is worth one drop of blood. That's where we really differ."

"Would the slaves in Jamaica share that point of view?", Brendan asked.

Stephen laughed. He admired Brendan's skill in argument and always enjoyed their verbal jousts together. But somehow or other, Brendan always got the last word.

⁓⁓⁓⁓ ● ⁓⁓⁓⁓

One evening, Brendan invited Stephen to supper in a private room over the *White Bull Inn* on Thomas Street, where Stephen, to his surprise, found that several others had been invited to join the company.

"May I introduce Mr. Stephen Allen," Brendan said, after Stephen had thrown off his coat.

"You may remember Mr. Dowdall," said Brendan, "whom you met in Paris. Next, two good men you should know, Mr. John Hevey, who brews the finest ale in town, and Mr. Denis Redmond, who has the best coals. This is *Mr. Miles Byrne whose name may be familiar to you. And finally, Mr. Philip Long, the most important man here. We are his guests tonight."

Everyone laughed. Mr. Long was a wealthy wine importer.

"Who are all these people?", Stephen asked Brendan in an aside as soon as he got the opportunity.

"Oh, nothing special," replied Brendan deviously. "Let's say they're all interested in the state of the country. You'll enjoy talking to them."

Stephen was intrigued. He guessed Brendan had something up his sleeve but couldn't decide whether it was a prank or something serious. Nor, at first, did the conversation give him much of a clue.

Mr. Long was discussing the extraordinary case of the late Bishop Butler, Lord Dunboyne, which had just been before Lord Kilwarden at the Trim Assizes, and the pros and cons of the late prelate's bequest to Maynooth College were debated as hotly across the supper table as they had been in court.

"Bishop Butler," Brendan explained to Stephen, "had been the Roman Catholic bishop of Cork for twenty-three years when, by unusual circumstances, the estates and title of the eleventh Baron Dunboyne devolved onto him. He thereupon renounced his creed and married a Protestant lady, by whom however he had no children. He died in August 1800 aged ninety-six, but not before he had been reconciled to the Roman Catholic Church by the celebrated Augustinian friar, Dr. William Gahan, and had bequeathed the Dunboyne estate to Maynooth College. The will was contested at the recent Trim Assizes and, on Dr. Gahan refusing to disclose the secrets of the dying Bishop's confessional, he was sentenced to a week's imprisonment for contempt of court by Lord Justice Kilwarden.

"Quite right too," interjected Mr. Dowdall. "The whole business was disgraceful. Butler himself was the most contemptible of all, trying to buy his way into heaven."

They all laughed.

"But what is the final outcome?", asked Stephen.

"It has been referred to the High Court," said Brendan. "The lawyers haven't finished with it yet. They'll probably have most of the estate before they get through with it."

Stephen was puzzled the whole way through supper. Mr. Dowdall was obviously a gentleman, but Stephen couldn't quite understand where the others fitted into the company. Brendan's friends were evidently closely acquainted and sometimes exchanged amusing or what appeared to be irrelevant asides to each other which went over Stephen's head. And it wasn't till late in the evening, when the table was about to break up, that the whole purpose of the supper suddenly emerged.

"Stephen, we have a favour to ask you of a most confidential nature," Brendan said as he took him aside to light a cigar. "But before I mention anything, let me assure you that a refusal on your part will be entirely understood. My friends need a most important message conveyed personally to Paris. Would it be possible for you to take it on your next visit there?"

Stephen was dumbfounded.

"Me?", he asked incredulously. "A confidential message?"

"Yes, a most important communication to Mr. Thomas Addis Emmet," Brendan confirmed. "You remember you met him at the Hotel d'Etrangers in Paris?"

"What sort of communication?", asked Stephen, who barely knew how to hide his surprise.

"It's confidential," Brendan repeated, "and need not concern you at all. It's just that, with your connections, you would have no difficulty in getting to Paris. Our friends might be intercepted."

"Intercepted? What are you talking about?", asked Stephen.

Brendan looked over his shoulder towards the table.

"I know we can trust you," said Brendan." And you are entitled to know. But the less you know, the better it is for all of us. And the safer. Let's just say that we are all friends of Ireland and pledged to..."

"You mean you are plotting something?", Stephen asked incredulously.

"Well, planning something, yes," Brendan confirmed.

Stephen's first reaction was to laugh out loud but he managed to restrain himself. A more unlikely bunch of conspirators it would be hard to imagine. Yet they were all mature men.

"Are you serious?", was all he could ask.

"Deadly serious," Mr. Dowdall interrupted as he joined them. And, for the first time, Stephen realised that there was indeed something serious afoot.

"And you want me to be part of it?"

"We only want you to carry a message," said Mr. Dowdall quietly. Stephen got the impression that he was the leader of the group.

All sorts of danger signals now began to flash through Stephen's mind. A bunch of amateurs were attempting to involve him in a most dangerous mission. They must be amateurs, he thought, as they were exposing themselves to him without knowing anything at all about him – anything really essential that is. He could be a spy. Half the country was in the government's pay. Brendan often said as much. Hadn't the men of 1798 been betrayed by spies? Even Lord Edward, the finest of them all. But more to the point, there could be a spy here amongst them. Stephen's own future could be in jeopardy. And for what? He decided to settle the matter quickly and moved abruptly to collect his coat.

"I'm afraid it's out of the question, gentlemen," he said in a strong voice. He wanted to leave not a shadow of a doubt in their minds. "I could not be a party to any such communication. But be assured that everything that has passed between us tonight will be treated as confidential by me – as I trust it will by you."

With that he strode out of the room, noting, as he passed, the look of deep embarrassment on Brendan's face. On the way out through the bar downstairs, Stephen brushed against a figure leaning on the counter. He glanced into the face, which was florid and weathered and partly covered with a cloth cap. But

Stephen could have sworn afterwards that it was Hugh O'Malley, the fisherman from Westport.

<p style="text-align:center">~~~~~~~ • ~~~~~~~</p>

The following morning Stephen sent a note to Brendan asking him to meet him in the front square of Trinity College at noon. Brendan arrived a bit late and appeared to be suffering from his drinking of the previous night, but Stephen came to the point straight away.

"You endangered my reputation last night in front of those strangers."

"They are good men and one hundred per cent trustworthy," Brendan replied with some heat.

"They may be to you, but I know even less about them than they know about me. Was anyone else aware that I was to be approached in that fashion?"

"No."

"Are you certain?"

"I am absolutely sure."

"Good."

They walked on in silence for a while past the long library and out around the playing fields.

"Brendan, do you realise what thin ice you are skating on?", Stephen asked.

"I know what I am doing," Brendan replied evasively.

"I wonder do you? I don't want to hear your plans. I don't want to be a party to any bit of them. But I know enough already to recognise treasonable conduct."

"Spoken like a patriot," said Brendan sarcastically.

"Don't be a fool," said Stephen. "I am stating my honest opinion."

"I'm sorry," said Brendan. "I didn't mean to offend you. I know we see things differently, which is only to be expected. I should never have asked you last night."

"Forget that for the moment," said Stephen. "It's unimportant. What is important is the real danger ahead of you. Have you forgotten '98? Do you imagine that your activities are not already under observation? Do you think *Major Sirr is any less efficient today than he was five years ago? I'd warrant he has the names of every man at that dinner last night on his desk this very morning."

"Nonsense," cried Brendan. "I know every one of them. I'd trust them with my life."

"Maybe so," replied Stephen, "but remember this. Out of every ten conspirators, on average, at least one of them will be a spy. Two or three of your friends are pretty sure to be under surveillance already. Conspiracy is a dangerous occupation. More dangerous than you seem to realise."

"Of course it has its dangers, but how else can we organise an insurrection?"

"An insurrection is it?", Stephen gasped." You must be mad! Have you learnt nothing from '98 then?"

"Certainly we have. And we will avoid their mistakes. Indeed the experience of '98 is a great help to us now."

"And to the authorities, no doubt! I wish I could dissuade you from this madness. Does Margaret know anything of your plans?"

"Of course not. And I know you will respect my confidence."

"She would talk some sense to you."

"She is a woman."

"And she's a realist. She would advise you against such a crazy escapade."

"We've been through all this before. My decision is made and there is no going back on it now."

They walked on for a while in silence till their route brought them back to Front Square. Stephen felt sorry for his friend. He would have liked to help him. He certainly didn't want to be the cause of any embarrassment to him. But neither did he want to encourage him in the least degree.

"I'll take your message to Paris," Stephen said with a sigh as they approached Front Gate once more.

"You will?", said Brendan who was genuinely surprised.

"Yes, I have to go anyhow. But there are three conditions," Stephen added. "The first is that the message is verbal. I will not risk anything in writing. The second is that only you must know that I have agreed to convey it."

"And the third?", asked Brendan.

"The third is that you promise never to ask me such a favour again."

Brendan felt the reprimand in this last condition. But still he was delighted.

"The verbal part should create no difficulties," Brendan said, "and I can understand your reasons for preferring it that way. But Mr. Dowdall, at least, will have to know about it. He is in command. But have no fear of any indiscretion. He is a gentleman and a true Irishman."

⁓⁓⁓⁓ • ⁓⁓⁓⁓

Stephen sailed for Bordeaux within the week with the message for Mr. Thomas Addis Emmet. It was simply to the effect that his brother Robert would be celebrating on the last Sunday in July. As Stephen recalled, that is also the date for the annual pilgrimage to Croagh Patrick above Murrisk.

Stephen delivered the message and attended to his business with the Ministry of Marine. But he was worried about the rumours of a renewal of war. He accelerated his arrangements to get the last of his barges across the channel and hurried back to Ireland as soon as he could.

⁓⁓⁓⁓ • ⁓⁓⁓⁓

William Dowdall always took his breakfast in Thornton's coffee-shop at the bottom of Grafton Street and, being a regular customer, his favourite table in a quiet corner was always reserved for him There he perused every item in the *Freeman's Journal* before facing out into the day. On Thursday, 19th May, 1803 he read that *The Jealous Wife* was playing at the Theatre Royal and made a mental note to see it. Also, that a colleague at the Bar, Bartholomew Canning, had passed away and his funeral service was to take place at St Catherine's church on Thomas Street. However, his breakfast was rudely interrupted when he read the following announcement of the news from London:

London. 14th May 1803

"All hopes of Peace have vanished. A letter received this morning by the Lord Mayor from Lord Hawkesbury in Downing Street will sufficiently prove that Bonaparte has rejected our Ultimatum and our ambassador, Lord Whitworth, has received his passports and may be expected in London this evening or tomorrow"

Dowdall quickly finished his breakfast and rode out to Robert Emmet's place in Rathfarnham where the news was not entirely unexpected. Talks on the Amiens agreement had been dragging on since Christmas, with both sides accusing the other of bad faith and breaches of the terms of the Treaty. Nevertheless, confirmation that the talks had finally broken down had massive implications for Emmet's plans.

"This is the best news we could have received," Emmet declared having glanced at the *Journal*. "Now we are certain to get the support from France. This makes all the difference. We must accelerate our plans immediately. And we must step up our efforts in Paris. Call a meeting for tomorrow evening here at seven o'clock. There is much to be planned but at least we can now proceed with greater confidence."

The authorities had been slow to pick up young Emmet's trail. Having been abroad for so long, even his appearance was unknown to the police in Dublin – which gave him a head start of at least a few months free from surveillance. But with the renewal of hostilities with France, the British authorities dispatched General Henry Fox (he who had been active at the Races of Castlebar) to Ireland as Commander in Chief. In Ireland, as in England, the Militia was alerted once again to the danger of invasion from the ever-threatening French, and police spies were again set loose on dissidents and known critics of the government.

Chapter XXV

MORNING

Dublin: Saturday, 23rd July, 1803

ROBERT EMMET'S plans for a Rising in Dublin were dependent on, and were to follow after, a new landing of troops from France. Once the British forces were engaged against the Soldiers of the Republic, Emmet planned to seize Dublin Castle and the city. After that, he was confident the country would follow. Emmet's strategy was simple too. Enlist the support of the best of the '98 men that still remained. But keep the numbers small. The treachery of '98 was not to be forgotten. This time it was to be different. Secrecy and surprise were the key elements in all his plans.

Emmet's plan to seize control of Dublin was concentrated on three key points in the city. The attack was to begin at the Pidgeon House – the point of entry from the sea to the city – and two hundred men, including Miles Byrne and Thomas Brangan, both '98 veterans, were assigned to this task. The place of assembly was the strand between Irishtown and Sandymount. The time: low water.

The seizure of Dublin Castle was also assigned to only 200 men. It was to begin with the entrance of six hackney coaches with two footmen and six persons inside, driving through the upper gate into the Castle yard. They would then debouch and overcome the guard. At the same time, scaling ladders were to be used to gain entry over the walls at other points. The third main point of attack was to be the Islandbridge barracks which controlled the vital bridge across the Liffey. Four hundred men were assigned to this objective.

Thanks to his employment of a Scotsman called John McIntosh, who had previously worked in the East India service where he frequently prepared fireworks, Mr. Emmet had also developed a system of signals using rockets. Three rockets were to be the signal that the attack on any part had been made; and afterwards, a rocket of stars in case of victory; a silent one if repulsed.

All these plans were proceeding extremely well until an unfortunate explosion took place in the Patrick Street depot on the 18th July where McIntosh had been preparing the rockets and ammunition. That afternoon, Robert Emmet called a council of war in the Thomas Street depot. Tom Russell was there, as was William Hamilton, Jeremy Hope, William Dowdall, and several others. They all knew that the police must have been alerted to the incident and would put two and two together. Of course, all Emmet's plans had been based on the assumption of receiving French support, and Thomas Addis Emmet had been working incessantly in Paris to secure this. But now that the authorities had been alerted, it was generally agreed that the Rising must go ahead even without the support of the French.

And so, the date of the Rising was advanced by a week to Saturday, 23rd July, 1803.

Early on the morning of Saturday, 23rd July, 1803, Brendan dropped a note into the letter box of the *Dublin Evening Post*, addressed to the editor and marked "Urgent". It read simply:

Dear Mr. Magee.

Urgent business, which I am not at liberty to disclose at this time, has called me away for the day. However I expect to have some very interesting information for the Post before this day is out. Please excuse me."

Your obedient servant,

Brendan O'Reilly.

Brendan had spent many hours trying to refashion Robert Emmet's *Proclamation of the Provisional Government to the People of Ireland*. Emmet attached great importance to this and had written out the first draft in his own hand. But it was much too long and detailed. There were some good passages in it, like: "We war not against property – we war against no religious sect – we war not against past opinions or prejudices – we war against English dominion". And: "We solemnly declare that our object is to establish a free and independent republic in Ireland and that the pursuit of this object we will relinquish only with our lives". But these were the exceptions. Emmet had included a long list of instructions to (theoretical) provincial commanders and even the outline of a new democratic assembly. Brendan had been trying to edit it down to a more suitable size.

As soon as he arrived at the depot on Thomas Street, William Dowdall ordered Brendan to "get the Proclamation down to Stockdale's or we'll never have it ready." Stockdale's was a small printing-works in Abbey Street sympathetic to the cause.

"How many should we print?" Brendan asked.

"Five or six thousand I'd say," said Dowdall, who to Brendan's surprise was attired that morning in a smart blue, cut-away coat. Brendan thought it inappropriate.

"We want them all over the city," Dowdall said. "And we must have a few thousand for the country too. This is an historic document! Better be on the safe side. Make it ten thousand."

"I think I'd better give him a last look at it," said Brendan, referring to Emmet.

"Impossible," said Dowdall. "Those Kildare men are giving him enough trouble as it is. Off with you quick. And bring back the first copies off the press."

Brendan made his way across the river to Stockdale's in Abbey Street. Everything seemed so quiet and normal in the town that he had to keep reminding himself that this was THE DAY – the day that could change the course of Irish history – the day that could change his own life. It was a lovely clear dry morning. He felt extremely happy.

Arriving back at the depot with the first copies of the Proclamation, Brendan found a scene of considerable confusion. One contingent of the Kildare men were threatening to quit the Rising because there were not enough guns. Others were shouting at them, even accusing them of cowardice. Then, suddenly, Robert Emmet appeared, resplendent in an impressive green uniform. Brendan was stunned. He had never seen Robert Emmet in uniform before.

Taking aside a few of his confidants, Emmet said in a low tone: "Our greatest need is for more guns. Send to Philip Long immediately. Tell him we must have £500 urgently. And buy what pistols and blunderbusses you can. Devereux in Blackhall Row will ask no questions. He has pistols. And try Mulveys in Parliament Street for the blunderbusses. But be careful to raise no suspicions."

Dowdall asked Brendan to help in raising some cash.

"You will attract the least attention," he said.

Philip Long was a small, foreign-looking gentleman whose appearance exactly suited his business, which was in the importation of Spanish wines. He lived, and carried on his business, from Number Four Crow Street, which was just off Dame Street – a stone's throw away from the Castle. He had already proven to be the most generous of Emmet's supporters, but at short notice he was able to produce only £100 of the £500 so urgently required.

Brendan collected £100 from his own lodgings and was heading towards Mulvey's when he suddenly thought of his sister. Margaret would give him the necessary funds. Margaret never let him down. He hailed a hackney and headed for Hatch Street.

At first Brendan did not tell Margaret what he wanted the money for – only that it was urgent and essential. But Margaret was not so easily duped.

"You know I'll help you in any way I can," she said. "But you must trust me. You must tell me what trouble you're in."

"I'm not in any trouble."

"Then why do you want three hundred pounds? And so urgently?"

"I'd tell you if I could. But my lips are sealed."

"Are you being blackmailed?"

"Nonsense!"

"Have you been gambling?"

"You know I don't gamble."

"Then what is it?"

Brendan paced the upstairs drawing room, while Margaret sat, sympathetic but implacable.

It wasn't that he didn't trust her. But he couldn't be sure of her reaction.

"You know I wouldn't ask you if it wasn't absolutely essential," he said.

"Of course."

"And that you are my last resort."

"I can believe it."

"Then you must trust me. All I can say is that there is nothing dishonourable involved."

"Well, even that is something," said Margaret, feeling that she was making a little progress at last.

"In fact it's not a personal matter at all," Brendan added suddenly, and Margaret sensed that she was about to hear the truth.

"Not a personal matter?" she prompted.

"No."

"Is it a public matter then?"

"Yes!"

"What sort of public matter?"

"A political matter."

A silence fell in the elegant room, and for the first time Margaret felt a tinge of real apprehension. The business had begun to sound serious. What sort of a mess could her brother be caught up in? Margaret was concerned. And she was more than ever determined to get to the bottom of it.

"Brendan, I'll be frank with you," she said. "You're wasting your time. I have no intention of parting with three pounds, not to mention three hundred, until I am fully informed of the necessity for such a large sum. Now, either you tell me straight out – or you don't get a penny."

Brendan knew when his sister was serious.

"There's a Rising planned for to-night," he blurted out.

"A rising?", repeated Margaret incredulously.

"Yes, tonight. They're going to take the Castle," he added enthusiastically.

For a moment Margaret could hardly believe her ears. A rising! To take the Castle! And her own brother involved.

"You must be mad," she said.

Brendan was taken aback. It was word for word with Stephen's reaction.

"No, it's deadly serious," he assured her. "There are thousands involved. The city will be in our hands before dawn."

Margaret rose from her seat, a look of absolute horror on her face.

"You don't mean to say you're involved in such a mad-cap scheme?", she demanded.

"You don't understand," he explained. "The plans are well-advanced. We have ten thousand pikes…"

"And no money – obviously," she cut in. "Who is behind this madness?"

Brendan regretted having told her anything. It was getting him nowhere.

"I'm going," he said, heading for the door. "I'm off if you won't help me."

"Help you?", she cried and her voice was rising. "Help you to get killed? Is that what you want? Is that what you want me to do? For God's sake don't be so foolish! Think of the family." She was clinging to him now and she was becoming almost hysterical.

"I've got to go," he said calmly. "I shouldn't have mentioned this business at all."

"No, don't. Don't go," she begged.

But Brendan had opened the drawing room door only to find Charles immediately outside. Evidently he had been listening to the entire conversation.

"Charles!", Brendan exclaimed in surprise.

"What's this I hear?", Charles demanded. "Do my ears deceive me? Or are you gone out of your mind? Do you want to destroy us all? Desist immediately from this madness, or I will take steps to ensure you do."

"This is not your affair," Brendan said firmly. "And I'll thank you to mind your own business."

"It certainly is my business," Charles answered hotly, "and not for one moment will I tolerate it. I give you this solemn warning. Either you desist immediately, or I will be forced to inform against you."

Brendan looked at his brother-in-law in horror. He had never liked the man. Now he felt like punching him in the face.

"What a despicable specimen you are," he said. "Do as you please – and to hell with you." And with that he pushed past him and down the stairs.

Charles ran after him, shouting as he descended to the landing.

"I warn you," he said. "I'll not be ruined for the sake of your adventures. I'll go to Major Sirr forthwith. I'll not be smeared with this disgrace. You fool. You bloody fool…"

Margaret, in alarm, followed the two men downstairs, but before she could catch up with them, Brendan had let himself out the front door which he slammed loudly behind him. Charles went straight into the small cloakroom off the hall, muttering aloud all the time.

"I'll not be ruined for the sake of this fool… I tried to warn him… but he wouldn't listen to reason…"

"You wouldn't report him to the police?", Margaret pleaded as she followed him into the small cloakroom.

"I am about to do so," Charles confirmed in a righteous tone, and Margaret knew he meant it.

"Not my brother?"

"To hell with your brother," Charles spat out. "He doesn't give a damn for us. Why should I care for him?"

Margaret recoiled in horror. Her own husband was about to betray her brother; her Brendan. But her mind was clear. She knew immediately what she had to do. While Charles was still putting on his coat, Margaret stepped back into the hall, pulled the door sharply behind her, and turned the key in the lock. Then, ignoring the shouting from within, she sent Patsy running down Hatch Street to bring back Brendan.

"What's happening?", Brendan asked, alarmed on his return by the thumping and shouting from within the cloakroom.

"I've locked him in, and there he'll stay until this day is over," Margaret answered with a wry smile. "It's too good for him, it is. If he doesn't quieten down I may have him committed."

"Here," she said to Brendan. "Here's two hundred pounds. It's all I have in the house. I don't approve of what you're doing. I only beg of you to be careful – for mother's sake if not your own. Come back here tonight. I'll be waiting – and praying."

And with that she threw her arms around her brother and hugged him close to her. There were tears too in Brendan's eyes as he hurried off with funds for muskets.

That same morning, Alexander Marsden (he who had conducted the most secret part of the Union negotiations) came into town at about eleven o' clock. Mr. Marsden was the most senior civil servant of the British administration in Dublin Castle that day, the Chief Secretary being in England on official business. One of his first callers was a Mr. Edward Clarke of Palmerstown, a few miles up the Liffey. Mr. Clarke employed a great many men in his factory there and had heard rumours of seditious activity for the past several days. But that very morning, the men had asked for their money early and his friend Mr. Wilcock had learned that they intended going into the city to create trouble. On hearing this alarming information, Mr. Clarke had immediately ridden into town to warn the Under-Secretary personally.

Mr. Marsden's second caller was a Mr. Atkinson of Belfast, who had arrived that morning from the north with the certain information that a rising was to take place that very evening, both in Dublin and in Belfast.

A little later, a Mr. Nason Browne, who had overheard a breakfast conversation between three men in a tavern in Islandbridge, came to advise Mr. Marsden that they spoke of a rising in the city that was to take place that night.

And so the morning went on. Not all of this came as a surprise to Mr. Marsden. He had had plenty of information that something was afoot from the ever-vigilant Major Sirr, the chief police officer of the city. It was only a question of how best to handle the situation.

Soon after mid-day he called Major Sirr to his office.

"How serious do you think it is?", he asked the police chief.

"Well, there's something brewing. There's no doubt about that. I have it from more and more quarters. And a lot of strangers have come into town, especially on the canal from Kildare."

"Who's behind it then?"

"We don't fully know. But I suspect several of the men of '98. Certainly Russell and Henry Hamilton have been in circulation again. And that fellow Dowdall has been keeping some strange company."

"Dowdall?"

"Yes. William Dowdall. You remember he had some contact with Colonel Despard who was hanged in London."

"Of course. Unfortunate business. Came from very respectable people."

"Should we alert the Yeomanry?", asked the major, whose own resources were extremely slim.

"We'll have to think about that," Marsden replied cautiously. "If we do, the troublemakers will know that we are appraised of their plans"

"And if we don't, they may seriously embarrass us," said the major.

"I will decide a little later," said the Under-Secretary who was already thinking of the political implications. "In the meantime, put your own men on the alert. But quietly so."

As soon as the major left his office, Mr. Marsden wrote, in his own hand, a short note to *Lord Hardwicke, the Lord Lieutenant, who was then in his residence in the Phoenix Park.

"My Lord,

On coming to town I find a considerable degree of alarm in the apprehension of a rising this night or tomorrow morning in Dublin. I have reason to think that something serious is intended. I wish Your Excellency would come to town with General Fox in your carriage which I would not request on light grounds."
Alexander Marsden.

Lord Hardwicke, who had been joined for luncheon by General Fox, the recently appointed Commander of the Forces in Ireland, received this communication at about 2pm. He immediately set out for the Castle accompanied by the General.

~~~~~~ • ~~~~~~

It was a little after three o' clock when they arrived at the Castle and immediately went into consultation, where General Fox was for calling out the troops but Mr. Marsden had different ideas.

"Without the assistance of the French," he said, "this conspiracy poses no real threat to us. Of course we can suppress it now, or later, as suits us best. But my opinion is that it should be later. This nasty boil must ripen to maturity before we lance it.

Otherwise the leaders may again escape us. Let them show their hand before we crush them. Once these remnants of the '98 trouble are well and truly purged, the French will find themselves friendless on these shores."

"That sounds all very well in theory," said the general. "But who will take the responsibility for allowing the situation to develop so?"

There was a pause and both men glanced at Lord Hardwicke.

"I take the Under-Secretary's point. If we alarm them now, we may never know the extent of the conspiracy or indeed the identity of the leaders. At the first sign of an alert, they would run to ground. However there is a risk involved in delay."

"Our bigger consideration is the French," Mr. Marsden repeated. "We must keep that factor uppermost in our minds when deciding how to handle the present trouble."

"Yes, I agree with that of course," said the Lord Lieutenant, who was feeling his way through the unexpected crisis. "How many troops do you have in the city?", he asked the general.

"About three thousand."

"Have we any estimate of the insurgents?"

"Nothing precise," said Mr. Marsden. "But they are likely to be armed only with pikes. And, of course, they have no artillery."

"You think they pose but a small threat then?"

"I am sure we can contain whatever presents itself," replied Mr. Marsden although he was less confident than he tried to sound. He was most anxious that no general alarm be raised.

"Well, let's review the state of play then," said Lord Hardwicke.

"We must increase the Castle guard at least," said General Fox. "Men can be moved up quietly from the old Custom House barracks."

"Agreed."

"I'll also double the guard at Your Excellency's residence."

"Certainly."

"What of Sir Edward's reception in the Castle this evening? Should it be cancelled?"

"Certainly not," said Mr. Marsden emphatically. "To do so might arouse suspicion."

"And the Privy Council?", asked Lord Hardwicke.

"Yes, it should be alerted. It may be necessary to convene a meeting at short notice."

"Very well then," said Lord Hardwicke at last. "I will return to the Park now. But keep me constantly informed during the evening. It promises to be an interesting one."

Mr. Marsden had a final word with general Fox. "Please be very cautious in not creating any alarm," he said. "I think we have a lot to gain from this day."

Chapter XXVI

AFTERNOON

Dublin: Saturday, 23rd July, 1803

ROBERT EMMET'S plan called for the attacks to be launched at dusk. But twilight in Dublin in the month of July lingers on and it was a long wait – especially for the countrymen who had made their way into town early in the day. By late afternoon every tavern along the length of Thomas Street, and around into Meath Street and Francis Street and down Bridgefoot Street, was full of thirsty men charging their courage. Mr. Emmet took some supper at the *White Bull* around six o'clock, but the mood was not too confident. Several of the Kildare leaders had deserted the cause and gone home within the previous few hours.

At the depot on Thomas Street, however, there was a comforting smell of freshly baked bread. Twenty dozen loaves had just been delivered for the famished countrymen who were now crowding all through the depot, filling the yard outside and even spilling out into Bridgefoot Street. The atmosphere was carnival more than rowdy – not unlike that at a country fair. It had been a very warm day.

Brendan, who had been on the move all day, arrived back at the depot in time to see Mr. Emmet reading out the Proclamation to the boisterous crowd, not many of whom could hear – let alone understand – him. But at least he looked the part. He had donned a deep green military coat with white lapels and heavy golden epaulettes over a white waistcoat. His breeches were of creamy-white cashmere and he wore a strong pair of Hessian riding boots. In the crimson sash around his waist were a brace of pistols, and by his side hung a sword. On his head he wore a tricorn hat with feathers.

"You are now called upon", Emmet announced, "to show the world that you are competent to take your place among nations: that you have a right to claim their recognisance of you as an independent country by the only satisfactory proof you can furnish of your capability of maintaining your independence – by wresting it from England with your own hands…"

Brendan winced. He wished he had cut it much more. Proclamations need short, sharp sentences – and simple words. It was all wrong. But somehow it didn't seem to matter what Mr. Emmet said. The men had come up to strike a blow for Ireland. Robert Emmet was going to lead them out against the old enemy. Very few of the men present had ever seen him before, but there was no doubting his sincerity. And when he came to the bit about the establishment of an independent republic, and "that the pursuit of this objective we will relinquish only with our lives", there was a great cheer from the men closest to him which was re-echoed at the back and resounded out into the yard. It wasn't that anyone wanted to die or had even thought about dying. They were really cheering Mr. Emmet because they believed that he, at least, was willing to die.

Emmet was still reading the long Proclamation when Michael Quigley pushed into the depot in great alarm.

"The redcoats are coming," he shouted. And immediately the whole place was thrown into confusion. It turned out to be a false alarm, but Emmet gave the order for the distribution of arms and men started throwing down the pikes into the yard from the upper loft. Michael Quigley and Nicholas Stafford donned regimentals similar to Mr. Emmet's but with only one gold epaulette, and Felix O'Rourke appeared from nowhere, dressed in a scarlet coat and a military cocked hat and white feather. John Fleming, the hostler at the *White Bull Inn*, was dispatched to nearby taverns to order that no more drink was to be served and a detail was sent to take possession of Costigan's distillery in Thomas Street. The big yard there was to be a point of assembly for some of the men.

A short time later Mr. Emmet emerged onto Thomas Street, flanked by his principal officers in their uniforms, and a great cheer went up from the men all round. A single rocket flared over the rooftops and Lord Moira's bell on the quays struck the first chime of nine o'clock. Robert Emmet drew his sword and called on his men to follow him, and Brendan found himself swept along with the others down Thomas Street, heading straight for Dublin Castle the walls of which could be seen in the distance. Emmet certainly looked the part, and Brendan even wondered why his hero was not astride a white horse.

As the uniformed leaders marched down Thomas Street, they were followed by about a hundred organised supporters, of whom about thirty had guns. But behind them were perhaps two hundred stragglers who surged out from the taverns to join the action. Soon they filled the whole street, cheered on by the spectators who waved out of every window along the way. Most of the men carried pikes or heavy clubs. William Dowdall was shouting to them to close up and keep order, but they paid little attention to him. When he came to the Market House on High Street, within sight of the Castle, Robert Emmet halted his march in an effort to reorganise the ranks. But there was no sign of any rockets from other parts of the city.

Brendan had fallen back from the front and was distributing copies of the Proclamation as he went along. He thus happened to be at the corner of Vicar Street when he saw the approach of a gentleman's carriage heading into town along Thomas Street. The postillion was calling for the way to be made clear and was even foolish enough to swish his whip in a threatening fashion. But the crowd was in no mood for such arrogance. At first they jeered the driver. Then they deliberately upset the horses. Then some brazen fellow banged on the side of the carriage.

"Make way for Lord Kilwarden," the driver shouted again, but to no avail.

Soon the carriage was completely surrounded by the rabble. The horses were playing up in front and the mood had changed from boisterous to threatening. The mob was getting out of control. Some young fellows were trying to heave the carriage from side to side. Then, someone threw a brick at the driver which, instead, hit the carriage window, shattering the glass and raising an ugly roar from the crowd.

At this point the carriage door was thrown open and Lord Kilwarden appeared, half peering, half leaning out of the door. He had been summoned to a meeting of the Privy Council and had come into town from his country residence accompanied by his daughter and by his nephew, the Reverend Richard Wolfe.

"It is I, Kilwarden," he said, "Chief Justice of the King's Bench."

The poor man was relying on his reputation, which was well deserved, for fairness and humanity on the bench. But the crowd only jeered him all the more. Part of the mob was just drunken and loutish, but there were evil elements at work too.

Hugh O'Malley, who had been drinking all day, had just joined the crowd outside the *White Bull Inn* when he saw the judge appealing from the step of his carriage. The image was blurred to the red-head, but strangely familiar. He had seen it all before – in Paris on the Rue de Bac in '95. And he remembered what had happened in Paris. Almost unconsciously he took hold of one of the long pikes and hurled it like a javelin towards the judge. The heavy pike plunged deeply into Kilwarden's chest and released a gush of blood all over his frock-coat.

"*Mort a tout les traites,*" O'Malley heard himself yell out.

"*Mort, Mort, Mort,*" he chanted, just like they did in Paris.

Like blooded foxhounds, the mob now surged forward and joined in the laceration of Kilwarden's body, driving thrusts through every part of his corpse.

The coachman meanwhile had jumped down from his box and disappeared into the crowd, soon to be followed by the Rev. Wolfe. But the clergyman did not escape the fury of the mob and was quickly cut to bits like his uncle.

It was at this point that Brendan saw the terrified visage of Kilwarden's daughter cowering at the back of the carriage and, pushing his way through the crowd, he came around the far side of the carriage.

"Quickly," he ordered, "come with me," as he almost pulled her from her seat and forced a passage towards the *White Bull Inn*.

"Here, put on my coat and say nothing. You will be safe now," and he guided her into the snug at the back of the bar.

Brendan ordered two brandies from the proprietor and then took him aside.

"I want a hackney out the back and I must have it immediately."

"You must be joking with all this going on."

"It's worth half a sovereign to you and the same for the cab driver," said Brendan as he produced two half sovereigns from his waistcoat.

"Well, I'll do my best," said the inn-keeper, duly impressed by the gold coins, but it was a full ten minutes before he returned with the cabbie.

"Take this lady to Mrs. Bourke at Number Eight Harcourt Street. Go by the back streets and avoid all the area around the castle. Look after her with your life. Come to my office tomorrow at the *Dublin Evening Post* and I'll reward you further. Now be off."

He had spoken hardly a word to Miss Wolfe who was still in a state of shock, but as helped her into the cab he assured her that she would be safe with his sister, Mrs. Bourke.

And as he closed the door to the carriage she raised her eyes to his and said in a low voice, "I will remember your kindness for as long as I live."

Chapter XXVII

EVENING

Dublin: Saturday, 23rd July, 1803

STEPHEN HAD agreed to accompany Margaret to the reception in the Castle that evening, and it was almost seven o'clock when he called for her at Hatch Street. But, to his surprise, he found Margaret not yet dressed. They had passed a few minutes in polite if strained salutation when Stephen heard a ferocious hammering from downstairs but, to his amazement, Margaret pretended to ignore it completely. The noise was coming from the cloakroom where Charles was still incarcerated.

"Do I hear something, or are my ears deceiving me?", Stephen asked with heavy irony.

Margaret assumed a worried air.

"It's Charles," she said. "He's been drunk again. I had to lock him up. He was really quite violent."

Stephen realised that he had arrived in the middle of a domestic *fracas*.

"Obviously you're not going to the Castle," he said.

"Oh yes, of course, I am," Margaret insisted. "I'll be ready in a few minutes."

Stephen felt obliged to sink back into the armchair, but before another word was exchanged, a splintering crash was heard in the hall and Charles came shouting and swearing up the stairs and burst into the drawing room.

"So, you're part of the plot too," he shouted at Stephen, looking about him in a wild fashion. "You're in with the rest of them are you? As for you," he said, turning on Margaret, "mark my word, you'll rue this day."

He then stormed out again, slamming the hall door hard behind him as he rushed into the street.

"What on earth was he talking about?", asked Stephen.

"Oh nothing. He's raving again, he's drunk."

"But the plot? And traitors? He said I was in a plot?"

"There's no plot really. But there are rumours of trouble in the city tonight."

"What do you mean trouble?", Stephen demanded directly.

"Some of Brendan's friends," she said, and Stephen's mind flashed back to that supper in the *White Bull Inn*. "Apparently, there's something afoot."

"Is it serious? I want to know."

Margaret caught the edge in his voice.

"Yes, I think it may be. Brendan talked of a rising."

"My God!"

"They say they're going to take the Castle."

"The Castle!", Stephen exploded. "Tonight?"

Margaret saw the hard look on his face.

"I have to go," he exclaimed, striding fast for the door.

"Where are you going?", she demanded in alarm. "Don't leave me now." Margaret had caught his arm and was clinging to it, desperately.

"I must go. I must," he said and there was no restraining him.

"No! Stay with me. Please stay this night. I need you," she pleaded.

But Stephen pulled himself free and ran down the stairs two at a time.

"It's Pamela," he called back. "Pamela Preston. She's due at the Castle too. I must warn her."

Margaret staggered back into the drawing-room. She felt faint, as if the blood had drained out of her every vein.

"So that was it," she sighed to herself. "Pamela Preston. But of course. Why didn't I guess? There had to be some other woman. But I would never have thought of Pamela Preston."

And, for the first time in her life, she collapsed into a fit of sobbing.

～～～～～ • ～～～～～

Stephen ran the short length of Hatch Street into Leeson Street where he found a hackney coach at the stand.

"Can this nag gallop?", he demanded of the alarmed jarvey as he jumped up to the driving seat. "There's a gold coin for you if you gallop the whole way to Merrion Square."

But the old driver didn't respond fast enough and Steve grabbed the reins himself.

"This is an emergency," he shouted, as he cracked the whip over the horse's rump. "A matter of life and death."

"My God, you'll be the death of me," cried the old driver, who was clinging to the side-rail with his left hand while holding on to his hat with the other.

"You'll kill that beast on me too," the jarvey wailed, as they finally swung into Merrion Square.

"Is Miss Preston at home?", Steve demanded of the maid immediately he arrived at Number Ten.

"No sir. Doctor Wilkinson and Miss Preston have just left for the Castle."

"How long have they gone?"

"Not more than five minutes sir."

Stephen turned on his heel.

"I hope we can catch them," he said to himself.

It was not yet 7.30 pm.

Sweating as she was, Stephen pushed the hackney mare at a gallop down Nassau Street, along the side railings of Trinity College and into College Green. But here the crowd was so dense that it was impossible to proceed. The whole length of Dame Street, which stretches from the front gate of Trinity College at one end to the Castle entrance at the other, was packed solid with an extraordinary assortment of countrymen and labouring classes that were seldom seen in that part of the town. Standing up on the driver's seat, Stephen could see some carriages further ahead in Dame Street, marooned in a sea of heads. But, in the fading light, he could not distinguish the Wilkinson carriage.

Stephen passed a half sovereign to the jarvey as he spotted a rough-looking fellow astride a big black horse over to his right near the Parliament building. He pushed his way on foot towards him, panic mounting with every moment lost. There was no doubting the ugly mood of the crowd. One group, he heard, had broken into the Lord Mayor's residence in Dawson Street and taken its stack of guns. God only knew what they would do next.

"A word with you sir," he called up to the man on the black horse.

The man frowned down at him but automatically leant down to hear what Stephen had to say. Stephen grabbed his arm and with a heavy jerk unseated him from the saddle. In the same instant, he hoisted himself lightly onto the surprised animal. Then, grabbing a short rein, he pulled the big horse round and galloped furiously down Westmoreland Street away from the crowd and swung into Fleet Street, which runs parallel to Dame Street. Within minutes, he had completed the square and returned into Dame Street at that point where the carriages were stranded.

"Redcoats," he roared repeatedly at the top of his voice. "The soldiers are coming." And the crowd opened before him like the Red Sea for Moses.

Stephen reached the first carriage only to find it empty. The second was likewise empty and badly damaged. Stephen pushed the excited horse forward again until he recognised the dark blue Wilkinson carriage, although the coachman was nowhere to be seen. And at first glance his worst fears were confirmed. The door on his side had been pulled off one hinge, and hanging out of the opening were the unmistakable legs of poor Doctor Wilkinson.

Stephen roared as he reared the big black horse and thrashed around him in all directions. A blind rage welled up inside him. He felt like a man possessed. But then he saw Pamela. She was cringing at the back of the carriage with blood spattered all over her creamy white silk evening dress. She was petrified.

195

"Pull him in," Stephen ordered roughly. "And hold on." And with that he vaulted onto the coachman's bench and grabbed the reins.

As Stephen brought the long whip down across the bay's rump, a blunderbuss was discharged close to the animal's head. The bay reared and plunged forward while Stephen struggled to control her. The crowd tried to scatter but several were knocked down and some even driven over in the confusion. Stephen was shouting and roaring at the top of his voice – an involuntary reaction which successfully added to the general terror. The mare galloped on into Aungier Street and Stephen let her tire herself out until he had escaped the mob. He slowed her down then but didn't stop for even a moment until he had returned to Merrion Square. Only then did he discover for certain that Doctor Wilkinson was dead.

Chapter XXVIII

NIGHT

Dublin: Saturday, 23rd July, 1803

ROBERT EMMET halted outside the Cornmarket within sight of the Castle. He was beginning to have grave doubts about the situation. There was no sign of the six cabs that were meant to carry the first men into the castle. Nor were there any signs of rockets from Islandbridge or the Pidgeon House. The Kildare men had already deserted him. Behind him was an unruly mob and ahead there was an ominous silence. He knew the military must be alerted by now. But where were they? He had lost the element of surprise on which his plans had depended. And, worst of all, he had just received word of the fate of Lord Kilwarden. His own father had known the judge well. He was a very decent man.

This was not how Emmet had dreamt of it. He had thought of something glorious. A great national awakening and uprising. Something noble and romantic. Instead, it was reduced to this. He looked back down the length of Thomas Street, where the crowd now seemed totally out of control. But what should he do? He knew there was little hope left of taking the Castle by surprise. They probably had artillery in place by now.

Emmet called his closest advisers to him: Michael Quigley, Nick Stafford, John Hevey, and the two Perrott brothers from Kildare and, for a few moments, they discussed the possibility of continuing on. Some of them were still for pressing on to the castle and wanted to fire off more rockets as signals to men in other parts of the city. And Henry Howley, who was standing nearby, cried out that only a coward would hold back now. But Emmet faltered in this moment of truth. The reality was that he had no stomach for the dirty deeds of revolution. He had never been on a field of battle; never faced a bloody encounter. In all his young life he had never even seen blood spilt. Now, the image of Lord Kilwarden, pierced through with a pike, blood spouting from his bowels, physically sickened him.

"If we disperse now," he concluded, "blood need not be shed uselessly and the rest need not be involved at all."

Reluctantly, many of them agreed although a lot of confusion remained. The word was passed back to the men, most of whom melted back into the drinking houses. Emmet himself slipped away from Thomas Street in the direction of Rathfarnham. He later headed for Wicklow before the military arrived to sweep the streets.

Brendan wandered aimlessly through the Coombe and the Liberties for some time. He refused to believe that Robert Emmet had quit the scene of danger. He thought he must be fighting somewhere else in the city – perhaps at Ringsend or Chapelizod or the Canal Harbour. Brendan knew he was in the thick of the struggle somewhere. But where?

He wandered down into Dame Street and pushed his way through the crowds there, past overturned carriages and broken shop windows, past King William's statue, down as far as the College itself. But nobody had seen Mr. Emmet in that part of the town.

He retraced his steps until he came up with a large body of men – perhaps as many as one hundred – besieging the Coombe barracks. A detachment of the Twenty-first Fusiliers was drawn up in front of the barracks and shots were being exchanged in the gathering dusk. But the action was desultory and, after some time, the men moved off without having made any really serious attempt to take the barracks. When they had gone, Brendan counted four dead men and saw others being carried away into the night. But he felt no sense of involvement, or even of tragedy. He recognised no-one; saw no leaders that were known to him. He felt strangely detached – almost disinterested in the proceedings. He only knew that everything had gone terribly, terribly wrong. He suspected now that Mr. Emmet had been taken and perhaps the other leaders too. All was lost – irretrievably gone. Had all their work been for nothing?

———— • ————

Around midnight, Brendan made his way back past St Patrick's Cathedral and into Kevin Street, heading for Margaret's house in Hatch Street. The military were now out in force and he had to keep to the back streets and the laneways. But just as he approached Aungier Street, he was challenged by a group of men hiding behind a rough barricade.

"It's a bloody spy," he heard one of them saying.

"It's me. Brendan O'Reilly," he called out. "I'm one of your own."

In the poor light Brendan could not make out the faces of the men behind the obstruction, but one big fellow emerged with a musket pointed menacingly straight at him.

"He has the look of a spy alright," the man called out. "Look at his fancy boots."

"Hang him up. Hang him up," came the chorus of voices from behind the barricade.

"No. I'm a friend," Brendan shouted in a firm voice. "I'm with Mr. Emmet. Ask any of your leaders."

Brendan tried to remain calm. He knew the men were drunk. He mustn't excite them.

"So what's your name again?", the big fellow asked, raising the musket to his shoulder.

"O'Reilly. Brendan O'Reilly," came the reply, but Brendan immediately regretted that his accent was not that of the Coombe or the Liberties.

Happily, at that moment, a pail of dirty water was splashed down onto the street from a window above and the sudden distraction gave Brendan his chance to make a run for it, zig-zagging back in the direction from which he had come. But a military platoon had advanced up Aungier Street and saw this fugitive in the semi-darkness. A shot rang out. Was it from the men or the soldiers? The effect was the same. Brendan was hit and tumbled heavily onto the cobbled street. He had been mortally wounded.

~~~~~~ • ~~~~~~

Brendan lay on his back with his mouth ajar. He felt no pain but his mind wandered as he gazed up at the darkened sky. He thought of his sister Margaret. He had promised to return there before dark. Now she would be worried. Could he get a message to her? But where exactly was he? Why was he lying here? He thought he could see some men above him, looking down at him. But his vision was blurred. And who were they anyhow? He thought he heard them murmuring. Or was that some other noise? And what did they want? He felt very tired and confused. He wanted to close his eyes. He wanted to sleep.

Eventually, the men lifted him onto a board and carried him to the hospice. A short time later, some doctor declared that he was dead.

On the following Monday, a Special Notice appeared in the *Dublin Evening Post*, surrounded by a heavy black margin. It read as follows:

"We regret to announce the death of our distinguished colleague, Mr. Brendan O'Reilly, of Westport, County Mayo, who was fatally injured last Saturday while covering the recent disturbances in Dublin for this paper, of which he was the Deputy Editor. Funeral arrangements will be announced later. May he rest in peace."

Mr. Magee had done Brendan one last service.

Chapter XXIX

PIDGEON HOUSE REUNION

AFTER DR. WILKINSON'S funeral, Stephen was invited back to Number Ten and he stayed on after the other mourners had gone home. A light supper was served in the study and he listened to Pamela talking on about the good doctor while they consumed another bottle of claret and the evening shadows gave way to darkness. Then the maid put a light to the coal fire and pulled the heavy curtains.

"What a turnout for the funeral," Pamela said as she poured Stephen another glass of wine. "The people around here really loved him. Of course, he brought many of them into the world. But what a senseless loss of life! Brendan too. What a tragedy! Brendan was more than a friend to me, you know. He was a companion when I needed one so desperately. I will never forget his coming to rescue me when I was almost suicidal. Completely out of the blue, he wrote to Aunt Olive asking could he accompany me to Westport. So typical of him. He was one of those rare souls who thought more about others than about himself. Margaret is inconsolable. Her only sibling. The body is being brought back to Westport for interment. Poor Mrs. O'Reilly. Her only son struck down in the prime of life. Where is the justice in all this?"

Pamela continued on in this vein for some time and Stephen thought it best to let her air these memories without interruption. But quite suddenly she changed the subject.

"Death changes everything," she said enigmatically as she poured herself another glass of wine. "It puts life into perspective, doesn't it?".

She took a large draught of wine before continuing.

"I have been trying to tell you something since you returned," she began, "but I have difficulty in finding the words."

Unusually for her, she looked Stephen straight in the eye.

"There is something that has been troubling me. Something that I should have told you about long ago."

Stephen felt distinctly uncomfortable. Her tone was ominous.

"But I know all about Bingham," he blurted out, wanting to forestall any embarrassment.

"You only know the half of it," she replied dismissively. "I have prayed for the strength to tell you, but even now the effort is almost too much"

Stephen moved his chair closer to Pamela.

"Nothing that you say now – or at any time in the future – could possibly alter my feelings for you," he assured her, speaking very deliberately. "You must know how I feel about you."

Pamela blushed. The candles were flickering and she seemed to hesitate again.

Stephen instinctively knew that whatever she was about to say was better left unsaid.

"Before you say anything," he continued, "please listen to me. There is no imperative for you to tell me anything. If it hurts you to tell it, it will certainly hurt me to hear it."

"But I feel compelled to tell you. To get it off my chest."

"To what purpose?", he asked. "It cannot be to please me – for evidently it will not. And if the telling of it is so difficult for you , then it cannot be something that I want to hear under any circumstances."

"But it worries me. It has come between us since your return."

Stephen was delighted to hear this. This was the first indication he had that his feelings for Pamela were reciprocated. And this strengthened his resolve to prevent her from spoiling this happy development.

"A lot of things have happened since we both fled from Murrisk," he said. "Things which neither of us could have anticipated. Some of them good and some of them not so good. But that's all in the past. Surely it is best to leave all that behind us now? To look to the future?"

Stephen could see that Pamela was weakening. She wanted to believe him. She too wanted to leave the past behind her.

"Please trust me," he said tenderly and his hand, almost involuntarily, covered hers which was resting on the arm of the chair.

Pamela let it lie there for a moment but she was still confused.

"I am so tired," she said. "I don't seem to know my own mind anymore. I'll have to think about it. About everything."

"Yes, of course," said Stephen, anxious not to lose the little victory he had gained.

"You know I have some business in London that has to be finalised. Please put all this out of your mind until I return. We've all had a most traumatic time."

Before he left that night Stephen kissed her hand for the first time. He had wanted to put his arms around her and to let her feel the strength of his warm embrace, to re-assure her, to comfort her. But he was conscious too of the sensitivity of the moment.

Very reluctantly he took his leave, pulled the heavy door of Number Ten behind him and went out into the night.

<p style="text-align:center">~~~~~ • ~~~~~</p>

While in London, Stephen wrote to Pamela every day and sometimes twice a day and soon Pamela found herself looking out for the arrival of the postman. She had not imagined that she could feel so lonely – but then she had never been so entirely on her own before. Now she found herself thinking constantly of Stephen and recalling every detail of their conversations in Dublin, of his kindness and tact, of his strength and comfort. Indeed she could think of nothing else.

In his absence, Stephen's character moved onto a higher plane in her estimation. She remembered only his qualities and even these, in her imagination, soon became larger than life. He had always been close to her when she needed him most – in times of danger and of tragedy. He was always so kind and generous, so undemanding and yet so totally reliable. And he loved her. Yes, she was certain of that, as she was of so little. She remembered asking Margaret what it was like to be in love and Margaret had warned her of infatuation. But Pamela knew that what she felt now was no infatuation. It was something much deeper than that. Something that consumed her waking hours. Something that she had never felt before.

<p style="text-align:center">~~~~~ • ~~~~~</p>

It was not until early in October that Stephen managed to return to Dublin. Out in the bay an autumnal mist shrouded the view of the Wicklow hills to his left and the protective hump of Howth Head to his right, as Stephen came up on deck of HM *Bessborough* after a sleepless night in the bunks below. He had sailed from Holyhead and now he joined Captain Edmund Brown at the wheel.

"The tide turned a few hours ago," the Captain told him, "but we'll have to ride at anchor here 'til the water is high enough for us to tie up alongside the Pidgeon House harbour. Then the hobblers can tow us in."

Peering ahead through the mist, which the rising sun behind them was beginning to disperse, Stephen could see the bulk of the Pidgeon House hotel standing out at the end of the newly constructed South Wall.

"I'm looking forward to a right good breakfast," said Stephen, rubbing his hands and pulling his greatcoat tighter around him.

"Well, you can count on Mrs. Tunstal for that. She's running the place now. Ask her for the black pudding, smoked rashers and three fried eggs on top of her Dublin cobble. That'll set you up for the day."

"Why is it called the Pidgeon House?", Stephen asked.

"Well it has nothing to do with pigeons," the captain laughed, "but it's a good question. During the construction of the South Wall, which was completed about ten years ago, the Ballast Office built a Block House which serviced the construction work and in which lived Johnny Pidgeon and his family. Johnny was the resident supervisor and caretaker for over twenty years, and a decent man he was too. During the summer he took boating parties on the river and the Missus made a few bob for herself with refreshments and all that. Everybody in the harbour knew Johnny and liked him. But one night four gougers broke into the Block House and beat poor Johnny unconscious and almost cut off the hand of his son with a cutlass. Johnny died soon after and his son followed him within the year. That must have been around '86 or '87. So when they came to build the fine new hotel to replace the Block House, it was named the Pidgeon House after Johnny. It's probably the only building in Dublin that is named after one of our own. And here come the hobblers."

The captain was now all activity, seeing the ropes thrown out to the tow-boats, shouting orders on all sides and enjoying the importance of the moment. Within twenty minutes they were alongside the new harbour wall and securely tied up. A porter carried Stephen's bags onshore while he negotiated the gangplank and headed for the Pidgeon House through groups of bare-footed young beggars who importuned him on all sides.

And then he saw her.

Stephen had written to Pamela to appraise her of his return but had received no reply before sailing. Now he saw her standing beside the door of her cab, dressed in a long cape and bonnet against the morning chill. Behind her the morning sun was breaking through the mist and overhead the gulls were swooping and squawking in that noisy aerial ballet so characteristic of Dublin. For a moment he hesitated. But then he quickened his pace towards her and, as he did, she too started forward, first holding her skirts in front of her, but then stretching out her arms to receive him.

That moment remained forever in Stephen's memory. He felt as if all his life had been leading up to this very moment although, as he moved to meet her, he felt he was advancing in slow motion. And flashing through his mind were multiple memories of Murrisk and Pamela as a young girl: of the day he rescued her from the wasps on Leckanvy; of the awful death of her father and Captain John, and of their escape together to Dublin and of his loneliness in Jamaica and of his longing for her all that time. But then he was holding her tight to him, his arms encircling her body as he breathed in the scent of her *Rose of Damascene*. And for the first time in his life he knew what it was to be loved.

Chapter XXX

EPILOGUE

IN THE DAYS immediately following the insurrection, hundreds of suspects in and around Dublin were rounded up and thrown into prison. About five hundred men were packed into Major Sandy's prison at Arbour Hill alone. Their trials started in September and the executions followed almost immediately.

Thomas Russell, the United Irishman and friend of Wolfe Tone, was found guilty of high treason at Downpatrick on 19th October, 1803, and executed the following day. He was thirty six.

Denis Redmond, the coal merchant, aged twenty five and engaged to be married, had fled after the 23rd July and embarked on the Wexford brig '*Tarleton*', bound for Chester. Bad weather, however, forced the vessel to put into Carlingford Bay where the authorities seized Redmond and brought him back to Dublin. Here he attempted to take his life with a pistol smuggled into the prison, but he survived to face trial and execution. He was hanged outside his own yard on Coal Quay.

Henry Howley didn't go so quietly. When they came to arrest him, he shot dead one of Major Sirr's assistants, a certain Hanlon, before he was overcome. Later at his trial he admitted to having killed Colonel Browne, who had stopped the six cabs heading for the Castle. He was hanged opposite the new prison at Kilmainham. He was twenty eight.

There were many others hanged or imprisoned – but some escaped. William Dowdall happily escaped to France and joined the French army.

Thomas Brangan, who was to take the Pidgeon House at Irishtown, escaped to Portugal but was killed in a duel in 1811.

John Hevey, the brewer, spent many years in prison until his mind was deranged. Shortly before his death he ran into the lower Castle Yard and fell to breaking Major Sirr's windows. He was seized and sent to the lunatic asylum where he died in utter destitution.

Michael Quigley, who had been close to Emmet at every step of the way from Paris to Thomas Street, was a spy. He had been a rebel captain in 1798 in Kildare, and was imprisoned in Kilmainham until 1802. At what point he became a traitor, no one knew. He lived and died in the government pay, happily tending his acres in County Kildare.

Miles Byrne escaped on an American vessel to Bordeaux and was able to report on the disaster to Thomas Addis Emmet in Paris. He later took part in Napoleon's campaigns of 1804–1815, and was appointed a Chevalier of the Legion of Honour. His *Memoirs* were published in Paris in 1863.

<center>~~~~~ • ~~~~~</center>

On Sunday, July 24th, Robert Emmet escaped to the Wicklow mountains to a place above Rathfarnham called Ballinascorney. Obviously he could have fled farther afield – to France or to America – but there was one restraining factor. Robert Emmet was in love.

All during his intense preparations for the rising, young Emmet had been secretly courting the only daughter of the celebrated barrister and former MP, Mr. John Philpot Curran. The secrecy was essential because Mr. Curran had indicated his disapproval at the first sign of Mr. Emmet's interest. So most of Mr. Emmet's courtship of Sarah had to be conducted through letters smuggled into her family home in Rathfarnham. But now that he was on the point of quitting the country altogether, he wanted Sarah to elope with him. That forlorn hope brought him back to Dublin – and to his death.

Who it was that betrayed him at his secret lodgings in Harold's Cross (despite the usual hidden cupboards and trapdoors) is still a matter of conjecture. But Major Sirr apprehended him there on August 25th and he was sent for trial on September 13th. He was defended by *Mr. Leonard McNally, the senior counsel who – as it turned out many years later – was also in the government's pay. In fact, it was probably McNally who betrayed Robert Emmet, as he had betrayed so many of his former clients over the years.

The result of the trial was a foregone conclusion and the jury did not even bother to retire. After a whispered consultation the foreman stood and addressed the court.

"My lords," he said, "I have consulted my brother jurors and we are all of the opinion that the prisoner is guilty."

The clerk of the court repeated the indictment and the verdict of the jury and the judge, Lord Norbury, then asked the usual question of the prisoner.

"What have you therefore to say why judgement of death and execution should not be pronounced against you according to the law?"

Robert Emmet's reply has gone down in history.

"My lords," he said, standing forward in the dock, "as to why judgement of death and execution should not be passed upon me according to law, I have nothing to say; but as to why my character should not be relieved from the imputations and calumnies thrown out against it, I have much to say. I have no hopes that I can anchor my character in the breast of this court. I only wish your lordships will suffer it to float down your memories until it has found some hospitable harbour to shelter it from the storms with which it is at present buffeted. Were I to suffer only death after being adjudged guilty, I should bow in silence to the fate which awaits me; but the sentence of the law which delivers my body over to the executioner consigns my character to obloquy."

Mr. Emmet was constantly interrupted by Lord Norbury, but despite this, and his obvious fatigue after a full day in the dock, Emmet persisted in reviewing his reasons for looking for French help and then passed on to a statement of the general objectives of the rebellion.

Lord Norbury continued to interrupt him until he came to his conclusion.

"Let no man write my epitaph; for as no man who knows my motives now dares to vindicate them, let not prejudice or ignorance asperse them. Let them rest in obscurity and peace. Let my memory be left in oblivion, and my tomb remain uninscribed, until other times and other men can do justice to my character. When my country takes her place among the nations of the earth, then, and not till then, let my epitaph be written. I have done."

The following day Robert Emmet was brought to his place of execution. In front of St Catherine's Church on Thomas Street, just across the road from the entrance to his assembly depot, a crude kind of gallows was created on a platform laid on empty barrels. The prisoner's hands were tied and he had to be helped up the ladder to the raised platform. Mr. Emmet had wanted to make a speech to the dense crowd gathered to see his last moments on this earth, but he was not allowed to do so. Instead he uttered but a short valedictory before the black cap was pulled down over his head.

"My friends," he said, "I die in peace and with sentiments of universal love and kindness towards all men."

When it was over, the executioner cut him down and carried out the second part of the sentence. With a long heavy knife, he severed the patriot's head from his body and holding it aloft by the hair of the head, chanted out to the crowd:

"This is the head of a traitor, Robert Emmet. This is the head of a traitor."

Some years later, the poet, Thomas Moore, who had known Emmet intimately in College days, had this to say of his friend: "Were I to number those men who appeared to me to combine in the greatest degree fine moral worth with intellectual power, I should, amongst the highest of the few, place Robert Emmet."

Of all the members of the former Irish Houses of Parliament, only Lord Castlereagh positively benefited in his career from the passing of the Union. He filled various high offices of responsibility in the British cabinet until 1812, when he was appointed Secretary for Foreign Affairs – a post he held continuously until he took his own life, by cutting his throat in 1822. But he was as unpopular in Britain as he had been in Ireland. As his hearse was drawn to Westminster Abbey, the mobs pelted his coffin with rotten fruit and dead cats. Of his public life, Sir Jonah Barrington remarked that "Its commencement was patriotic, its progress was corrupt, and its termination criminal." He was fifty three.

Lord Cornwallis died in the traces. In 1805 he was sent out again to India as Governor General and Commander in Chief, but the rigours of the long hot voyage were too much for him and he expired at Ghazepore towards the end of the same year. He was sixty six.

John Foster, the last Speaker of the Irish House of Commons, was one of the few anti-Unionists to secure a seat in the Imperial Parliament. Elected as a member for Louth, he was appointed Chancellor of the Exchequer for Ireland and was created Baron Oriel. He died in 1828 aged 87, opposing Catholic emancipation to the last.

Only a few weeks after "The Races of Castlebar", General Humbert and his small band was confronted by 13,000 troops under General Lake at Ballinamuck and sensibly capitulated. The French force was subsequently "exchanged" and repatriated to France, while Humbert's Irish supporters were "butchered without mercy", according to the account by Bishop Stock of Killala. General Humbert later took an active part in the Mexican War of Independence and died at New Orleans in 1823, aged sixty seven.

John Denis Browne, third Earl of Altamont, first Marquess of Sligo, died in Lisbon in 1809. He was fifty three. He was succeeded by his only son, Howe Peter Browne, the second Marquess, who was appointed Governor of Jamaica in 1834 and presided over the Negro Emancipation in that colony. Howe Peter lived a charmed life and died on the 25th January, 1845, on the eve of the ultimate tragedy in Irish history – the Great Famine of 1845-50.

The Union of 1800 lasted until 1921 when it was repealed as it applied to twenty-six counties of Ireland. The remaining six counties, Antrim, Down, Tyrone, Fermanagh, Armagh and Derry, remain in the Union with Great Britain to this day.